CLUE
KREWE

A Miss Fortune Mystery

NEW YORK *TIMES* BESTSELLING AUTHOR
JANA DELEON

MISS FORTUNE SERIES INFORMATION

If you've never read a Miss Fortune mystery, you can start with LOUISIANA LONGSHOT, the first book in the series. If you prefer to start with this book, here are a few things you need to know.

Fortune Redding – a CIA assassin with a price on her head from one of the world's most deadly arms dealers. Because her boss suspects that a leak at the CIA blew her cover, he sends her to hide out in Sinful, Louisiana, posing as his niece, a librarian and ex–beauty queen named Sandy-Sue Morrow. The situation was resolved in Change of Fortune and Fortune is now a full-time resident of Sinful and has opened her own detective agency.

Ida Belle and Gertie – served in the military in Vietnam as spies, but no one in the town is aware of that fact except Fortune and Deputy LeBlanc.

Sinful Ladies Society – local group founded by Ida Belle, Gertie, and deceased member Marge. In order to gain membership, women must never have married or if widowed, their husband must have been deceased for at least ten years.

Sinful Ladies Cough Syrup – sold as an herbal medicine in Sinful, which is dry, but it's actually moonshine manufactured by the Sinful Ladies Society.

CHAPTER ONE

I LEANED FORWARD IN THE PEW AND STUDIED PASTOR DON. He'd been hoarse before church when he'd greeted me, and one of the ladies who was helping set up the trays for the Lord's Supper had passed him a coffee mug of the grape juice that Baptists use as a substitute for wine—because of that whole no drinking rule. He'd sipped at it while continuing to greet until the congregation was in and it was time to get the church show on the road...or the altar. He'd gotten a refill on the grape juice before he'd headed for the pulpit, and I'd hoped his voice would hold out.

Now, over halfway into the service, I was praying for something entirely different.

"And so God spoke to Moses from a burning bush," Pastor Don said. "Apparently no consideration given to wildfires or that s'mores wouldn't be invented for thousands of years."

And that wasn't even the first odd thing he'd said. I looked at Gertie, who had suddenly developed a coughing fit.

I leaned over and whispered, "You swapped out the grape juice for Sinful Ladies booze, didn't you?"

The day before, I'd spent hours helping Ida Belle and

Gertie bottle up Sinful Ladies Cough Syrup—street name High Octane Moonshine—in preparation for the Mardi Gras festivities coming next weekend. We'd tested so much of the product while flavoring and bottling that Walter and Carter had taken one look at us and left us all sleeping on Gertie's kitchen floor. We'd barely made it up in time for church and I was feeling sketchy on running afterward, especially since at the moment, banana pudding didn't sound all that great.

Gertie glanced at me before doubling over, her shoulders shaking from the laughter she was holding in, and I held back a groan. The new flavor of 'cough syrup' they were introducing this year at their Mardi Gras booth was grape. And while just a little of it packed an alcohol-induced stupor, it was smooth and sneaky, catching you by surprise. Hence our sleeping on the kitchen floor.

"Bottoms up with the blood!" Pastor Don yelled, then tossed back the rest of his 'grape juice' and slammed the glass upside down on the pulpit.

The rest of the congregation looked confused, but drank. Then the coughing began and everyone sitting at the ends of the pews grabbed the remaining shots from the deacons' trays and started passing them around as if we were at a fraternity party. Ida Belle, who was in the loft with the choir, sniffed her glass, then looked at the ceiling. I figured she was praying there wasn't a lightning storm headed our way.

"And the Lord Jesus said," Pastor Don continued, "this is my body. Eat it in remembrance of me. Hmm, that sounds really bad. Too many episodes of *The Walking Dead,* probably. Hey, Jesus was sort of the first zombie, right?"

He popped the unleavened bread into his mouth and started to munch.

"These are pretty good, actually," he said and took another. "And more blood to wash it down."

He hurried down to the altar and grabbed the last remaining shot of 'grape juice' from the tray, barely beating out Old Mrs. Cline for it. She gave him a good whack with her cane, but he ignored her and downed the shot as though he was at the Swamp Bar.

"Okay, I'm calling it," Pastor Don said. "I've got the munchies and these bits of crackers aren't going to cut it. Thanks, God, for everything. Amen. You can all sing the last hymn on the way home. It's 'Nothing but the Blood of Jesus'—naturally."

And with that, he headed out the side door, humming.

I checked my watch and saw we were finishing up ten minutes early, which wasn't allowed, per se, at least not in relation to the banana pudding race. The rules were both churches had to dismiss at the same time, or the race was null and void. Heck, the café didn't even open until church let out, but a forfeit suited me well enough. I didn't feel like running and banana pudding lacked its usual allure. Everyone else jumped up and started out the doors, apparently not about to look an early dismissal gift in the mouth.

I picked up my tote bag that contained my tennis shoes and motioned to Gertie.

"Come on, Satan," I said. "Let's get out of here before the whole place explodes in fire."

Gertie's face was red from laughing and she clutched the pew in front of her as she rose, still shaking with merriment. "He called Jesus a zombie," she said. "When everyone sobers up, they're going to crucify him."

"Seems appropriate. At least I don't have to run."

But as the words were leaving my mouth, the chimes at the Catholic church went off, signifying they'd let out for the day... nine minutes early.

"Do you think they saw us leaving?" I asked.

Gertie collapsed back on the pew again, this time laughing so loud they could probably hear her in the next parish. Ida Belle walked up, took one look at Gertie, and frowned.

"You gave that nun a bottle, didn't you?" she asked.

'That nun' was a regular at the Catholic church and since Gertie had defrocked her at a cemetery and wrestled her in the street for Mardi Gras beads, giving her a bottle of booze didn't appear to be her biggest offense against the woman.

Gertie nodded and managed one word in between gasping. "Communion."

"Good Lord, the whole town is going to be in the drunk tank," Ida Belle said.

"I thought Catholics drank on the regular," I said. "They should be better off than the Baptists."

Ida Belle waved a hand in dismissal. "Everyone drinks. Baptists just keep it to themselves. But very few people drink the likes of that mega grape syrup. You saw what it did to us, and the congregation only had one shot and then went snatching and grabbing for more. It might be too strong to sell. I think—"

"Race is on if the Catholics are out," Gertie interrupted.

I pulled my tennis shoes out and handed them to her. "You're up. If Celia had a shot of that booze, even Sheriff Lee could beat her today."

Gertie let out a *woot* and pulled on the tennis shoes, then dashed—or some version of it—out of the church, shoving exiting drunks aside as she went. Ida Belle and I hurried after her, because a drunk Celia meant an even more spiteful and illogical Celia, if one could imagine that.

But it wasn't going to be left to imaginations.

Gertie and Celia raced out of their respective churches and both stopped at the edge of the street. Like two gunslingers in an old Western, they stared at each other, arms out from their sides, each waiting for the other to flinch.

"It's like two cats waiting to pounce," Ida Belle said, then did a single clap.

That was all it took.

"May the force be with me!" Celia yelled and slashed at the air with her Bible. "And also with you."

"Good Lord, she's toasted," I said.

"Well, Gertie's hungover, so it seems fair enough," Ida Belle said.

The two of them took off—sort of. Celia had a bit of an edge as the Catholic church was on the same side of the street as the café, but Gertie went for the diagonal cross to cut some of the advantage. Unfortunately, her diagonal also took a diagonal, and it looked more like she was trying to dodge a pursuing alligator than win a race. Fortunately, Celia was faring no better. She'd run out of one of her granny pumps and was now limp-trotting.

Until she hit a post.

She clawed the post and made her way back to standing, then noticed a bicycle propped on the other side. She hopped on the bicycle and set off in a wobbly race down the sidewalk. Ida Belle leaned back against the brick wall of the church and pulled a bag of peanuts out of her pocket.

"Want one?" she asked as we watched the show.

"I'm more of a Junior Mints sort of gal."

She nodded. "But they melt in pockets and I don't carry a handbag of death like Gertie."

Gertie had now spotted Celia on the bicycle and was yelling 'foul' as she ran for the sidewalk.

"Uh-oh," I said. "Gertie's spotted a moped. I hope the owner didn't leave the key in it."

Ida Belle snorted. "It's Sunday in Sinful. Of course the key is in it. This is supposed to be a safe place and a sacred day."

"Do people here *know* Gertie?"

"And there she goes."

I looked over to see Gertie take off on the moped, which was moving as wobbly as she'd been running.

"This isn't going to end well," I said.

Ida Belle shoved the peanuts in her pocket and we set off down the street, but there was no way we were going to catch up with them before they reached the café. The only plus was that the rest of the congregants were too tipsy to be in the way. Instead, they all clustered on the sidewalk and in the street, watching the show, which made our passage slower.

We'd just broken through the last of the church stragglers when I noticed the Open sign on the café was lit up. I pointed as we ran and saw Ida Belle frown. What was up in Sinful today? Protocol was being broken all over.

By that time, Celia and Gertie had almost reached the café. Celia was pedaling furiously, the entire bicycle shaking with the effort, and it looked as if she was going to win the race. But apparently the moped had a little more to give. Gertie cranked the throttle and shot forward.

Then hit a pothole.

The pothole launched the moped up and a bit sideways, then the front tire hit the curb and sent Gertie over the handlebars and right into Celia. They both went soaring straight through the plate glass window of Francine's Café.

And landed right on Carter's breakfast.

Then the table collapsed.

"Good Lord, they almost got my apple Danish!"

"Those religious folk are crazy!"

"At least there's a tablecloth over that one woman's butt. It will spoil your breakfast!"

All the patrons jumped up yelling at once as Ida Belle and I looked into the café through the giant hole in the wall that used to be a window.

Carter took one look down at his collapsed table and ruined breakfast and sighed.

"I was here first!" Celia yelled as she wrestled around on the floor with the tablecloth, only succeeding in wrapping herself in more. "She cheated! I want you to arrest that woman."

"There's a shocker," Carter said.

"You cheated first," Gertie said. "You got on a bicycle."

"And you got on a moped. That has an engine."

"Thanks, Captain Obvious."

Carter cleared his throat. "Am I to understand that one of you stole a bicycle and another stole a moped and then you proceeded to destroy the stolen vehicles and Francine's picture window?"

The entire café went so quiet you could have heard a fork drop.

"Uh," Gertie said. "Well, I suppose, maybe..."

"The moped is mine." A young man seated in the far corner rose.

Late twenties. Six foot even. A hundred seventy pounds. Great muscle tone. Didn't look like much of a scrapper as he was kinda pretty, but those pretty boys could fool you. Still, he was on a moped, so I was going with threat level low but not necessarily determined. For all I knew, he could have an arsenal in that big storage trunk on the back as it was bigger than Gertie's purse.

The young man stepped forward and waved his hand at Gertie, who had finally made it into a standing position. "I told Ms. Gertie that she could borrow it anytime."

Carter narrowed his eyes at the man. "Dixon Edwards? Is that you?"

The man nodded. "It's been a minute, Carter. Good to see you. Well, not necessarily at this exact moment as I seem to be part of some trouble, but overall. You know what I mean."

Carter extended his hand and Dixon shook it.

"Good to see you as well. And trust me, the only thing you're on the hook for is telling the real trouble that she could borrow your moped. You might want to reconsider that offer. Not that the moped will be usable with the front wheel out."

"I'll pay for the repairs, of course," Gertie said. "I'm so sorry, Dixon."

He nodded. "Is Scooter still fixing things around here? Maybe I can get it to him and he can look at it."

"He moved in with his grandfather to help him out. Same house," Carter said. "Just leave it right there for the time being. I need to get some photos for the police file I have to open."

"Yes, sir," Dixon said and gave Gertie an apologetic look.

"You're arresting me?" Gertie asked.

Carter shook his head. "Nope, I'm arresting that Celia crepe rolled up on the floor."

Celia, whose head was now the only part sticking out of the tablecloth, looked up at Carter and glared. "What are you arresting me for?"

"For stealing a bicycle," Carter said. "Unless someone else wants to come forward and claim they gave Celia permission to use their property."

Everyone looked down at the floor or up at the ceiling. A few people started whistling.

"Okay, then," Carter said and motioned to Deputy Breaux, who'd apparently been notified of the event and was now hurrying across the street.

"Help me get her up and into a cell," Carter said.

Deputy Breaux didn't so much as raise an eyebrow—just

leaned over and grabbed Celia's shoulders and helped Carter haul her out. You had to love a man who really understood his town and his people. I could hear Celia screaming about the 'fake sheriff' all the way down the street. The rest of the café patrons cheered.

"Mommy! Mommy!" A child ran down the sidewalk crying. "The mean old lady with the ugly dress stole my bicycle. And look! It's ruined."

"We can fix it," the woman said, casting a nervous glance at the window, then at the screaming Celia. "You shouldn't say it was stolen."

Ida Belle leaned toward me. "She's Catholic."

"But it was!" the child insisted. "You told me lying is wrong and it's Sunday. I can't lie on Sunday or God will punish me."

The mother looked apoplectic but just forced a smile. "That's right, dear. But maybe we'll get you a new bike, okay?"

The mother practically dragged the child away from the café, the child still complaining loudly as they rounded the block.

"I'm really sorry, Francine," Gertie said. "I'm happy to pay for the window and the etching."

"And the table," Ida Belle said. "And Carter's breakfast."

"And that tablecloth," I said. "No one is going to want to eat on it now."

Everyone in the café nodded.

Gertie waved a hand as she sank into a chair. "Just send me a bill. It was worth it."

Francine gave her a critical eye as she snapped a finger behind her back. A couple seconds later, a busboy appeared with a broom and dustpan. She took them from the busboy and handed them to Gertie.

"You can start with cleanup," Francine said and waved a hand at the window. "And all of this was for nothing by the way. My refrigerator is totally taken up with ingredients for pies for the Mardi Gras festival, so there's no banana pudding. That's why I opened early. I thought maybe I'd get you lot fed, then close up and give myself a break. Not like I have to make a hundred pies or anything this week."

She gave the shattered window a frown, whirled around, and headed back to the kitchen.

"Ouch," Gertie said. "She's mad."

"Look at her café," Ida Belle said. "She should be mad."

"Are you all right, Ms. Gertie?" Dixon asked.

"Some breakfast, a bottle of aspirin, and a heating pad, and I'll be fine," Gertie said. "Thanks for the cover."

He shrugged. "You know how I feel about Celia."

"If you're hoping Carter dumps her in the bayou still wrapped in that tablecloth, then you feel the way most of us do," I said and stuck out my hand. "Fortune Redding."

He raised one eyebrow and shook my hand. "I've heard a little about you. Nice to put a face to the reputation. Good to see you too, Ms. Ida Belle."

Ida Belle nodded. "Surprised to see you, though. I thought your mom was going to keep the house as a rental. Is she selling now?"

"No ma'am," Dixon said. "Actually, she passed a month ago. Heart finally got her."

"I'm so sorry."

"Sorry to hear that."

Gertie and Ida Belle replied at once.

"She was a good woman," Ida Belle said. "She deserved a better body."

"Yes, ma'am, she did."

"Are you seeing a doctor regularly?" Gertie asked.

He nodded. "So far, I'm clear, but I'll keep a watch my whole life, I guess."

"So are you here to sell the house?" Ida Belle asked.

"Actually, I'm a bit in between things—job, life, you know—and I think I'm going to live there a while and figure stuff out."

"Well, let us know if you need anything," Gertie said.

He smiled. "I could use a ride home. You can have my table. I'm going to pop back to Scooter's place and ask about the moped. I'll be back."

"A ride is no problem," Ida Belle said.

"Good," Gertie said. "I'm starved."

Ida Belle pointed to the broom. "You are on cleanup duty first. The last thing you want to do is order food from Francine when her café looks like this."

Gertie sighed. "Order me eggs, toast, bacon, pancakes, and a blueberry muffin. And coffee. A whole pot of coffee."

"You are not going to eat all of that," Ida Belle said.

Gertie picked up the broom. "I'm going to try."

CHAPTER TWO

IDA BELLE SHOOK HER HEAD AS WE MADE OUR WAY TO THE table Dixon had vacated.

"If she gets sick in the café trying to eat all of that, Francine's going to be even madder," I said as we sat.

"She's just ordering a lot of food to try to placate Francine because of the window. She'll end up boxing up most of it and taking it with her."

"Makes sense."

The server stepped up with coffee and we gave her our orders. She raised an eyebrow at the amount of food but then just smiled and headed off.

"So how's Carter doing with his new 'fake sheriff' position?" Ida Belle asked.

I shrugged. "Technically, he's been doing the job for years. He just finally has the title."

"By appointment, and from Marie, hence Celia's animosity. He'll be in a better position once the election is over."

"You sure the sheriff isn't going to use that wheelchair to climb onto his horse and run again?"

"No. His climbing and riding days are over, and that horse

should have been out to pasture a decade ago, at least. I have no doubt Lee will be walking before summer, but his heart isn't going to last forever, and his brother has been harping on him to retire and fish."

"You don't think there will be any problems with the election, do you?"

Ida Belle shook her head. "Like you said, Carter's been doing the job for years, and everyone around here knows it. Plus, there's no one else with even half the qualifications. The guys who were waiting on him to retire so they could make their run have gotten old as well. They haven't been doing much besides chair warming for years, and voters know that. The locals want someone who gets results, especially with the increase in crime we've seen lately."

"Carter has been getting results even though he wasn't sheriff."

"True, but people will assume—right or wrong—that he'll be able to do even more if he has the title."

"Big shoes."

"Carter can handle it."

"I have no doubt he can."

Ida Belle must have picked up on something in my voice because she gave me a pointed look. "Are you worried his relationship with you might throw a kink into things?"

I shrugged. "I'd be lying if I said it hadn't crossed my mind. I've pissed off a lot of people around here."

Ida Belle snorted. "And most of them are either dead or in jail—including, at the moment, the one you piss off the most."

"The ADA doesn't like me."

"He only gets one vote, just like everyone else."

I slumped back in my chair. "I guess you're right."

Gertie finished cleanup duty just as our breakfast arrived. She slid into the seat looking far too energetic for someone who was hungover and had just participated in a footrace and been tossed through a window.

"Thank God," she said as she grabbed a piece of toast. "All that cleaning made me hungry."

I shook my head. "I'm not sure if you're still alive because of genetics or sheer stubbornness."

"God has a sense of humor," Ida Belle said.

"She does," Gertie agreed. "Or we wouldn't have Celia. What did I miss?"

"Just talking about the 'fake sheriff,'" I said.

Gertie made a face. "Celia is going to have to get some new material after the election."

I nodded. Everything pointed to Carter winning the election, but I couldn't help that tiny feeling of apprehension. Things in Sinful rarely went the way they were supposed to, and I knew just how important this job was to Carter. Not because he was dying to be sheriff, because he wasn't an authority-hungry kind of guy, but he knew if anyone else was made sheriff, they'd see him as a threat to their position and would make his life miserable. I didn't even want to think about what he would do if he couldn't stay with the sheriff's department.

And then there were the phone calls. I'd already caught snatches of conversations as he bowed out of the room and away from my hearing. It was a recent development, and it didn't take but a few key phrases for me to guess that those calls were from the military. They were trying to coax him back—whether it was full time or consulting, I had no idea— but either way, if he accepted, it would likely mean him disappearing. Force Recon didn't exactly do the accounting for the Marines and if they needed him, it was because of his knowledge on a previous mission.

"So what's the story on Dixon Edwards?" I asked, trying to

shift the conversation and, hopefully, my thoughts. There was no use concerning myself with all that until Carter said something.

"Nice young man," Gertie said. "His mother was an angel."

Ida Belle nodded. "But married to the devil. There was never anything official, mind you, but people talked and there were long sleeves in the summer and the like."

"That sucks. Did you guys finally run him out of town?"

"No," Gertie said. "He set out himself. Right about the time Dixon started high school and had a growth spurt. Put on five inches and a good forty pounds of muscle in one year."

"And wasn't going to let his mother take the brunt of things anymore," I concluded.

"Exactly," Ida Belle said. "His mother inherited the house from her parents before she married, so the husband couldn't touch it and he didn't have any people around these parts. We figure he headed back to Mississippi, where he was from."

"Or just crawled back under that rock," Gertie said. "Either way, no one was sad to see him go. Dixon's mother had worked at the hospital in the billing department forever, so she was good as far as money went, especially having no house note."

"Heck, she was better off as far as money went once that loser was gone," Ida Belle said. "He never held a job more than a couple weeks. Couldn't keep his mouth shut or his hand off a bottle."

"So Dixon went to school here? With Carter?"

"Yep. Dixon is a bit younger, so they weren't friends," Gertie said. "And even if they'd been closer in age, they ran with two different groups. Carter was an athlete and Dixon was a big fisherman."

"Isn't most everyone around here?" I asked.

"I'd say Sinful lends itself to a higher-than-average number of weekly hours spent holding a fishing pole," Gertie said. "But Dixon took it to another level. He broke curfew to fish, cut class to fish, 'borrowed' other people's boats to fish. He tried to make a career out of it, but didn't have the capital to compete with the big dogs."

"Interesting," I said. "So what does he do now?"

"Marine welder, last I heard," Gertie said. "Works on oil rigs mostly."

"That's a dangerous job," I said.

"But the fishing is excellent," Ida Belle said. "So is the pay. The life expectancy, however..."

"So he moved off after high school?"

Ida Belle shook her head. "He stuck around for a year, while he was trying the pro fishing thing, then his mom got worse, and it was clear she wasn't going to be able to manage living here. Her house is really old—steep, narrow stairs and all the bedrooms on the second floor. No way to add on or modify without spending a fortune, and the house just wasn't worth the investment. She had a sister who was widowed and lived in New Orleans, so they moved there. One-story house and closer to specialists and all that."

"Dixon gave up the fishing thing and took up welding," Gertie said. "His mother leased the house to have a bit of extra income, and well, because I think she wanted to leave it to Dixon rather than sell it. Family history and all."

"We never thought he'd come back here," Ida Belle said. "If it hadn't been for his mother, he would have cut out sooner, but she needed his help. He barely showed his face around here in the years after they moved. Honestly, I'm surprised he's sticking around now."

"The town was never the problem," Gertie said.

"Let me guess," I said. "A woman."

"Ha!" Gertie said. "You're catching on to this small-town stuff."

"I think that's just regular people stuff," Ida Belle said. "After all, people in cities have relationship issues as well."

"But they don't have to see the person every day after they get dumped," Gertie said. "You can't drive through downtown here without seeing half the population."

"So who was this evil woman who broke Dixon's heart?" I asked.

"Athena Durand," Gertie said.

"Sounds fancy."

"And she was, especially for Sinful," Gertie said. "Her parents were NOLA money. Her dad was some kind of investor, but then there was a scandal and he lost his business—went to prison, too."

"There was some distant cousin of theirs who lived outside Sinful," Ida Belle said. "Athena came to stay with her to finish up high school. Her mother stayed in New Orleans. I don't know the story behind that. They weren't really from here, so no one had a line on the details."

"And the cousin didn't talk?" I asked. "That's surprising."

"The cousin was the angry hermit type and was tight-lipped about everything, but even more so about that," Gertie said. "And people didn't figure quizzing a teen on the break-down of her family was the right thing to do, so everyone just let it go."

Ida Belle nodded. "I don't think I saw the cousin but a handful of times all the years she lived here, which was probably ten or better. She didn't socialize with anyone and didn't go to church. She stocked up every couple months at the General Store, which was the only time we happened to cross paths. Walter said she barely said a word to him either."

I frowned. "The whole thing sounds odd. Why would a mother send her child to live with someone like that?"

"It *was* odd," Ida Belle said, "but who knows why people make the choices they do. Rumor was the mother was the delicate type. Maybe Athena was too much for her to handle."

"Or could be Athena was better off getting out of New Orleans and off somewhere where everyone wasn't talking about her father," Gertie said.

"I suppose so, but that had to be hard on her," I said.

I'd lost both parents before I was an adult, so I knew firsthand how it felt to have everything in your life shifted at once.

"If you ask me, it was a crap move," Gertie said. "But at least in Sinful, she was able to finish school without the drama she probably would have had in New Orleans."

"And I'm assuming she met Dixon and decided it wasn't so bad after all?" I asked.

"That's what it looked like at first," Gertie said. "They started dating shortly after she arrived. He was a year older and just out of high school and doing the fishing thing. It was clear he was over the moon about her, but apparently, she was sneaking out with someone else on the sly. Some rich kid from Mudbug. Dixon caught them together at a festival and it was all over. He was completely torn up about it. Rumor was he was just waiting for her to graduate and was going to ask her to marry him."

Ida Belle nodded. "Once his mother was convinced to change living arrangements, he packed them up and never looked back. Gave up the fishing pursuit and started with the welding. The sad thing is, he could have stuck around and made a longer go at fishing because a couple months later, Athena graduated and left town. That's the last we saw of her. Except for in the newspapers, of course."

"The newspapers?"

"Yep," Ida Belle said. "The Mudbug kid didn't work out—but she snagged another rich one in New Orleans and wound up in the newspapers."

Gertie nodded. "Beckett Rousseau. Oldest son of a state senator and heir to the family business and political throne."

"Also rumored to be engaged to another woman at the time, but I never got any details on that," Ida Belle said.

"Yikes," I said. "I guess Athena was determined to get back to her rich and powerful roots."

"Looks like," Ida Belle said. "Married him not long after news of their romance hit the wires. And it all looked like the fairy-tale romance."

"Until?" I asked.

"Until she killed him," Gertie said.

CHAPTER THREE

I STARED. GERTIE'S DECLARATION WAS ONE I HADN'T SEEN coming. Even though the story involved a sort-of Sinful resident, financial shenanigans, cheating, and a politician, this tale had moved right from the starting line and to the locker room. But before I could manage to run down the list of questions that had already formed, Dixon dropped into the remaining empty seat.

"I talked with Scooter and showed him a picture of the moped," Dixon said. "He thinks he can fix it, but he'll have to order some parts. Might be a week or so."

"Gertie can rent you a car in the meantime," Ida Belle said.

"That's not necessary," he said. "I have my truck with me. The moped was just something I won in a card game. But it's kinda fun and works great for places like this. I didn't take it out much in New Orleans. The roads there are terrible, and the drivers are even worse."

"Sinful is not exactly stellar in either of those categories either," I said.

"That's true, but it's good for getting from my house to

Main Street. At least, it was until today." He shot a grin at Gertie.

"Well, we appreciate you keeping Gertie out of the clink," Ida Belle said.

"Anything to get a dig at Celia," he said. "And to help you ladies out. Your group always looked after my mom, even when she tried to keep you from doing it. She appreciated you more than you'll ever know."

"She was a lovely woman," Gertie said and patted his hand. "We would have done more if she'd have allowed it."

He cast his eyes down and shook his head. "She was too embarrassed, you know? I hate that man for what he did to her. Hate that half of me comes from him."

"That's just skin and bones," Gertie said. "Your heart came from your mom, and that's the important part."

"You ever hear from him?" Ida Belle asked.

"No. He cut out and stayed gone. Not so much as a peep. I heard through extended family that he finally managed to drink himself to death some years back."

"And no one notified you?" Gertie asked.

He shrugged. "His family was just as bad as he was. Nothing about those people will ever surprise me."

"Well, none of that matters now," Gertie said. "Your mother is in a place with no pain and her son turned out well. I'm sure she was proud of you."

He looked a little embarrassed but nodded. "I suppose she was, even though she wished I would have done something less dangerous."

"Are you thinking of changing things up now?" I asked. "Because I'm not so sure that coming back to Sinful will accomplish that. I mean, I thought I was going from CIA missions to a sleepy small town, but just this morning, I've been party to getting the whole town drunk and the theft and destruction of private property."

He laughed. "Yeah, Sinful has a lot more going on than most people think, but I've got an opportunity I want to dwell on. That new shipbuilding outfit up the highway is looking to hire some welders when they get going, and they've made me an offer. It's less than I was making before, of course, but I'd be guaranteed to go home every day, so there's that. And it's a short commute from Sinful, so I wouldn't have rent to worry about."

"That sounds like a great option," I said.

"It is, but I have some time to decide. I never figured on moving back here and need to see if it feels right. Me and Sinful weren't exactly on good terms when I left."

"Well, the people who made it intolerable are long gone," Ida Belle said. "Except Celia, of course, but every town has a Celia."

Gertie put down her fork and waved at the server for some to-go boxes.

"If I eat one more bite, I won't fit in my front door," she said.

"Then let's wrap this up," Ida Belle said. "We still have two hundred more bottles to get packaged before next weekend."

Dixon laughed. "You guys are still selling that whole cough syrup story?"

"What do you think caused all the problems today?" I asked and gave him a rundown on the morning's activities while we settled up our bill and packed Gertie's containers.

"I have to admit there are some things I've missed about this place," he said, chuckling as we rose.

We followed Gertie out the door, and when she turned onto the sidewalk—her food containers blocking her view—

she almost collided with a woman. We all drew up short behind her and I heard the intake of breath behind me.

"Athena," Gertie whispered.

———

As I stared at the woman who had killed her husband, all I could think was, *Holy crap, this might be one of the most interesting Sundays I've had in Sinful.* Then I wondered why a murderer was about to stroll into Francine's Café. I mean, it wouldn't be the first time, but it might be the most obvious one.

Midtwenties. Five foot six. A hundred fifteen pounds. Blonde, beautiful, and angelic-looking. Withholding final assessment until I knew how she'd killed her husband. Threat level undetermined.

Apparently, I wasn't the only one stunned because we all stood there staring, no one saying a word after Gertie's whisper. Finally, Athena forced a small smile.

"Good morning, ladies," she said.

I felt someone move behind me and inch out the door, and her eyes widened.

"Dixon?" she said.

"I'll walk home," he said. "I need the air."

Before any of us could respond, he headed off down the street without even a backward glance. The tension was thicker than the mud at the bottom of the bayou.

Athena watched Dixon walk away, her eyes sad, before turning to face us. "I'm so glad I found you here. Since it was Sunday, I hoped you'd be observing old traditions."

"You wanted to find us?" Gertie asked. "Why?"

She looked at me and stuck out her hand. "You're Fortune, right? I'm Athena Durand, and I want to hire you."

My mind raced. A murderer wanted to hire me? I wasn't exactly in that line of work anymore.

"For what?" I asked.

"To find the person who killed my husband," she said.

"Pardon me for saying so, but I thought I was looking at her."

Her mouth opened just a bit and she stared, then she let out a single laugh. "Thank God. You're as direct as the rumors said. It's refreshing to have people say what they're actually thinking, especially when you've been through what I have."

"Are you saying you *didn't* kill your husband?" I asked.

"That's exactly what I'm saying."

"Then why not go to the police?"

She shook her head. "They didn't believe me then, and they won't believe me now."

"If they don't believe you, then how are you walking around in Sinful?" Ida Belle asked.

"My attorney got me out on a technicality, but that doesn't get me a pass in the court of public opinion."

"I can't believe we didn't hear about this," Ida Belle said. "When did it happen?"

Athena shrugged. "A few days ago. They just did the sign-here thing, handed me a bag with my personal items, and rushed me out the door. I was relieved that reporters weren't waiting outside. But it's all bound to come out soon, and unless the real killer is caught, I'll have to live with this hanging over my head."

"And you think I can figure out who killed your husband when the police couldn't?"

"You're not owned or influenced by the Rousseaus. That makes you one of the few in this state that might be capable of objectivity."

"Carter LeBlanc is the sheriff now," I said. "His middle name is objective when it comes to his job."

"Carter's a good man, but he's still beholden to the rules and the whims of the DA and has no jurisdiction besides. You're not beholden to anyone and the consensus is that you're not afraid to think and act outside the box to get results. I need results. I can pay you—I'm not asking for a favor here."

I looked over at Ida Belle to get her read on the situation, because Gertie would investigate stink in a fish-cleaning shed. But if Ida Belle thought this was something best left alone, she wouldn't hesitate to let me know. She was studying Athena, frowning, then she glanced over at me and raised one eyebrow. That sealed it. If she'd given me the headshake, I would have politely sent Athena on her way, but clearly, there was enough amiss about her situation that Ida Belle found merit into looking into it.

"I think we need to have a much longer conversation than should be had here on the sidewalk," I told her. "Can you come back to my house so that we can talk in private?"

"Well, not completely private," Gertie said. "We're her assistants."

Athena smiled. "I'd heard that as well, and of course, I'm happy to tell you whatever you need to know. So you'll consider it?"

"Let me get the facts," I said. "If I think there's something I can help with, then we'll talk about the investigation. If there's not, then I'll have to opt out."

"Fair enough," she said. "Where do you live?"

"Marge's old house," Gertie said.

Athena nodded. "I'm going to grab a coffee and muffin to go, then I'll meet you there."

As she walked away, Gertie bounced up and down, causing

the containers to slide. Ida Belle and I clutched at the stack, steadying it before the birds got the benefit of all of Gertie's leftovers.

"We have a case!" Gertie exclaimed, unable to control her excitement.

"We *might* have a case," I said. "I want to hear what she has to say."

"And then we'll take the case?" Gertie asked, sounding like a five-year-old begging for ice cream.

"We'll see," I said, sounding like the parent of the five-year-old.

But I had to admit, I was already intrigued.

———

WE HEADED FOR IDA BELLE'S SUV AND SET OFF FOR MY house. Gertie elected to bypass dropping all the food off at her own place in favor of taking it to mine—in case we needed a snack later. I knew good and well she was hoping to spot Godzilla in the bayou behind my house. No matter how often we got onto her, no one had been able to curb her habit of feeding the gator, who'd formed an unhealthy attachment to humans' food.

And the occasional human. But only the bad guys.

Athena showed up about ten minutes later, and when we were all seated in the kitchen, I opened my laptop.

"Why don't you tell me a little about yourself first," I said. "Maybe start with a summary of your life here and how you met Beckett."

She looked momentarily taken aback. "Why do you want to know about me?"

"Because if I don't know who you are, I can't make a decision on your innocence or guilt. I don't take jobs without questioning the merits of them. Not anymore."

"I thought you were former CIA."

"Which is exactly why I question everything."

Her eyes widened. "Oh. Well, there's nothing interesting to tell, really. I was born in New Orleans and I'm an only child. My father was an investment banker—from Toronto originally—who was extremely successful until he wasn't. My mother was a NOLA socialite with family money, but my father managed to run through it, and his clients' money as well, and got himself ten years for fraud."

"Is he still inside?"

"No. Got out early for good behavior. Stupid, right? Not like he could steal retirement accounts from prisoners, so of course his behavior was good."

"Where is he now?"

She shrugged. "No one knows. People assume he headed back to Canada."

"He never tried to contact you after he got out?"

"No. But then, we were never close."

"How old were you when he went to prison?"

"A very angry seventeen."

"Tough time for your family to fall apart."

She nodded. "The house was taken along with everything else that wasn't leveraged to the hilt. My mother was never a strong woman, so she took to pills and her bed. She moved in with her parents, who were ancient by that time as she'd been a surprise baby after years of her mother not being able to conceive."

"You didn't go with her?"

"I wasn't welcome there. My grandparents never approved of my father, and therefore never approved of me. They foisted me off on a distant cousin in Sinful. She was old and broke and wanted the money that I came with."

I stared. "But you were their only grandchild."

She shrugged as a flash of anger crossed her face. "They never saw my mother when they looked at me. Only my father."

"But surely your mother wanted you with her."

"My mother never wanted kids. I didn't understand that when I was young but as I got older, things started to make sense. She was required to produce an heir, you see. That was why my father married her—someone with a family name and contacts that could help grow his business. But social climbers want a son, and my grandfather wanted a grandson since his only child was a girl. My mother had trouble with my birth and couldn't have any more children. The day the doctor told her that was probably the happiest and most relieved she'd ever felt."

I took a couple seconds to absorb all of that. I could certainly relate to the uninterested parent thing. My father had faked his death to get away, albeit that was for the mission and not because of me. But it didn't stop the thought from crossing my mind. I couldn't help feeling sorry for Athena, who knew absolutely that both her parents and grandparents resented her in some way.

"Are your mother or grandparents still alive?" I asked.

She flashed a look at Ida Belle and Gertie. "You never heard?"

They both shook their heads.

"I figured the cousin would have talked eventually, but then, there was probably a gossip clause in the will. There was in her agreement to keep me. To get my paltry share, they told me I'd have to sign a nondisclosure concerning any family business, past or present. I told the attorney to get lit. I had no intention now or then of keeping quiet about the things my family did. They left the bulk of their estate to charity anyway."

I shook my head, trying to absorb that level of callousness. "What happened to them?"

"My mother killed them all. Best anyone can guess, she spiked their drinks with sedatives, then turned on the gas and started a fire. The whole house went up in flames, but they were all found in their beds and didn't appear to have tried to move. That's why the police suspected drugs."

"Were they able to run tests?"

She nodded. "There was enough left to test on my mother because a wardrobe fell over her when the wall came down. Positive for sleeping pills—one of the many drugs prescribed for her. No sign of forced entry, I mean, other than the firemen breaking down the front door."

"But why did they assume it was your mother who'd done it?" I asked.

"She told her therapist she wanted to die and insisted she was just waiting for my grandparents to bring me back home and then we'd all leave this horrible life. The therapist had to tell my grandparents and they told the cousin, who told me."

"And you think it was true?"

"At the time, I figured it was just another excuse to leave me in Sinful, but by then I didn't care. I was better off here anyway. But then after the fire, I talked to the therapist and realized she'd insisted they pass on the information as a warning. You know, in case my mother got out of their sight and managed to find me."

"I have to ask..." I said. "Was your father still in prison at that time?"

"Yes. And trust me, he had no one who would have done him that kind of favor or the money to pay someone to do it."

"And none of this was ever in the papers?" Ida Belle asked.

"My grandfather was a big donor to the police and firemen," Athena said. "I think it was their way of protecting his granddaughter from a future of side-eyes and whispers. Besides, what good would it have done for the rest of it to come out? They were all dead, and no one really knew for certain what happened. It was all just theories."

Gertie patted her arm. "No use causing more pain when there was nothing to be done about it."

"I didn't think of it like that at the time," Athena said. "I wanted her to pay, you see, even in death. Not for the fire so much as for tossing me aside like a nuisance and always only caring about herself. But then the cousin cautioned me that if people suspected what my mother had done, they might think of me like her. A hereditary thing, you know?"

"But you've never had any issues in that regard?" I asked. "I'm sorry, but I have to ask."

"I'd be asking too before I took on myself as a client. I've had bouts of depression, but I never needed prescription meds. Counseling, meditation, and yoga really helped. I'll admit to a lot of unresolved anger, but I don't think you can blame me given that I just spent a year locked up for a murder I didn't commit."

"I'd be angry," I agreed. "Did the Sinful cousin move away?"

"Yes. The fire happened right before I graduated from high school. I'd just turned eighteen and didn't require a guardian anymore. And with my grandparents dead, the monthly checks were replaced with a fat payoff. She sold her house before the bodies were cold and lit out of here the same day, telling me I had a week to pack my things and get out. I never heard from her again."

"Good Lord," I said. "What did you do?"

"Talked to my teachers and tested out early. Got my

diploma and headed to New Orleans to find a job and a place to live. It was hard but I managed, even though I regretted not taking the money from that lawyer a couple times. But I met a couple girls I hit it off with at the hotel where I worked, and we got an apartment together."

"Do you know if the cousin is still alive?"

"She's dead. Passed away at a senior home in Florida. An attorney tracked me down in prison. She hadn't left a will, and as her next of kin, I inherited. Wasn't anything left but some clothes and personal items that I told the home to throw away or donate, and a couple thousand dollars in a bank account."

"Tell me about your husband," I said. "When and how did you meet him?"

"About two and a half years ago, his family hosted a party at Château Cassard, the hotel where I worked. It's one of the historic boutique hotels in the French Quarter that books a lot of ritzy private events. His family was having a fancy dinner and auctioning off some items for their charity of the month. I was usually scheduled to work the high-end events because I knew how to handle rich people...upbringing, you know?"

I nodded. Being raised in a wealthy, known family meant Athena knew all the social graces required to move silently and appropriately among the guests.

"Anyway, I stepped out back on break—I used to smoke. Awful habit and so expensive, but it helped with stress. He came outside and bummed a cigarette from me, saying how he'd stopped but those kind of events got on his nerves. We chatted for a bit, and I felt a connection right away."

She looked down and sniffed, then wiped tears from the corner of her eyes as she looked back up.

"He was a really nice guy—not at all like his family or the other rich guys I'd met at the hotel. They'd hit on me and offer to throw money or jewelry at me, but they didn't see me as a person. He talked to me like I was someone, not just a pretty girl holding a tray of champagne glasses. I watched him leave that night and thought myself an idiot for not giving him my number. But then he came back to the hotel two days later and asked me out."

"You must have made quite the impression," Gertie said.

"I guess so," she said. "It was a whirlwind romance. We dated for six months, then he asked me to marry him on New Year's Eve. He knew his family would want a big production but neither of us wanted that—especially since I had no family to attend. And we were afraid the press would drag up my dad's conviction."

"But surely that was going to happen regardless, given the family you were marrying into," I said.

"Yes. But we were hoping that a quick wedding in another country would eliminate months of articles and speculation. That they'd get it all out at once and then some other scandal would pop up and we'd be old news. So we eloped to the Bahamas and issued a press release when we returned."

"And did everything work according to plan?"

"Pretty much. They all dredged up my father's dirty laundry, but since I had nothing to do with it, the court of public opinion couldn't really come down on me. And the fire had been deemed a tragic accident and I didn't live there besides."

I nodded. "So let's move on to your husband's death, and I'm going to warn you now that I will have a lot of questions because I hadn't heard of this crime until this morning. So I'm starting at ground zero."

"Okay."

"Let's start with how your husband was killed."

"That's the problem—no one agrees on that."

CHAPTER FOUR

I STARED AT ATHENA, CONFUSED AT HER STATEMENT.

"What do you mean?" I asked. "The determination had to be foul play, or the DA wouldn't have even pursued it."

She nodded. "The questionable issue was the blow to the back of his head. He was on a boat, you see, so it could have happened multiple ways. The coroner said homicide with the blow caused by persons unknown. But my attorney pushed for a separate review, which came back indeterminate because the head injury could have been caused by falling and striking his head on any number of objects on the side or back of the boat."

"Were you on the boat with him?"

"No one was. When Beckett was tired of playing the role for his parents, he'd take his father's boat out into the Gulf. Sometimes he'd stay for days."

"Days? On a boat?"

She shrugged. "I guess I should have called it a yacht, but it sounds so pompous. It had a full kitchen and living room, two bedrooms, and a full bath. It even had a hot tub on the front. It was as nice as our penthouse."

"I see. So how did you realize something was wrong?"

"He wouldn't return my calls. It was normal for him to ignore them for a while—he usually did some heavy drinking once he anchored—but when I hadn't heard from him by the following afternoon, I called his father. They hadn't heard anything, either, but were able to track the boat with GPS. It hadn't changed positions since the day before when he'd first anchored. His father has friends everywhere, so the coast guard went out to check, but the boat was empty."

I stared. "But I thought the coroner examined his body."

She shook her head and grimaced. "He examined parts. The back of the skull, some of the torso, and part of a leg. He must have been casting for bait when it happened because they were caught in a net tied to the side of the boat. But the rest, well, they assumed ocean predators..."

Gertie covered her mouth with her hand. "Oh my God. None of that was ever public."

"His family managed to keep it quiet," Athena said. "Quentin was coming up for reelection, and it was horribly gruesome, even just the description. I didn't see him...I mean..."

"Of course not," Gertie said and reached over to squeeze her hand.

"Anyway, as you guys know, the trial was closed," she said. "It would have been a circus otherwise, and my attorney told me that more gag orders were issued for my case than in the previous twelve months total. The DA gave the media a roundup of the key points at the end of every day, but they managed to keep some of the worst details out. Like the condition of the body."

"I assume they matched him by DNA?" I asked.

She nodded.

"Where were you when it happened?" I asked. "Or could they even establish a time of death?"

"Not really," she said. "They just left it as sometime after he left the dock at midmorning the day before and up to possibly a few hours before he was found. Apparently, it doesn't take long for...things to happen."

"So roughly a thirty-hour window to alibi."

She nodded. "I had a charity event the day he left, so I was out of the house before he even crawled out of bed. I set up for the event that morning, then hair, nails, and dress. The event ran until almost midnight. Then I was at home alone from then until the next afternoon when I went to his parents' house to wait and hear from the coast guard."

"Are there security cameras in your building?"

"Yes. And there's a doorman 24/7. We had to use cards for our doors, the elevator, and the parking garage. Unless I was Spider-Woman, I wasn't getting out of that building without a person or technology knowing about it."

"Then I don't understand how you could have committed a murder. And that's assuming you even had access to a boat, knew how to use it, no one saw you, and a host of other things that had to fall perfectly in line."

"They said I paid someone to do it. There was twenty thousand dollars wired out of our checking account the week before. I swear, I didn't do it or know anything about it. Beckett handled the money. I had credit cards to use."

"Surely someone had to go to the bank and wire the money."

"No. Beckett was a manager at his father's investment firm, but he wanted to break out on his own. He moved money around a lot, buying this and selling that to come up with the capital—stocks, gold, real estate. He could wire direct from the account, even from his phone."

"But the money had to go somewhere."

"It went to a bank account in the Bahamas that was emptied and closed the same day. And all while a known hit man just happened to be vacationing there. The FBI had been watching him, but he gave them the slip a couple days later and they didn't catch up to him again until after Beckett's death. But they claimed they had an eyewitness who placed him in New Orleans when Beckett was killed."

"Did anyone have access to the checking account besides you and Beckett?"

"No."

I shook my head. "This is all very circumstantial. I assume the DA claimed your motive was money."

"Yes, but the truth is, there wasn't really much in it for me. Beckett wasn't a great investor like his father—they were always fighting about it. Beckett handled our own finances, for what it was worth, but he lost more often than he gained. That twenty thousand was over half of every penny we had."

"What about life insurance?"

"He had a life insurance policy worth two million, but with bonus, his salary was close to eight hundred thousand a year. And since he wasn't due to inherit until his father's death, to put it in a very crass manner, the longer Beckett remained alive, the more he was worth to me."

"People have killed for *far* less than two million," I said.

She nodded. "I once saw a man stabbed on the sidewalk outside of that first apartment for the five dollars he had. But the guy who stabbed him wasn't in love with the man. I loved Beckett and more importantly, he was my best friend. No amount of money could ever replace that."

She swiped at the tears running down her face and shook her head, her expression shifting from sad to angry. "I don't know who killed him—or if he was even killed—and I don't know what happened to that money. But I know one thing for certain; I did not kill my husband. And more than anything, I want to know the truth of what happened because whether it was murder or just a horrible accident, it clears my name."

"What if I can't find concrete evidence?" I asked. "It's been almost a year. The crime scene is long gone, and the FBI has far more resources to track that money than I do. I'm not sure what you expect me to find."

"I want you to create another narrative. One that doesn't cast me as the bad guy. Beckett's father is a politician, and politicians always have enemies. The family business is finance. My father showed me how easy it is to create enemies when you're responsible for other people's money. There have to be people who benefited from Beckett's death. I just wasn't one of them."

"Even if I find other suspects, without evidence, the DA won't move forward, especially since his case with you fell apart. He won't stick his neck out again unless it's a sure thing."

"But the police will reopen the investigation, right? Even if they don't try very hard, I can still make that fact known. I know some will always believe I did it, and I'll live with that. But if I ever want to have a decent job, friends, or God forbid, fall in love again, I can't have this cloud of doubt hanging over me. And I can't spend the rest of my life not knowing something."

I looked over at Gertie and Ida Belle to get their stance on the matter, but their expressions clearly said do it. I had to admit, my curiosity was piqued. I loved a challenge and this definitely fit the bill.

"Okay," I said and told her my hourly rate. "If you'd like, I can get started with a retainer of two thousand. That buys you a few days of work. If I don't find anything, then we can call it quits. I'm not in this to drain people's bank accounts when I can't offer anything in return."

"That's fair," she said and pulled a stack of bills out of her purse. She counted out two thousand and pushed it across the table to me.

"I'll go get a contract and a receipt for this," I said.

"Athena Durand on that contract please," she said. "I changed my name back while I was in prison. I didn't want the name without Beckett, and the Rousseaus don't want me to have it."

I returned with the paperwork and she signed.

"I'll get you a copy of this," I said. "Are you staying at your penthouse in New Orleans?"

She let out a single laugh. "No. The penthouse and most everything in it was owned by Beckett's father. Like I said, Beckett didn't have the skill set his father did. He lost a lot trying to hit the big one."

"Where are you staying?" I asked.

"I checked into a hotel in NOLA when I got out. That's when I overheard a conversation about you in a bar and did some poking around and decided you were just the person who had the backbone to take this on. Since you've agreed to look into things, I'll probably get a weekly rate at the motel up the highway, so I can be closer. If you don't turn up enough to keep going, then I guess I'll have to rethink everything. I don't have the capital to just lounge around hotels all day."

"What about the insurance money?" Ida Belle asked.

She shook her head. "They refused payout because I was convicted. My attorney is working on that now, but the insurance company's new angle to hold things up is the suggestion that Beckett committed suicide."

"Do you think that's a possibility?" I asked.

"No way. Beckett was frustrated but he wasn't depressed."

"So how are you managing things now?" I asked, wondering about the stack of cash she'd just given me.

"My car was in my name only. It was new and actually paid for, so my attorney sold it for me. And since the judge wouldn't give me bail, I went straight from jail to prison, so he also collected all my personal property from the penthouse. I went through pictures of it and pointed out the designer items that could easily be sold on consignment sites. And I had a few pieces of nice jewelry, including my wedding ring, and he sold those for me as well. Anyway, it was enough to cover his bill and that old car in your driveway, and to pay my way until I can figure out what I want to do."

"That sucks," Gertie said. "But you can do it."

She sighed. "It's hard to imagine starting over again. I feel like I've already done it more times than a person is supposed to."

I nodded. I'd had several do-overs myself and understood how unsettling it was.

"Here's my card with my cell number. Text me when you get a room, so I'll have your number and know where to find you."

We all rose and she extended her hand. "Thank you for taking this on. And I know you're far more qualified than the average PI, but I would feel guilty if I didn't warn you to be careful. Beckett's family doesn't play nice, and his father has a lot of power."

"Don't worry about me," I said. "Politicians don't have anything on arms dealers."

———

THE DOOR HAD BARELY CLOSED BEHIND ATHENA WHEN IDA Belle and Gertie both started talking. I whistled because my talents didn't include listening to two conversations at once, but I could tell they were all amped up.

"I take it you two are excited about the new case," I said.

They nodded.

"You both realize this stinks to high heaven, and she didn't even give us the whole story, right?"

"Who does?" Ida Belle asked.

"True," I agreed. "But that means I'm counting on you for the local gossip, so let's start with Athena. What do you know that she decided to leave out?"

"Not much, except for what we told you over breakfast about her and Dixon," Ida Belle said. "But that isn't related to the case, so no harm no foul."

"But she definitely hedged on her own pursuit of money," Gertie said. "And her history with Dixon would have exposed that, especially when combined with the fact that Beckett was engaged to someone else when they met. Which she didn't mention."

"That's hardly odd if you're trying to play down your pursuit of someone else's fiancé," Ida Belle said. "Assuming Athena's childhood story is true, she comes across as a sympathetic party."

Gertie nodded. "The poor girl from unfortunate circumstances who's bullied by the rich family who considered her unsuitable. It's the plot device for a million stories, all with Athena cast in the heroine role."

"Unless you know about the gold-digging angle," I said.

"Exactly," Ida Belle said. "What was your take on her story? Was she telling the truth about her parents and grandparents?"

"I think so," I said. "I mean, it was all lumped together and we only got the highlights, but I have no reason to believe she made it up."

"It wouldn't be the first time a woman married a man her

parents didn't approve of and turned out to be right about," Gertie said. "Or the last time a woman had a child she didn't want."

"So her childhood probably wasn't a Hallmark movie," Ida Belle said. "But there's no doubt she was looking to improve her life with someone else's pockets. I'm not saying she didn't love Beckett—at least, it seems she might have—but I can see where the family might have different thoughts on the matter."

I nodded. "But like she said, she benefited more if he was alive. Her max gain was two million. Nothing to sniff at, certainly, but if he made eight hundred thousand in a year..."

"Not to mention he'd have had far more coming in if he'd made it up the ranks in politics like his father," Ida Belle said. "At her age, two million is only a lot of money if you know how to have it make more."

"With her desired standard of living, I don't imagine it would have lasted long," Gertie said. "But she was guaranteed the cushy life being married to Beckett."

"All true," Ida Belle agreed. "But it hinges on one thing—whether or not she was truly happy with him. Plenty of relationships look good in the paper or on social media, but what goes on behind closed doors is an entirely different story. She might have viewed the insurance money as enough to tide her over until she found the next mark, because with Quentin holding the purse strings and Beckett making bad investments, it doesn't sound like there would have been much for her to get in a divorce."

"And with her looks, it's not like she'd have trouble hooking the next rich guy," Gertie said.

I nodded. "So we all agree that the place to start is with background information on Beckett and Athena."

"Definitely," Ida Belle said. "I know we can't cover someone's entire life in one meeting, but I'm certain Athena is leaving stuff out. And my guess is given a thousand meetings, she still wouldn't admit to anything that makes her look bad. She's clearly casting political rivals and his family as the bad guys."

"Then we'll start with her," I said. "Because if we turn up enough sketchy stuff, then I can call the whole thing off before we get started."

"As much as I hate to say it, we should start with Dixon," Ida Belle said. "If anyone here knew Athena's secrets, it would have been him."

————

WE HAD JUST FINISHED CLEARING UP THE KITCHEN AND WERE about to head out to accost Dixon when my phone rang. Carter. I hesitated for a moment because it was hours before he got off, which meant he wouldn't be planning dinner yet. So whatever had him ringing me now was probably something I didn't want to hear.

Gertie leaned over and looked at the display on my phone.

"God hates a coward," she said.

I sighed and answered the phone, wondering how my resolve had gotten reduced to childish threats by a two-hundred-year-old woman.

"Did something happen to Celia in jail?" I asked hopefully.

"I wish. She's alternated between yelling and sobbing from the moment I brought her in. Deputy Breaux has given me his notice twice already. I just keep refusing to take it."

"Why don't you turn her loose? You can't charge her without coming down on everyone else in town over this sort of nonsense. And you don't have room to house all those nonsense providers."

"It just so happens, I'm calling you about a huge nonsense problem that I'm hoping to get some help with. Is Ida Belle with you? I tried calling her, but she didn't answer."

"We were having a meeting," I said. "Let me turn you on speaker."

"Is anything wrong with Walter?" Ida Belle asked.

"There's a situation down at the store," Carter said.

"The store's not open today," Ida Belle said. "He's doing inventory."

"Yes, well, Sheriff Lee decided he needed to be open and rode his horse in through the back door."

"Sweet Jesus!" Ida Belle said. "I thought he was still at that rehab facility."

"Apparently, he thought it best to check himself out this morning. Something about the toilet paper being cheap."

"Sounds reasonable," Gertie said, and Ida Belle and I nodded.

"So he thought once he'd gotten a softer wipe in, it would be a good idea to ride his horse into town?" I asked.

"Appears so," Carter said. "And he's refusing to leave until Walter sells him some cigars that he doesn't even carry and never has. Walter and I have tried everything we can think of, but he's not budging."

"Why not just lead the horse out of there?" I asked.

"That horse doesn't listen to anyone but Sheriff Lee," Carter said. "I've tried to get him going, but he's dug his hooves in. And I'm afraid to scare him into motion because the horse is even older than Lee. If that horse or Lee drops dead in the store, Walter will have an even bigger problem on his hands. Less if it's Lee, but still."

"Well, what the heck do you expect me to do about it?" Ida Belle asked.

"We thought maybe you could convince Lee to get off the horse and back into bed where he belongs."

"You need a better plan," Ida Belle said. "You do realize that I've been unable to curb Gertie's behavior for the past hundred years, right?"

"Yeah, well, Lee's not as stubborn."

Gertie glared at the phone, hands on her hips. "I am *not* stubborn!"

"It's Sunday," I reminded her, as Gertie had a strict personal policy concerning lying on Sunday.

"Oh yeah," she said. "I am not more stubborn than Sheriff Lee. Only Celia can wear that crown."

"We all have our limitations," Carter said. "But Walter and I would appreciate it if you tried. Sheriff Lee has always had more respect for Ida Belle than most people around here."

"Fine," Ida Belle said. "I'll see what I can do, but I think I'll be wasting my breath."

I shoved my phone in my pocket and we headed out, Ida Belle grumbling all the way.

"What the heck is that old coot thinking?" she asked as we climbed in her SUV.

"Doesn't sound like his thinker's running correctly given that he wants Walter to sell him something he's never carried," Gertie said. "His mind is probably messed up from the heart attack."

"His mind's been questionable since Jesus was teaching man to fish," Ida Belle said. "Too bad Walter didn't take Rambo with him. Lee wouldn't have gotten that horse in the door."

"Why didn't he?"

"Can't keep an eye on him and work, and if he's in the crate and you're within hearing distance, he won't shut up. Last time Rambo was there during inventory, he got into a shipment of cereal. Chewed the corner off twenty-two boxes before he was spotted. And you don't even want to know about clean-up...it went on for days. All that sugar and puppies do not mix well."

I could hear yelling inside the General Store as soon as we climbed out of Ida Belle's SUV. Given that the door was closed and the windows were thick, I wondered how Sheriff Lee was managing the energy to project so well. Carter must have been checking for us because he had the door open motioning us inside as soon as our feet hit the pavement.

"Hurry! He's got Walter cornered," Carter said.

"Why haven't you done anything?" Ida Belle asked.

"Walter has no cover, and shooting Lee probably wouldn't look good on my annual review."

"I'm not leaving here without my bounty!" Sheriff Lee's voice boomed through the store. "I know you pirates took it and if you don't return it, I'll lay a curse on you."

"Pirates?" I asked.

"He was watching *Pirates of the Caribbean* when I visited him the other day," Gertie said.

Ida Belle shook her head. "If his mind is crossing things up with the television, you best get to his house and clear out his stash of war movies."

Carter paled just a tiny bit before dashing out the door.

"What about streaming?" I asked.

"Lee's so old he would think 'streaming' had something to do with fishing or peeing," Gertie said.

We headed into the storeroom, wondering what we were about to encounter. And it was a doozy. Sheriff Lee was still on the horse, but his ancient steed had decided it was past time for a nap and was now leaning against a stack of pallets that looked like canned goods. Thank God it was something heavy enough to support a horse, even though he was as much skin and bones as Sheriff Lee at this point. Lee's leg was pinned between the horse and the pallets and since he wasn't yelling about it, I figured it had either gone to sleep or his circulation was so poor he didn't even realize it.

But the more urgent matter involved a lasso and a sword.

"Looks like he's been watching Westerns as well," Gertie whispered.

Walter was indeed trapped in the far corner of the stockroom, just in front of Lee, his arms secured with a rope tied off to the sleeping horse's saddle. Sheriff Lee brandished a sword above him, wearing a uniform that looked as if it came from the Civil War.

I pulled out my cell phone and sent Carter a text.

Get Tombstone *too.*

CHAPTER FIVE

I SLIPPED MY PHONE BACK INTO MY POCKET AND ASSESSED the situation. The lasso had eliminated my original plan, which was to get the horse out of the storeroom. I'd seen that horse spooked before. and despite being older than Lee, he could work up a decent run. If he did, Walter would be dragged along in whatever world the horse and Lee were opting for at the time. And given the proximity, even if Walter could shrug off the lasso, he couldn't make a dash for it without running underneath the sword. Even in his confused state, I didn't think Lee would intentionally hurt Walter, but I wasn't sure how long his arm could hold the sword up, either.

Walter looked over at us, his expression a mixture of aggravation and a hint of fear. I couldn't blame him. It was tenuous at best if we wanted the three of them to come out unscathed.

"Sheriff Lee?" Ida Belle called out as she approached the man and horse.

Lee looked over and frowned. "I don't know this Sheriff Lee. I am Blackbeard, most fearsome of all pirates."

"I'm pretty sure Blackbeard would be younger," Gertie whispered. "If he weren't dead."

"I'm going to go grab some carrots from the store," I whispered. "If we can wake up that horse without startling him, I can use them to get him out of the store. Preferably without a stampede."

"Good idea," Gertie said. "I think I have some smelling salts in my bag."

I didn't even bother to ask why she would be carrying smelling salts. I already had too much firsthand knowledge of some of the things she and her boyfriend, Jeb, got up to. And this smelling salt situation sounded suspiciously related to activities that Ida Belle forbade conversation about.

I grabbed a couple of carrots with the largest leaves on them, figuring if the carrot didn't entice the horse, maybe the greenery would, and hurried back into the storeroom. Gertie had moved into position to the side of the horse, where she couldn't be kicked but Sheriff Lee couldn't twist enough to see her, either. She had a bag in one hand and gave me a thumbs-up with the other.

Unfortunately, things were starting to get heated between Ida Belle and Sheriff Lee. Despite being friends with Gertie her entire life, Ida Belle had never developed what most people would call a good deal of patience. I thought she had plenty, but Carter said that was only because she had twice as much as me and I wasn't interested in getting any more.

"Get that horse out of this store, you old coot," Ida Belle said. "You'll be lucky if Walter sells you a gallon of milk after this. If the health department happened to come by here, he'd have to throw everything away. You've got that animal in here with food."

"I will not be ordered about by a wench," Sheriff Lee said. "Get back to work cleaning floors, or I'll make you walk the plank."

As soon as the word *wench* left his mouth, I clenched. It didn't take long.

Ida Belle yanked her pistol from her waistband and fired at the sword, making a direct hit in the middle of the blade. The sword flew out of Lee's hand and into the wall, where it stuck in the drywall. Lee was either too stunned or too befuddled to react immediately, but it didn't matter—the horse was on the job.

The old stallion bolted upright and backward, and Lee came alive and grabbed the reins. He attempted to stand in the stirrups to get more leverage, but the leg that had been trapped between the horse and the pallets was completely numb and not even in the stirrups. His aggressive move sent him falling over the side of the horse and crashing into a pallet of honey.

I rushed forward with the carrots, but it was too late. The horse was officially spooked and determined to get out of the building at any cost. He whirled around with more speed than I would have guessed he could muster, then bolted for the open back door.

And that's when I realized the rope around Walter was still tied to the saddle.

Walter's eyes widened as he twisted, trying to work the ropes loose. Ida Belle pulled out her knife and ran for the rope, and I prayed she'd make it in time.

"I got this!" Gertie shouted.

"No!"

All three of us yelled at once, but it was too late. Ida Belle's knife sliced through the rope, saving Walter from being dragged by the escaping animal. But Gertie had already made her action hero move.

She'd climbed to the top of a stack of empty pallets and as the horse ran by, she leaped onto the saddle. Unfortunately, the saddle had either loosened up with all the activity or had never been secured well in the first place. It twisted around, dropping below the speeding horse, Gertie still attached, as the horse exited the building.

Carter had apparently decided hay would be a good way to get the horse moving, but the fleeing beast hit him like an NFL linebacker and sent him sailing into the bushes in a flurry of hay. Ida Belle, Walter, and I rushed out after the horse. I gave Carter a glance as I passed but as he was thrashing about in the bush, I figured he was fine.

"If she lets go, she'll be trampled," Ida Belle said as we ran.

The horse, beyond panicked because of the saddle and Gertie dangling beneath him, ran straight down the pier and off into the bayou.

"She'll drown!" Walter yelled.

I turned up the speed, thinking if that horse started swimming, she was more likely to be killed by him flopping about before the water got her. Either way, every second counted. I raced to the end of the pier and jumped, pulling out my knife before I even surfaced, ready to cut the saddle off the horse.

As soon as my head broke the water, I heard Gertie laughing. I looked over and found her standing in the bayou at the end of the pier, the confused horse standing politely beside her, drinking muddy water. Walter and Ida Belle ran up to the bank, took one look at the situation, and joined in with the laughter.

I glared at all of them—including the horse—and stalked up the bank and back to the store. Carter, who'd run up with Ida Belle and Walter, followed, me dripping water and him dripping hay and leaves.

"Sheriff Lee fell into a case of honey when the horse took off," I said as we walked.

"That's Walter's problem," he said. "Guess he'll learn not to leave the back door unlocked. Thanks for your help. Sorry you took a dip."

"At least I fell in dirty water. That washes off. You'll be walking around itching from that bush for a week."

He sighed. "This used to be such a quiet town."

"How? Except for the time when Gertie was in Vietnam, how was it quiet?"

"I think when they were younger, they weren't as much trouble. Look at Lee. He's lost the plot."

"I think you need a word with his doctor. He's going to get himself or someone else killed. Did you get his DVDs?"

"Deputy Breaux was clearing them out when I went to grab the hay. Good call on the Western thing. He had a complete John Wayne collection. Breaux's rounding up his guns and any more swords he can find as well. We'll keep them locked up at the sheriff's department until we know it's safe."

"He'll be down there yelling every day. He'll become a bigger nuisance than Celia."

He put his arms up. "What can I do?"

"Give me a ride home? I should drip in Ida Belle's SUV just to pay her back for laughing, but I don't feel like waiting. Or listening to her laugh and Gertie exclaim over how awesome this all was."

He nodded and we headed for his truck.

"Oh, and I have a potential new client," I said as Carter drove off. "Figured you should know about it, because if I find enough to decide a full investigation is in order, it's going to raise some eyebrows."

"Who is it?"

"Athena Durand."

Carter's eyes widened. "Athena Durand is out?"

"Met her outside Francine's Café this afternoon. Her case

was overturned. My guess is on the extremely sketchy evidence. Sounds like they railroaded her."

"The Rousseaus are capable of most things and have the money and power to accomplish them. I'm not going to bother telling you not to take the case, but be very, very careful."

"Do you know them?"

"I know *of* them. That's enough."

"What about Athena?"

"She left shortly after I returned to Sinful."

Something about his tone made me take a closer look at him. Then I laughed.

"She hit on you," I said.

"She was still a kid," he said. "And from what my mom told me, had been through rough times. There were a million reasons why that was never going to happen."

I shook my head.

"What? You don't think other women besides you have hit on me?"

I rolled my eyes. "I *never* hit on you. I did everything I could to avoid you."

"You hooked up with Ida Belle and Gertie your first day here. That's the definition of not avoiding me."

"I didn't know that at the time."

He laughed, then grew serious. "Seriously, though. Be careful. The Rousseaus are dirty, and if they feel threatened, they'll find a way to come after you. If they can't get to you directly, they'll go after people you care about."

I frowned. I could protect myself, but if someone came after my friends, that might send me back to my old job mentality.

"I'll just have to be discreet," I said.

"That would be a first."

———

IDA BELLE AND GERTIE WERE ALREADY IN MY KITCHEN when I headed down after my marathon shower. Gertie had her wet hair in curlers and was wearing a bright pink tracksuit with fluffy matching slippers. At least they'd had the fore-thought to put on a pot of coffee and heat up some of Gertie's breakfast. I was starving.

Ida Belle slid a cup of coffee onto the table, and I plopped down in the chair. I hadn't even gotten a sip in when Ronald came bursting through the back door, waving his hands in the air, clearly agitated.

"This will not do," he said. "Not at all."

"What the heck are you in a snit over?" Ida Belle asked.

Ronald stared at us in dismay, then waved at Gertie. "Her hair, of course. You can't just leave your house before you're done cooking."

"I'm pretty sure she's moved past cooking and is well into decaying," Ida Belle said.

"There was an incident," Gertie said. "I had to wash and set my hair again and we've got a new case, so I couldn't wait around for it to set."

Ronald sighed. "Honey, that's why God made wigs. Even *she* has a bad hair day sometimes."

He placed a bag on the table, then narrowed his eyes at Gertie, moving his head from side to side. Finally, he nodded and reached inside the bag. "I think this bob would work wonders for you. It's platinum but the cut is updated and will make you look younger. You should really stop with the whole roller thing. That's so 1950."

"Which would be about the last time anyone cared about her hair but you," Ida Belle said.

Gertie shot her a dirty look, then gave Ronald an excited smile. "Make me younger."

Ida Belle shook her head. "Good. God."

"Let's get those rollers out," he said, and he and Gertie tackled her head, piling the rollers and pins on the table. Then Ronald pulled out a platinum wig cut in a straight bob and plopped it on Gertie's head.

"Okay, let's see what we've got," Ronald said as he got it arranged correctly and all the loose ends of her own hair tucked underneath. He stepped back and gave her a critical stare, then clapped his hands and smiled.

"Perfect!" he declared. "You look at least fifty."

"Fifty times two," Ida Belle said.

I had to admit, it did look nice. I didn't know about it making her look fifty, but she definitely looked younger simply because she was wearing a contemporary style.

"It looks good," I said.

"Really?" Gertie asked. "Do you have a mirror on you?"

I stared. "You're asking *me?*"

Ronald snorted and pulled a mirror out of his bag. "People who are naturally beautiful simply don't understand the importance of mirrors. The rest of us rely on them like air."

He turned the mirror to Gertie and her eyes widened.

"Oh, I like it!" she said. "I wonder if I could grow my hair out like this."

"I doubt it," he said. "Your hair has a slight wave to it and wouldn't hold straight in the humidity here. And it's thinner and finer than the wig hair. But you're welcome to keep this one. I could never pull off the platinum look. A shame, really. It's so glam."

Gertie beamed. "You hear that—I'm glam."

Ronald slid into a chair. "So now that the emergency is over, tell me about this hair-destroying incident."

"Technically, Gertie has been in two today," I said. "And you'll be thrilled to know that the first one ended with Celia being rolled up in a tablecloth and hauled off to jail."

Ronald threw his arms up in the air and cheered. "Oh my God! Spill the deets."

We filled him in on Celia's arrest and the Sheriff Lee event over coffee and Gertie's leftovers, then he sat back and shook his head. "You ladies sure do pack a lot into your Sundays. All I've managed so far is a pedicure. So what's this new case? Anything I can help with?"

"Not unless you have personal knowledge of Athena Durand," I said.

Ronald's eyes widened and he let out a quiet, "Oh."

"Your turn," I said. "Spill."

He sighed. "Most everything about Athena is a drama and not an uplifting one. Can I ask why your new case involves her?"

"She hired me."

He stared at me, clearly shocked. "Athena Durand was *here* —in Sinful?"

"At this very table just hours ago."

"Good Lord, I pride myself on being in the know, and that one completely escaped me."

"I don't think the DA has a habit of making it known when a case is overturned and a prisoner is set free."

Ronald nodded. "Of course not. That makes perfect sense, but what did she hire you for?"

"She insists she did not kill her husband and wants—at minimum—for me to find another viable option."

"She wants vindication with the public. Smart. She'd be unable to remain around here unless everything people think they know about her is brought into question."

I studied him for a moment. "Do you think she did it?"

"Obviously, she couldn't have personally. I followed the case, of course, and the theory of the expert hire is plausible, especially with that sketchy wire transfer."

"But?"

"I never thought she did it."

"Another fool for a pretty face?" Gertie asked.

"I'm certain her looks have swayed men in many ways," he agreed, "but this is more a gut feeling than anything. I knew the Durands, you see."

"You knew the Durands?" This was a perk I hadn't seen coming.

"Mostly from society events in NOLA, of course. I wasn't invited to tea or anything, but I supported several events with the family over the years. If you're an observant person, you can get to know a lot about people, even when they think they're hiding the worst of themselves."

"That's true," I agreed. "And what did you learn about them?"

"I think the Durands were very unhappy people. Clarisse Durand—Athena's mother—was weak and spoiled. Her parents ruled with an iron fist, and she married Gerard shortly after meeting him."

"She wanted to get away from her parents' rule," Ida Belle said.

Ronald nodded. "But I doubt Gerard was any better. In fact, by all appearances, she married her father, except for the financial thievery, of course. I have no doubt that Pierre Bourdeaux, Athena's grandfather, was brutal with his businesses and made his money off the backs of the less fortunate, but he wasn't a blatant criminal like Gerard."

"How bad are we talking?" I asked. "Abuse?"

"My guess is yes although I've never heard anything specifically," Ronald said. "The Bourdeaux are from a different era when such things happened often but were never spoken of, even if you were commoners. But given their elevated social status, even the hint of such things would be hidden away and they would have raised their daughter with the same standards."

"So why not divorce Gerard?" I asked. "This is modern times. She could have gotten a good bit of money before he lost it all."

"Clarisse lacked the aptitude for anything beyond what she was directed to do," Ronald said. "And even if she'd grown a backbone, it would never have been strong enough to go against Pierre. And Pierre would have absolutely forbidden a divorce."

"But I thought Clarisse's parents hated Gerard."

"They did, but they were Catholic, you see."

"And?"

"They were *Catholic*. Wealthy contributors to the church, personal friends with the archbishop. Pierre was actually invited to New York once to meet the pope. The only way Clarisse was going to get out of her marriage was death or prison."

"Which sort of happened," Gertie said. "Gerard went to prison, and Clarisse went running back to her parents."

"I doubt she saw any other choice," Ronald said. "Gerard had rendered them less than broke, and she had no money or skills and lacked the intelligence or fortitude to get either. She was a spoiled princess whose only talent was being at the beck and call of her husband and her father."

"But she didn't take Athena with her," I said.

Ronald nodded. "There was a lot of speculation about that, especially when Athena wound up in Sinful with a distant cousin whom the Bourdeaux hadn't spoken to in decades. Most assumed that Clarisse had gladly abdicated her responsibilities as a parent as it was a role she never took to anyway. A few of the nicer among us thought Clarisse felt Athena had the best chance for a future if she didn't live in the Bourdeaux household."

"What do you think?" I asked.

"At first, I think it might have been both. But after a short time of being back in her parents' home, it was clear that Clarisse wasn't right. There had always been rumors about her maternal grandmother, so it wasn't necessarily surprising, but definitely something the Bourdeaux would have kept quiet."

"But no rumors about Clarisse's mother?"

"No. Lisette was always the perfectly coiffed ice princess, but even if there was truth in the tales, sometimes such things skip generations. Or perhaps Pierre's control over Lisette was so extraordinary that the structure held her in role and prevented that breaking point."

"Well, clearly Clarisse broke. Athena says the police believe her mother drugged them all and intentionally set the house on fire."

Ronald's eyes widened. "Good Lord. The society buzz portrayed it all as a horrible accident, and given Clarisse's claimed health issues, no one thought it anything other than a tragedy. But if they were *all* drugged, then how can the police be sure it wasn't someone else?"

"No sign of forced entry. Nothing missing, that they could ascertain, anyway. And apparently, Clarisse had been talking to her shrink about how she was just waiting for Athena to come home and then they'd all leave this world."

Ronald shook his head. "That's awful. I knew Athena had been through rough times, but I never imagined...and her own mother. I guess Athena should be thankful Clarisse got tired of waiting, but what a horrible thing to be thankful for."

"Did you have any interaction with Athena—in NOLA or here?"

"A very limited amount in both places. She had to make an appearance at NOLA charity events, of course, but she was far too young to be interested in adult affairs. Other than a polite greeting, we never really interacted. When she first moved here, I ran into her downtown. She seemed surprised to see me here. I guess she never realized this was my home as I attended so many events in the city. She didn't say much then either, but she seemed different."

"Different how?"

"Broken? But perhaps that's a bit too dramatic. Defeated, maybe, is a better word. In the city, she'd been the usual sullen teen, forced to play a role for her parents, but underneath the polite facade was this sparkle. She was bored with her lot as the polite rich girl with societal aspirations. I saw her once smoking behind the hotel with the busboys. They were all laughing and making fun of the proper men and women inside. Athena said it was all just window dressing to hide how boring and awful they all were."

"But when you saw her here?"

"She appeared to be attempting to resign herself to the life of the commoner."

"I don't think she ever got there," Ida Belle said. "She went after status and money soon enough."

"And crushed Dixon in the process," Gertie said.

Ronald sighed. "Nothing says heartbreak like finding out your first love is a lie."

Something about his tone made me study him for a minute. As far as I knew, Ronald had never dated, although he talked as good a game as Gertie. I'd assumed that he was an eccentric and preferred to be alone, as he seemed perfectly happy with his life. But perhaps I'd been mistaken. Maybe Ronald had walked in Dixon's shoes and had never really taken them off.

"Does anyone know what happened to the other boy?" Gertie asked. "I heard he left the state."

Ronald gave her a sad smile and patted her hand. "You're a hopeless romantic, Gertie, which I appreciate a great deal, being one myself. You've cast this boy in the role of the hero, who is sent off to war but returns one day to claim his one true love. It's a great movie, but it's not reality."

"You know what happened to him?" I asked.

Ronald nodded. "His parents were particularly odious people. So full of their perceived importance and with their bit of money. As soon as Athena attached herself to their son, they made plans to send him far away for college. But what they didn't know was that the apple didn't fall far from the tree. Prior to Athena, his parents had been insisting he attend university in NOLA, where he could be kept under their eye and thumb."

"So he hooked up with Athena because he knew they'd send him as far away as possible," I said. "It's a crappy thing to do, assuming Athena wasn't in on it, but I have to admire his creativity."

Gertie slumped in her chair. "There goes my great idea for a Hallmark reunion."

"Maybe you should write a book," Ronald suggested. "Or a screenplay. A romantic tragedy. I've got it—you should write an old con movie, like *The Sting II*."

Gertie brightened up. "I could write a screenplay and then insist on a role in the movie when it's made."

"You jump right on that," Ida Belle said. "I'm sure there are no scripts in Hollywood for sale, or a line of aged-out women looking for work."

"You're a real party pooper," Gertie said.

"I'm a realist," Ida Belle said.

Ronald laughed. "You're sort of both, but I digress. Is there anything else you want to know?"

"Yes," I said. "Do you know anything about Athena after she left Sinful and hooked up with Beckett Rousseau?"

Ronald's expression shifted from amused to serious.

"No one *knows* things about the Rousseaus, or they don't last long," he said.

I blinked. "Are you saying they kill people who find out their secrets?"

He shrugged. "All I know is that a number of people surrounding the Rousseaus have disappeared over the years. Whether they're on the bottom of the bayou or paid off and living somewhere out of the Rousseaus' reach, I can't tell you. But what I do know is that they are not a family to be dallied with. If they feel threatened, they will come after you with everything they've got. And that's a lot."

"Like they did Athena," I said.

"I'm certain Beckett's family pushed hard for a conviction. They never considered Athena good enough for them."

"Unlike the secret woman he was rumored to be engaged to when he met Athena?" I asked.

"Ah, you've heard some of the dirt," Ronald said. "I'm sure the Rousseaus were very disappointed with the shift in Beckett's affections. Mind you, there was never an official announcement or talk of a ring but there was chatter. It was probably more of an agreement to become engaged—quite common in NOLA society."

"And do you know who the woman was?" I asked.

"Veronique Vidal," Ronald said.

Gertie sucked in a breath, and even Ida Belle looked a tiny bit impressed.

"I get the impression I should know who this is," I said.

Ronald patted my arm. "Goodness, no one expects *you* to know. The Vidals are fashion royalty and what you know about fashion would fit in my Gucci mini-bag."

"Rumored to be in the top three wealthiest families in NOLA," Ida Belle said.

Ronald nodded. "I've met their car caretaker. He has a mechanical engineering degree. You just can't make this stuff up."

"Wealthier than the Rousseaus?" I asked.

"Honey, the Rousseaus are practically vagrants compared to the Vidals," Ronald said. "The story is that the great-grandfather was one of the original designers for Coco Chanel when she first launched in France. When he immigrated to the US, he decided to invest his savings in his own boutique but took it one step further. He designed two lines—one couture and another more moderately priced and mass-produced—and he owned the factory producing the clothes as well."

"I take it his line was successful."

"Ridiculously so," Ronald said. "Probably half the women in the country have at least one Vidal item in their closet."

Gertie nodded. "The family is so important that none of the women change their last name when they marry. In fact, some of the men who've married into the family have changed their last names to Vidal."

"That's just practical," Ida Belle said. "If you're trying to make a run in the fashion business anyway."

"And Beckett was supposedly pre-engaged to Veronique?" I asked.

"That was the gossip," Ronald said. "They'd been seen at a few events, and there was talk that they'd left the country at the same time, so speculation ensued and grew and voilà—pre-engaged."

"I imagine the Rousseaus were really hacked when he

dumped Veronique for Athena," I said. "They were probably counting on all that fame and money backing their political aspirations."

"Without a doubt," Ronald agreed. "Quentin Rousseau has always had his eye on the White House. If he can't manage it, then he was going to ride his sons until one of them did. Beckett, being the oldest, the best-looking, and the most affable, was always expected to be that Rousseau."

"Until he married the broke, unconnected daughter of a criminal," I said.

"Exactly."

"Is Veronique the type of woman who would have sought revenge?"

"I'm not worthy of personal time with the Vidal staff, much less the royals themselves, so I can't speak to her character on a personal basis," Ronald said. "She's rumored to be as demanding in business as she is beautiful, and she's stunning. But risking her freedom and the family name over someone who didn't measure up to her family's standards to begin with is a hard sell for me."

"A woman scorned..." Gertie suggested.

"You're right, of course," Ronald agreed. "Anything is possible, and certainly Veronique had the funds to make most anything happen."

"But you don't see it," I said.

He shrugged. "If Veronique had actual feelings for Beckett, then I suppose nothing should be off the table. But she wouldn't have been the only one who could have taken action. It's well-known that her father was very protective of her and the pedestal he put her on, and the scuttlebutt is that he tasked her brother, Matisse, with filling his shoes in one of those deathbed agreements."

"So her dad is dead?"

"Yes. Her mother is still alive and still the figurehead for the business, although I doubt she has much to do with the day-to-day anymore. The grandfather is still with us but he rarely leaves the family estate. He's rumored not to be in great health. Veronique and Matisse have been groomed to rule the empire since birth."

Ronald reached across the table and squeezed my arm. "Honey, be very careful with this one. Those people have the means to make you disappear. I know you were CIA and all, but you were used to dealing with actual bad guys being bad guys. The ones hiding behind their social positions, money, and Botox are far more dangerous."

CHAPTER SIX

As soon as Ronald left, we headed out to talk to Dixon. I felt a bit of guilt course through me as Ida Belle parked in front of his house, but I pushed it aside. His teenage heartbreak wasn't as important as a murder. He might not feel that way, but he seemed like a reasonable enough person that I figured I could convince him to talk.

We headed up the sidewalk, armed with one of Gertie's casseroles and some cookies from Ally's bakery, figuring there was no way a single guy was turning down free food, even if it meant dredging up an old girlfriend to get it. Dixon surprised me by answering the door just seconds after we'd rung the bell. He gave Gertie's hair a doubletake but as a typical guy, didn't say a word about it.

"I was working on boxing up things in the living room and saw you coming up the walk," he said. "Come on in but pardon the mess."

"I thought the property was rented after you moved out," I said.

"It was rented furnished, and that included a bunch of books and knickknacks and stuff hidden away in drawers," he said. "It's probably a combination of my mom's things and a few items from everyone who rented over the years, but it's all my problem now. I get claustrophobic with all the clutter, so I grabbed some boxes and started tackling this room first."

He was slightly flushed, and I guessed his burst of domestic duty had more to do with needing to work off a good dose of shock and anger than it did needing to make the living area Zen. And here I was, about to work him up some more, but it couldn't be helped.

Gertie handed him the casserole and cookies and he grinned.

"If this is one of your chicken casseroles, you've made my day," he said. "I remember how good they were."

She nodded. "And the cookies are from Ally's bakery."

He perked up. "Ally has a bakery? Man, that's cool. I swear she was baking before she could even walk. Tasted professional even when we were little kids. Good for her."

I held in a sigh, hating that I was about to ruin his improved day.

"I'm really sorry to rain on the baked goods parade," I said, "but I was hoping you could help me out with a case I'm working."

"Me? What could I possibly help with?"

"Background investigation," I said. "Kind of a character reveal sort of thing."

He looked more than a little confused. "Okay. I mean, I guess I could try, but I haven't lived here in a long time. Who are you wanting to know about?"

"Athena Durand."

The flush rushed up his face so quickly, I wondered for a minute if he was going to tell us where to put the casserole and cookies and send us packing. But curiosity must have gotten the better of him.

"Are you investigating her, or did she hire you?" he asked.

"I'm not at liberty to answer that, but I'd like to ask you some questions, if you don't mind."

He blew out a breath and stared at me, completely silent. Finally, he shrugged. "What the hell. Might as well come back to the kitchen. I'm going to have a beer and you ladies are welcome to that or tea. I'm also going to have a shot of whiskey. Then you can ask anything you'd like. But I can't think of anything I know that would be valuable, and certainly nothing complimentary."

"I just want the truth."

"I got plenty of that."

We headed back to the kitchen and everyone opted for a beer, figuring it might relax him a bit if it seemed more like a group of friends hanging out and drinking. Dixon had his shot of whiskey, which we all declined, then he sat down and grabbed his beer.

"What do you want to know?" he asked.

"Background stuff, mostly," I said. "Did she ever tell you how she came to live here with a distant relative she didn't even know?"

"She told me her grandparents hated her father and her and she wasn't allowed to live with them. It's total crap that her own mother didn't stand up for her, but she said her mother wasn't right in the head, so maybe she landed where she needed to."

"When she left Sinful, she went to New Orleans. You'd moved there months before with your mother. Did you pick up the relationship again then?"

He snorted. "Are you kidding me? Athena had her sights set on money and an important name. I was just too young and stupid to see it at the time. And if there were two things I didn't have to offer, it was a family name and money."

"So you never ran across her again after leaving Sinful?"

"It's a big city. You could spend decades there and never see someone. And we didn't exactly run in the same circles."

"After she married Beckett, sure, but she was working the service industry before that."

"And I was working offshore and living with two women who didn't have anything better to do but cook and dote on me. I didn't spend much time out on the town. Didn't have the money or the need. When I had some extra, I spent it on local bar trips with my buddies, and believe me, she'd never have walked in the door of that place."

"Did you ever meet Beckett?"

"Nope. The Rousseaus weren't exactly my running crowd."

He answered quickly and averted his eyes. He was lying, but to what extent?

"Do you think Athena killed him?"

His eyes widened and he stared for a couple seconds, then slowly shook his head. "How would I know?"

"I'm not asking you if you have evidence," I said. "I'm asking you, as someone who knew Athena better than anyone else in this town, if you think she was capable of killing her husband."

"Jesus." He jumped up from the table and paced across the kitchen and back. "That's a hell of a question."

"It's a hell of a crime."

"I get that, but she was convicted, right? I mean, I don't know why she was walking around Sinful today like nothing ever happened, but she was. And since Louisiana pretty much owns you on a murder conviction, I have to assume it got overturned, right?"

"Yes."

"Then I don't know what to tell you."

"Did you follow the trial?"

"I might have seen some of it on the news."

I raised one eyebrow. "You lived in New Orleans and Beckett was the son of a state senator. It was probably on the news every day until the trial was over, and you used to date the woman on trial."

"Okay, so I watched. Not like I'm the only one."

"And did you form any conclusions?"

"Yeah. Rich people have more problems than poor people and don't even have the luxury of privacy when crap hits the fan."

"That's true enough, but I was looking for a more personal take since you were once close with Athena."

"'Close' isn't exactly the right word when someone's using you."

He was silent for several seconds, then sighed. "I don't know if she did it. Part of me wants to say that there's no way she could have done something like that. But then the other part remembers how ruthless she was about money and how she reacted when I caught her with the other guy. You know she didn't even apologize? Didn't even look remotely sorry or even a little embarrassed at being caught. Who does that?"

"A person driven by their own agenda and with a complete disregard for anyone else," Ida Belle said.

"But it still doesn't make her a murderer," I said.

"No," he agreed. "It doesn't. But if you're asking me if she's capable, I guess I'd have to go with yes."

———

CARTER FINALLY STROLLED INTO MY LIVING ROOM AROUND ten o'clock that night. He dropped onto the couch, looking as if he were ready to be put out of his misery.

"Do you want a beer, a shower, or a loaded handgun?" I asked.

"Hmmm."

"I'll start with the beer and you can consider the other options."

I grabbed us both a beer and sank onto the couch next to him.

"Long day," I said. "Especially considering it was supposed to be your day off."

"Ha! Day off. I've forgotten what those look like."

"Will Harrison be able to cover soon?"

My former CIA partner, Ben Harrison, had recently relocated to the area and was a flexible deputy, floating among the area's departments to fill the gaps left by vacated positions, vacation, maternity leave, and illness. For the last couple weeks, he'd been filling in for a deputy in Mudbug who'd had ACL surgery. Since Carter was only the temporary sheriff, he didn't want to hire someone permanently to fill his own deputy position until he won the election and was certain of maintaining the sheriff's job.

"The deputy will be back in a couple weeks, but he won't be fit for regular duty for a while yet. Still, they'll rotate him into desk work and let the others in the field more. Then maybe I can move Harrison over here to cover for me a couple days. Sheriff Lee might have been ineffective in the field, but he still managed to get a good amount of administrative work pushed through. The paper is getting pretty high down there."

I nodded. "Plus it seems that things have ramped up a bit in the crime department lately."

"Yeah. The big stuff has been on the rise for a couple years now—"

"Since I came to town, you mean."

He grinned. "As you're fond of saying—correlation does not equal causation."

"I'm glad you finally realize that."

"But covering Gertie issues has had a sharp uptick, and I absolutely blame you for that."

"Gertie was Gertie long before I rolled into town."

"Yeah, but she didn't think she was a private investigator with the body of a twenty-year-old back then."

"She didn't think she was a PI. She'll never be convinced she doesn't have the body of a twenty-year-old."

He frowned. "It's not just the big stuff, though. It just seems that there's a host of small crap now. Like everyone who's never been a problem has added it to their bucket list. Walter caught Sister Mary Catherine stealing at the General Store the other day."

"Why on earth?"

"She told Walter she'd seen it in a movie and just wondered if it was actually that easy. She has decided it's not, by the way."

"Did you arrest her?"

"I'm not arresting a nun for something she didn't even get away with. That's bad karma, even for a Baptist. She claimed she was just going to walk outside and then go right back inside and return it. Given what she took, I'm sure that's true."

"What did she take?"

"A package of condoms."

"Good. God."

"I don't think God was present for that one at all."

"Speaking of derelict Catholics, is Celia still in jail?"

He shook his head. "My people are too overworked to have to babysit her and her whining. Myrtle told me straight out that if Celia was still in the cell when she went on shift tonight, she was handing me her retirement paperwork and taking the next four weeks in vacation time due."

"So you just let Celia walk?"

"No. I told her she had to buy that kid a new bike and split the cost of everything broken at the café with Gertie. Then I fined her a thousand dollars for disturbing the peace and said if she didn't like it, I could press charges and ask for community service. The toilets at the park need cleaning."

I laughed. "I bet she broke her wrist getting her checkbook out. Did Walter get Sheriff Lee out of the honey?"

Carter sighed. "What a disaster. He hauled Lee out behind the store and Scooter came over with a big container of degreaser. It took an hour of scrubbing to make him suitable enough to transport home—which they did in the back of Scooter's truck. Then Walter and Scooter started on the mess inside. Lights were still on when I left the sheriff's department."

"Long day for everyone."

He nodded. "I think I'm going to take you up on that shower. I don't suppose you have any leftovers?"

"Pot roast and French bread."

"Perfect. Did you do any poking around into Athena's case?"

"There wasn't really a lot we could do today. I got everything I could from Ida Belle and Gertie, and Ronald popped in and was a real help in creating the bigger picture on the New Orleans society scene. Then we went and talked to Dixon."

He winced. "Ouch."

"Yeah, I felt bad about it, but I can't represent someone if I think they're guilty of something like murder, and I can't come up with alternate theories on what happened unless I understand all the people involved."

He nodded. "I wish I could help, but I don't really

remember much about her. When I first got back, I was caught up in my own future, trying to decide whether I wanted to plant roots here or move on again. Between that and the job and trying to deal with old demons, I had a good set of blinders on for anything else."

"I know the feeling."

He smiled. "And we both chose to stay right here in Sinful. Who would have ever guessed it?"

"No one who knew us before, that's for sure."

He leaned over to kiss me.

"Best decision ever," he said as he rose. "Let me grab that shower, then I want to eat, sprawl out on the couch, and turn on some awful movie that neither of us wants to watch."

"Why would you want to put on something neither of us wants to watch?"

He grinned. "So we're forced to find other ways to entertain ourselves. I'm never too tired for that."

―――――

THE NEXT MORNING, CARTER ONLY TOOK TIME TO PULL ON his clothes and give me a quick kiss before heading out. I went about the morning at a more leisurely pace, brewing up a pot of coffee and then sitting down with a full cup and my laptop to make some notes on the case. Or perhaps questions would be a better description, because I had a whole slew of them and not many facts. And a ton of my questions involved the initial investigation, because details on the internet were sparse. But before we headed out to investigate, it would help to know where we were going and what we were asking.

I'd texted Ida Belle when I got up, so I wasn't surprised when I heard her call out from the front door. A couple seconds later, she stepped into my kitchen with Gertie shuffling behind. She was wearing purple leopard-print bike shorts, a bright pink T-shirt, and Crocs with marijuana leaves on them. I noticed her real hair had returned, although it appeared to be unbrushed, and I assumed the wig was more trouble than she could handle first thing in the morning. She hovered over a chair before dropping into it, and I wasn't sure if she was too tired to make the effort to sit or her knees had finally given out on her. Ida Belle grabbed coffee cups and poured some for her and Gertie, then topped mine off before taking a seat.

"You having a rough morning?" I asked Gertie.

She took a huge drink of coffee and nodded. "Legs are killing me. Had to sit on the toilet to brush my teeth. Didn't even try to put that wig on. Would have required too much standing. I guess I was clenching so hard when I was under the horse that I overworked the muscles. Kinda surprising, really, given that me and Jeb—"

"No!" Ida Belle lifted her hand. "That conversation is never allowed and definitely not when I haven't had coffee and have a loaded gun at my waist."

Gertie rolled her eyes.

"Have you taken some aspirin?" I asked.

"Half of one," Gertie said and slurped more coffee.

"Half an aspirin isn't going to do much," I said.

"I got it from Nora," Gertie said. "She said to start with half and give it an hour and I'd be feeling right as rain. She gave me the shoes too."

"That explains a lot," I said.

Ida Belle stared at her in dismay. "You know better than to take anything Nora gives you."

"I had to call you to my house this morning to help me off the toilet," Gertie said. "You're lucky I was only sitting there to brush my teeth. Of course, if you're so concerned, I can take some Tylenol next time, but I can't guarantee teeth brushing will be the only thing I need help up from."

"Maybe just this once," Ida Belle grumbled and pointed to my laptop. "You been making case notes?"

"More like case questions," I said. "I got what trial information I could online, and I did a search on Athena and wandered down that rabbit hole for a while. But what I'd really like to know is the things that won't be in there—like avenues of investigation the cops took and all those random things that they don't figure are important."

Ida Belle nodded. "If the past has taught us anything, it's that everything matters when it comes to an investigation."

"Exactly," I said. "So I was thinking since the case is settled with the courts, then I might be able to convince Detective Casey to talk to me about it."

"You think she was one of the people who investigated?" Gertie asked.

"I know she was," I said. "She was quoted in a news article. Of course, there were others, and Casey wasn't the lead, but looks like she was part of the team."

"Doesn't hurt to ask," Ida Belle said. "Why don't you give her a call?"

I shook my head. "It will be harder for her to turn us down in person."

Gertie let out a weak *woot*. "Road trip."

"Are you up for that?" I asked.

"Sure. I'll be sitting most of the time. And the stuff Nora gave me should kick in before we get to NOLA. I might need a butt shove to get into the SUV though."

"I'm not putting my hands on your butt," Ida Belle said.

"I have a step in the laundry room," I said. "It's light and portable. I also have a cane and a walker. Gertie supplies."

"Why's it got to be Gertie supplies?" Gertie asked.

I raised one eyebrow.

"Fine." She waved a hand in dismissal. "I'll take the cane just in case Nora's fix doesn't work. The walker is for old people."

Ida Belle shook her head. "I'm not going with you dressed like that, either. Those shorts are meant for someone a century younger who runs as much as Fortune does. And you have to at least brush your hair. You look like a vagrant."

"Since when are you worried about fashion?" Gertie asked.

"Since we're on the job and might end up interviewing people other than Casey—people who aren't already familiar with your oddities."

"It's Fortune's case," Gertie said and looked at me. "What do you think?"

"I think it might be better if people being interviewed were concentrating on my questions instead of wondering what the heck you're wearing. If we need to follow someone, we have to blend and that's not going to happen unless we spend all our time on Bourbon Street. If we need to get away from someone, we have to run and you're not going to make it two steps before your sketchy knees and those just-asking-to-be-detained-by-the-cops Crocs have you eating pavement."

Gertie stared.

I took a deep breath. "That might be the most words I've ever said at one time about clothes."

Ida Belle nodded.

Gertie sighed. "Fine. I have one of those wraparound skirts that snaps on. It's easy to rip off, if you know what I mean—"

"Nope!" Ida Belle held up her hand.

Gertie rolled her eyes. "*Anyway*, it comes down to my ankles and I can change into black canvas sneakers. Will that work for the unimaginative among us?"

I couldn't exactly form a mental picture of the skirt Gertie was describing but wasn't about to ask. "Works for me. Let's finish up the coffee and head out."

"And if we can't meet up with Detective Casey?" Gertie asked.

"We still get po' boys and beignets," I said.

Ida Belle jumped up. "Let's get this show on the road."

CHAPTER SEVEN

WE STOPPED BY GERTIE'S HOUSE TO GRAB THE SNAP-ON skirt, then headed out. I reviewed the main points of the trial on the way, so we'd be as educated as possible if Casey decided to talk to us. When we got to NOLA, Ida Belle headed for one of our favorite cafés a couple blocks from Jackson Square. She found a parking spot in front of the café, and I called Detective Casey, who answered on the first ring.

"I hope I'm not your one allowed call," she said.

"Not this time, but the year's young."

She laughed. "So, to what do I owe my curiosity spike?"

"I caught a new case and was hoping to pick your memory. It's closed on your end, so no professional conflict."

"Got a name?"

"Athena Durand."

She whistled. "That's a name all right. You in NOLA?"

I gave her the café name.

"I'll be there in ten."

I opened the back door of the SUV and extended my hand to help Gertie out, but she hopped out onto the ground as though she was in a competition and gave me a big grin.

"Nora comes through again!" she exclaimed. "I don't know why you two don't trust her more. Look at me. I went from crippled to Olympian quality in an hour's time, and I didn't do anything but sit there."

"Uh-huh," I said, still wondering what the aftereffects of anything Nora prescribed were going to be. Hopefully, they wouldn't kick in until tonight and I'd hear about it tomorrow.

She reached back and grabbed the snap-on skirt, wrapped it around her and clicked, and just like that, she was ready for non-Bourbon Street consumption. We ordered coffee, and right at the ten-minute mark, Detective Casey strolled through the door and headed for our table in the back corner. She slipped into her seat and signaled the server for coffee.

"Athena Durand, huh?" she said after she'd taken a sip. "I wondered what she'd do when she got released, but I have to say, heading to Sinful and hiring you wasn't even on my list."

"It's a trial run at the moment," I said. "I have to make sure I'm not making a mistake taking this one. I agreed to do some preliminary investigating on her and the case, and then told her I'd make up my mind as to whether or not it was worth pursuing and I if was interested in doing so."

Casey nodded. "Smart. But with the whole case over-turned, what's she looking to do? Not like we can put her up again."

"She says she wants to find out who killed her husband so she's not on the public perception hook for it the rest of her life."

"Hmmm. I guess I can buy that, especially if she's hoping to land another rich guy. They'd shy away from a woman accused of killing her husband."

"I think even broke guys would shy away from that," Ida Belle said.

"You'd be surprised at the level of weakness in men over a woman who looks like Athena," Gertie said. "In both cases."

Casey laughed. "You're probably right. I just picked up a new partner—young guy and green as hell. He might make a good detective one day if he'd concentrate on the job instead of his girlfriend, who's yanking him around. So what is it you want to know?"

"Everything you can think of," I said. "But let's start with the most important thing—do you think she did it?"

Casey leaned back, considering.

"I worked the team that investigated the homicide, which I'm sure you already know since you called me. Our lead was one of the old-timers. He didn't get to pick his team and he wasn't a fan of women detectives, so I was left out of a lot of things. But one of the few things I was allowed a front-row seat to was notification. It was just the lead and me, and I'm guessing he thought a woman cop would make the family feel better."

"Because you've got *hugger* stamped right on your forehead," I said.

She laughed. "You would know." She sobered and shook her head. "The truth is, I never thought she did it, but I was the only one."

"Just gut instinct?"

"That and her expression when we informed the family. They were all together at the Rousseaus' estate. The 'real' Rousseaus were collected on one side of a parlor that looked like a Ritz-Carlton lobby, and Athena, clearly separated and alone, was on the other. When we told them we'd found body parts caught in the cast net, the family looked more...I don't know, frustrated with the news than shocked. Maybe 'put out' is a better description."

"So they were more taken aback by the unpleasantness of the situation than the fact that it meant he was dead."

"That's the way it struck me. I could practically see the wheels turning in Quentin Rousseau's mind. He was already trying to figure out how to spin it for public consumption."

Ida Belle rolled her eyes. "And get some sympathy votes for the next election."

Casey nodded. "Beckett's mother, Lena, just looked more mortified than anything—like she'd smelled Bourbon Street the day after Mardi Gras."

"She didn't appreciate a tasteless end to a family member," Gertie said. "The rich and powerful are supposed to die in an expensive bed, surrounded by servants and attorneys."

"That's it exactly," Casey said. "Athena was the only one who reacted the right way. She paled and dropped onto the seat behind her. Honestly, if the chair hadn't been there, I think she would have just fallen to the floor."

"I've seen some pretty good acting in my day," I said.

"I'd bet you've *done* some pretty good acting in your day," Casey said. "But you can't force the blood to rush from your face or your pulse to spike unless you've got serious skills. I checked after she did that dip just in case we needed to call the paramedics. Her heart was ready to leap out of her chest. She even started to hyperventilate until I told her how to control her breathing. I know some people might be capable of all of that, but her reaction struck me as genuine."

I nodded. "So why did the police and the DA make a case against her?"

"Political pressure."

"But your lead detective had to form theories and direct the investigation."

"You were CIA," she said. "You know the drill. You might not have gotten orders from politicians directly, but they sure as hell were filtering through your superiors and down the pipe. A high-profile murder drops serious pressure on the cops to get it handled fast. That kind of case makes or breaks careers, and the captain wasn't about to get crossways with the Rousseaus."

"So your lead picked the path of least resistance and pursued it without stretching his arms."

"In my opinion, yes," she said. "But it was more than taking the easy path. It was clear to me from the beginning that the Rousseaus had it out for Athena. They didn't even wait for her to leave the house before they started accusing her of having something to do with it."

"Bet that was a fun scene."

"You have no idea. Quentin started going off on Athena, then Lena and their other son, Tate, joined. The servants tried to calm them down, but they knew who signed their paychecks. My lead stood there like a deer in the headlights, and I knew he wasn't going to be able to manage the situation. I got Athena out of the house and left him to deal with the rest of them."

"Athena said a separate medical review of the remains was indeterminate. Seems like an accidental death would have been better for the family than the scandal of homicide. Why push for murder?"

"There was some circumstantial evidence that looked damning."

"The wire transfer?"

"That and a couple things that indicated the marriage might be on the rocks. There was an incident with Beckett, Athena, and another man at an event the week before. The claim was the guy was coming on to Athena, but stories differ on that part. Just not on the part where Beckett decked the guy. The Rousseaus insisted Athena had been cheating on him, but Beckett had taken a couple weekend trips without her a couple months before he died, so it might have gone both ways."

"But why push for a homicide investigation if they knew it would air their dirty laundry?"

"My honest opinion? Because if Beckett's death was accidental, then Athena remained a Rousseau."

"But if she was convicted of killing him, then the family got rid of her for good," I concluded.

"That's seriously harsh," Gertie said. "You railroad someone for murder just because you don't want them claiming space at the table on Thanksgiving."

"I think the last place Athena would want to be is anywhere the Rousseaus were," Casey said. "But I'm certain they didn't like the idea of her being able to run around New Orleans using their name. And if Beckett had died accidentally, they would have looked horrible if they kicked her out of her home."

Ida Belle snorted. "Yeah, 'family man' Quentin couldn't afford to be the guy who left the poor widow to fend for herself."

"That's rough," I said, "but you might be right. Which moves us on to the next question—do you think he was murdered?"

She stared at me for several seconds before nodding her head. "I think so. I can't give you any concrete reason why, except for a feeling that everything about the situation was off."

"So if we go with your instincts—which I'm perfectly willing to do—what do you think happened?"

"I think someone went out into the Gulf, clocked him on the back of the head, and tossed him overboard."

I nodded. "Suspects?"

"That list is long. Quentin has made plenty of enemies in politics and in finance—and then there's the brother to consider. It wouldn't be the first time one sibling took out another to pave the way for themselves. According to the local gossip, Tate had been nipping at Beckett's heels most of his life. With Beckett out of the picture, everything goes to him."

"What about the woman Beckett was rumored to be engaged to before he met Athena?" I asked. "Veronique Vidal."

"If Veronique Vidal wanted Elvis resurrected and riding a unicorn in Jackson Square, she has the money and connections to make it happen. But she's as untouchable as Jesus around NOLA."

"So you didn't question her?"

Casey snorted. "If I'd have gotten within a three-block radius of her, I would have been written up and demoted."

"Any chance they're reopening the case now that Athena's conviction was overturned?" I asked.

"Hell no. I brought it up yesterday during a departmental meeting about the DA having to issue a statement on her release soon and got a death stare from the captain. He said they would be revising the paperwork to reflect an accidental drowning to agree with the second medical opinion."

"What does the coroner have to say about that?" I asked.

"Nothing if he wants to keep his job."

I sighed. "All that crap is exactly why I left the CIA and went private."

"It's not the worst call," she said. "When I've got my retirement locked in where I want it, it's probably the direction I'll go. Can't see walking away entirely. Don't golf or fish, so I've got to find some way to spend the hours."

"I will admit it's nice answering to no one but myself."

Casey leaned in, her expression serious. "It is, and you'd be a hard one to touch, even for the Rousseaus and the Vidals.

But a lot of the people you care about wouldn't be. You need to stay low with this. Either one of those families has the ability to ruin lives, and there is nothing me, Carter, the Heberts, or even your fancy attorney could do about it."

"I don't suppose you remember the name of the guy Beckett punched?" I asked.

She nodded. "I don't think I've forgotten anything about that case. His name was Dixon Edwards."

———

AFTER CASEY HEADED OFF, WE HAD BREAKFAST AND MULLED over what we'd learned. It was clear that Dixon had some explaining to do when we got back to Sinful. He'd outright lied about not having any interaction with Athena in New Orleans. And since a man didn't generally go around punching someone for a single conversation with his wife, I wanted to know exactly what their relationship was at that time.

Because we were already in New Orleans, I decided to ignore everyone's advice about staying below radar and made an appointment to see Tate Rousseau at the family's business. I'd lied to get the appointment by saying I had just inherited a substantial estate and would only be in town for the day. That had gotten the assistant quickly finding a slot for me, but I had every intention of laying my cards on the table when I got there. Requesting audience with a Rousseau under false pretenses was one thing—and likely something that happened to them often—but perpetuating the lie would cause me more trouble in the long run. Better for me to tell them my agenda than for them to hear about it from someone else.

The office was in one of the refurbished buildings in the central business district and probably cost more to rent in a year than my entire house was worth. The lobby looked like a presidential palace, and a security guard greeted us immediately upon entering. After producing our IDs and him placing a call, the guard unlocked the elevator, selected our floor, and locked it again. Apparently, there was no claiming to visit one business while intending to hop off on another floor. I'd seen card readers on the stairwell at the end of the hall, and cameras covering every square inch of the lobby and hallways, so they were serious about their security game.

The elevator opened into a lobby on the top floor of the building and I had to admit, it was impressive. The white marble, gold fixtures, and huge chandelier in the waiting area set the tone for everything else. The furniture, rugs, and decor were equally impressive.

"Someone has some seriously good taste," Gertie said.

"*Expensive* taste," Ida Belle said. "Good is a matter of opinion."

It was a little garish for me, but that made sense given that it seemed the Rousseaus trended toward bold statements and a need for attention. Except when they would come off looking bad, of course.

A perfectly coiffed young woman gave us a completely blank stare as we approached the desk.

"Tate is ready for you now," she said, her voice as void of expression as her stare. "Take the hallway on the right to the end office."

"What's with Miss Personality there?" Gertie grumbled as we headed off.

"Maybe she hates her job," Ida Belle said. "But it pays too much to leave."

"Like a bad marriage," Gertie said.

As we reached the end of the hall, a door swung open and Tate Rousseau beckoned us inside.

Late twenties. Six foot one. A hundred seventy pounds. Decent muscle tone all derived from a gym—likely a home one. No physical issues that I could see, but this guy had never been in a fight. Threat level low unless you took into account his last name.

We took seats across from him as he slid into a ridiculously expensive leather chair, then gave me an expectant look.

"So I understand you have recently inherited and need an investment plan," he said.

"I have to be honest with you," I said. "I told your assistant that in order to get in to see you, but that's not why I'm here."

His expression shifted from eager to annoyed and he shook his head. "I don't have anything to do with our charitable donations. If you have a cause that you'd like us to support, you can submit your information on my mother's website. I'll give you the URL."

"I'm not here for a donation, either," I said and pushed my business card across the desk.

He picked up the card and his eyebrows lifted. "PI? What do you want with me?"

"Background information," I said. "I'm considering taking a case but before I sign up for work, I prefer to know exactly what I'm getting into."

His expression shifted, and I could tell his opinion was that if my case involved the Rousseaus in any way, it was better not to take it. But curiosity and a desire to know what his family might need to put up additional protection for won out.

"What kind of background information?" he asked.

"I'm looking into your brother's death," I said.

A flush ran up his face and he jumped up from his chair. "That bitch hasn't even been out a week, and she's already causing problems for my family again?"

"I'm confused—what kind of problems could looking into his death cause? Athena has always contended she had nothing to do with it."

"That's a lie. Everything that comes out of her mouth is a lie."

"But what if this time she's telling the truth? Her conviction was overturned. I've reviewed the case, and quite frankly, if the victim's last name had been something other than Rousseau, I don't think she would have even been charged, much less convicted."

"I don't care how weak the evidence was. I know what I know. That woman married my brother for money and status —the two things she lost when her father's sins came under public scrutiny. We all told him not to marry her—that she wasn't good for him or his future—but he refused to listen. Beckett never was one to toe the line."

The way he said it made me think that Tate *was* one to toe the line—his father's line—and he resented Beckett for having the backbone to do what he couldn't. Typical sibling rivalry, especially if the younger one was doing the better job obeying the patriarch's wishes but the older one always came first simply by virtue of birth.

He sat in his chair again and I leaned forward.

"What if she didn't do it? Are you okay with whoever killed Beckett getting away with murder?"

He stared at me for several long seconds, then sighed. "The truth is, I don't even know that it *was* murder."

I blinked, surprised at this shift in dialogue.

"I think Athena Durand is the worst thing that ever happened to Beckett and my family," he continued. "She was a gold digger and a low-rent one at that. Not only did she not bring anything to the table, their marriage hindered his political aspirations as well as cost this firm a few clients due to her father's history. And that was just at the onset. Then she got into his mind and turned him into her...you know what, none of that is your business."

Crap. He was just on the verge of saying something that I felt might have been important when he'd caught himself.

"But you're not convinced it was murder, why exactly?" I asked, hoping to prompt him back to what he was going to say.

"Look, my parents have insisted that Beckett was murdered, and I get it. No one wants to believe that the golden child screwed up his life and ran off to get a drunk on. He should have been back here cleaning up his messes, but instead he probably had way too much to drink, slipped on the deck of a boat, fell overboard, and cracked his head. There was half a bottle of whiskey open on the table when that boat was found and two more empties in the trash. He'd only been out there a day. You do the math."

"What kind of messes did he need to drink that much over?" I asked.

Tate's jaw clenched and his eyes darted toward the door. He'd said too much, and he wasn't about to unleash some scandal that clearly hadn't come out back when Beckett died.

"His wife was enough to drink over," he said finally.

"But you don't think Athena killed him?" I asked, confused.

"I didn't say that," he said. "Money was missing from their account and the only two people who could have moved it were her and Beckett. And the FBI said that hired gun was on location where that money was sent. Then they tracked him to New Orleans after, but it was too late. I get that it could be a lot of coincidences, but I don't buy it."

"So you *do* think Athena killed him?"

He put his hands in the air. "The truth is, I don't know how Beckett died. Maybe he *did* fall overboard, got tangled in the nets, and drowned. But that doesn't mean Athena didn't hire that man to kill him. It just means he got paid for a job he never had to do. Athena Durand is not a good person. Every bad decision Beckett made filtered right back to her. And despite giving her everything she wanted, she was cheating on him."

"That never came out in the trial," I said.

"Because we didn't have any proof and the DA thought if we made those accusations, it would look too much like a witch hunt. But Beckett told me that he wondered sometimes where she was all day because she didn't have enough shopping bags to show for it and you could only have your hair and nails done so many times a month."

"Who was the other man?"

"He never said, but he told me he had an idea. He was thinking of hiring a PI to get proof. But the DA said that conversation wouldn't hold water in court—not without someone else to back it up or proof of an affair."

"And you never could find that proof," I said.

"No." He leaned across the desk and looked me straight in the eyes. "I can't tell you what happened on that boat. But the one thing I *do* believe with absolute certainty is that if Beckett had never met Athena Durand, he'd still be alive. For me, that's guilty enough."

CHAPTER EIGHT

Tate claimed another meeting after issuing his last statement and ushered us out the door, but that was fine by me. I figured he'd said everything he was going to say about the matter and far more than his father would have approved of.

"That wasn't what I expected," Ida Belle said when we were back in the SUV.

"Me either," I said. "Quite frankly, I expected to be escorted out before we'd taken a seat."

Gertie nodded. "Daddy Rousseau wouldn't be happy if he found out Tate was talking to us about Beckett."

"No," I agreed. "Especially since Tate seems iffy on the hard line his parents are pushing on murder."

"He's still firmly on the blaming-Athena train, though," Ida Belle said. "Not that it's surprising. Families like the Rousseaus always give the side-eye to people who have far less to lose than they do."

"And Athena had nothing to lose and everything to gain," Gertie said.

I frowned. "That statement—that Athena got into Beck-

95

ett's mind and turned him into her...what? Combine that with the messes Beckett should have been cleaning up and what does that sound like to you?"

"Financial shenanigans," Ida Belle said.

"Do you think Tate was about to say Athena had turned Beckett into her father?" Gertie asked.

"That's the direction I'm leaning," I said.

"Well, if nothing came out during the trial, any indiscretions Beckett committed are swept so far under the rug, they're embedded in the floor," Ida Belle said.

I nodded in agreement. "So here's the bottom line—do we think Beckett was killed, or do we think he had a huge drunk on and got careless?"

"I'm sure he did the second based on the evidence of alcohol consumption alone," Gertie said. "But then what was that money wired for?"

"Could have been anything," I said. "Maybe Beckett had a girlfriend there, or was making a payoff, or a shady investment, or sending cash off to hide it from his wife or family. It seems the kids' lives are pretty much controlled by the parents. Maybe he had plans to jet at some point."

"And the hit man in the Bahamas and then in NOLA is coincidence?" Gertie asked.

I blew out a breath. "I know. I hate coincidence. But maybe this time it is."

Ida Belle snorted. "You know good and well you don't believe that. Detective Casey is sharp and if she says something was off about the whole thing, then there was."

"Yeah, but can we find it?" I asked. "Like you said, Casey is sharp. If she couldn't suss out the truth when it was all fresh, how can we manage it now that everyone has had time to cover their tracks?"

"Casey's hands were tied by the bureaucracy," Ida Belle said. "We don't have those limitations."

"We also have no authority. People don't have to talk to us, and the kind of people this case involves usually don't."

Ida Belle shrugged. "You got Tate to talk to you. Keep poking around and see if you can form an alternative theory, then present it to Athena. That's all she can reasonably expect you to do given the circumstances. And while your over-achieving self will see solving the murder as the goal line, that's not what she hired you for."

"She's right," Gertie agreed. "Beckett's dead and nothing's bringing him back. Maybe Athena still mourns him, but at this point, she's just trying to save herself."

"Which is understandable," I said. "But after talking to two people, Athena is still the most likely suspect. Tate claimed she was cheating, and Beckett was mad enough to punch Dixon. Something neither Dixon nor Athena bothered to mention, which doesn't help either of them as far as I'm concerned."

"It looks bad," Ida Belle agreed. "I assume you're confronting her and Dixon both when we get back to Sinful?"

"Without a doubt," I said. "I wish there was some way to talk to Veronique Vidal. I bet she'd have plenty to say about Beckett and Athena. Woman scorned and all that."

Gertie sighed. "If only we could get an invitation to her Mardi Gras gala."

"What gala?" I asked.

"Some charity thing," Gertie said. "There was an invitation on Tate's desk. Probably one of those things where they auction off a thousand-dollar handbag for ten thousand, then everyone writes it off on their taxes, and the Vidals get to claim credit for all the money going back into the community."

"When is it?" I asked, an idea forming.

"Wednesday night," Gertie said.

I pulled out my phone and dialed Ronald. "What are the chances you can get us into Veronique Vidal's gala Wednesday night?"

"Good Lord," he said, "why don't you just ask me to save the whales or eliminate world hunger? Maybe get you a lunch with Marilyn Monroe?"

"That hard, huh?"

"Let me make some calls. But fair warning—you won't get in without me, and I'm not going with you wearing anything currently in your closet."

"See what you can do. If you can get us in, I'll go shopping with you."

"Really?" He perked up.

"Do I have a choice?"

"Now that I think of it...no."

"Smart," Ida Belle said when I hung up.

"There's no way he can get invitations for all four of us though," Gertie groused.

"Let's see if Ronald and I can get in and then we'll figure something out."

"So what now?" Ida Belle asked. "It's too soon for lunch."

"Speak for yourself," Gertie said.

"You don't need more food shoved in your handbag," Ida Belle said. "And I don't want more food stinking up my vehicle."

I considered for a minute, then saw Tate walking toward us down the sidewalk. He was on his cell phone and he didn't look happy.

"Duck!" I said and it was a testament to the level of trust we had that Ida Belle and Gertie simply flopped over in the SUV without pause.

I waited a bit, then inched up and pointed to Tate, who'd walked by the SUV and had climbed in a Mercedes sedan.

"He was on the phone and angry," I said. "Which might mean nothing, but..."

Ida Belle started up her SUV and waited until Tate pulled away to enter traffic two cars behind him.

"Speed up or you'll lose him," Gertie instructed.

"Stop backseat driving," Ida Belle said. "If I get too close, he'll spot us and that will be worse than losing him."

"Traffic seems worse than usual," I said.

"A lot of people are here to prepare for Mardi Gras next week," Ida Belle said. "The krewes start well in advance and not everyone lives in NOLA, so they come early and stay. Then there's the tourists who book extra vacation time before the parade."

"Yep," Gertie agreed. "The energy is huge the week leading up to Mardi Gras. The feel is totally different after, so if you want the party vibe, you come before and avoid after."

"Tate didn't look like he was out for a party," I said.

Ida Belle changed lanes and put on her turn signal. "Looks like he's headed for Jackson Square, though."

"Crap," I said. "Even with the crowds, it will be hard to tail him on foot, especially since he just met with us."

"We keep hoodies in the back." Gertie reached behind the seat for a duffel bag. "And it's chilly enough today, so that will help."

"Hoodies won't hide our faces," I said. "We still won't be able to get close enough to hear anything or even lip-read, and if Tate spots me, we might score a ride on the family's enemy list."

Gertie grinned. "I have something that might allow you to get closer."

She reached in her purse and pulled out a wig with long, curly red locks. "Ronald said he couldn't pull off the red with his skin tone but thought I might have some fun with it. I was going to add it to our supplies since long hair makes my neck itch. Try it on."

What the heck. My hair was already in a ponytail, so I pulled on the wig and shoved my hair up under it.

"Perfect!" Gertie said. "Now the sunglasses."

I pulled on my sunglasses and slipped the hoodie on. I pulled up the hood and pulled some of the long red hair up front and let it drape down onto my chest. I flipped the mirror down and looked. It actually wasn't bad.

Ida Belle looked over at me and nodded, then pulled a knife out of her pocket. "Cut some holes in your jeans. With your skin, you can pass for a teenager. You just have to dress the part."

"These are brand-new jeans," I said.

"So are the ones the kids are wearing with the holes in them," Ida Belle said. "And you don't even want to see the prices on them. Walter put some in stock with the T-shirts, and they sell out as soon as they hit the shelf. Cost more than a good reel."

I sighed and cut some holes in my perfectly good jeans, then ripped them a bit and let the threads dangle.

"Perfect," Ida Belle said, "especially since you're already wearing that sullen young adult expression. You'll blend completely."

"If he ever stops," I said.

"Looks like you're up," Gertie said.

Tate put on his blinker and turned into a parking lot close to the Square. Ida Belle sped up and into the parking lot but drove past him as he secured a space close to the entry. She found a spot several cars down with a clear view and pulled in. He didn't exit immediately, but I figured he was doing the same thing I was doing, which was paying the parking fee on his phone. About the time I got ours paid, I saw him jump out of the car and start across the lot.

We climbed out and hustled after him, making sure we had some cover with cars or hedges. He headed for the street, then crossed into Jackson Square. The Square was busy already, so we had no trouble disappearing in the crowd while maintaining surveillance. I was a bit surprised when he never once turned around, but instead, strode directly through the Square.

I stopped behind a jazz group and continued watching as he headed toward St. Louis Cathedral. Gertie limped up beside me, huffing with the effort.

"He picks now to go to church?" Gertie asked.

"Maybe he needs to confess," Ida Belle said. "If we're making a list of people with motive, he's at the top of mine."

"What's wrong with you?" I asked Gertie.

"Pill must be wearing off," Gertie said.

"It didn't last very long," Ida Belle said.

"Nora told me to only take half, remember?"

"Well, take the rest now before we have to rent one of those horse carriages to get you back to the car."

I stared at the church, trying to decide if my disguise was good enough to get by in close quarters.

"I'm going to go inside," I said, mind made up.

"I'd like to say he wouldn't give you a second glance," Ida Belle said. "But if he's paranoid and has something to hide, it's still a risk."

"He'd have to catch me to be certain who it is, right?" I said. "I can definitely outrun him."

"True enough," Ida Belle said. "But I don't like you going in there without cover."

"Who said she is?" Gertie asked.

We turned around and saw Gertie wearing a nun's habit, an

enormous cross hanging around her neck that looked more suited to a rap video than a place of worship.

"Where the heck did you get that getup?" Ida Belle said.

"My purse," Gertie said. "I saw it online and thought the nun thing has worked before so it might come in handy for an investigation. And what do you know—I just took it out of the box this week and here we are. Skirt off, habit on, and now, Fortune can go in with cover."

"Where's your purse now?" I asked.

"Cross-body strap," Gertie explained. "I just look like a nun who likes her wine and snacks."

"You can barely walk," Ida Belle said. "And it looks like you're going to kill vampires with that ridiculously huge cross."

"Limping just makes the old nun thing look authentic, I've got plenty of weapons in my purse, and the cross is big because I might need to put someone up on it." She gave Ida Belle a pointed look.

I shook my head and said to Ida Belle as I was walking off, "Stick near the door in case I have to flee and need a distraction."

"On it."

There was no time to argue with Gertie. Tate had already gone in the church, and I could only hope he hadn't disappeared into a private room. I figured families like the Rousseaus didn't wait in line for confession like regular people. I did a quick survey as I walked inside. Several people were in pews praying and I saw a row of candle holders, with a couple of lit candles, at the front of the church. I walked down the center aisle, lifting my head only enough to scan the nave—which I knew the correct name for because of the History channel—as I went. I finally spotted Tate up front, lighting a candle.

Then it hit me. Today was the one-year anniversary of Beckett's death.

Crap! Of all the days to not go stirring up the Rousseaus, it was today. I should have been paying better attention to those police reports. No wonder Tate was so angry. I slipped into a pew at the back of the church and watched as he lit a candle and placed it beside the other lit ones in the holder. Then he headed for a pew close to the front of the church and sat next to a man wearing a suit. I could only see his back, but I was going to guess by the silver hair that it was his father, Quentin.

Tate leaned over and whispered something, then the man turned and looked at Tate. Bingo. It was Quentin. But there was no way to get close enough to hear them and no way to stand in front of them and read their lips without drawing attention. So I did the next best thing. I turned my phone to Record, then hurried up front. I lit a candle, then entered the pew behind them, depositing my phone on top of a songbook in the rack positioned on the back of the pew where they were sitting. Then I kept going to the end of the pew and knelt down as if praying.

I cast a glance over and neither of them was looking my way, so I figured I was in the clear. Now, if they were talking loud enough for my phone to pick up their conversation, we might get something. I risked a few furtive glances over and could see Quentin's face as he turned toward Tate. He didn't look sad, which would have been the emotion I expected to see on the anniversary of the death of his son while sitting in a church to remember him.

He looked angry.

The church was so silent that the click of a camera lens echoed throughout the building, and I wasn't the only one who heard it. Quentin and Tate both jumped up and started scanning the church. I ducked my head but it was too late.

"You!" Tate said, his voice booming in the nave. "Do I know you?"

"Ssssshhhh!" A voice sounded from the front of the church, and I looked over to see Gertie standing there, holding a candle.

"This is a place of peace to remember those we have lost," she said.

"You took a picture of me," Tate said to me, completely ignoring Gertie's statement.

"Screw off," I said, modifying my voice and hoping I sounded young-adultish.

"If you publish anything in the papers, I'll sue you," Tate said.

"Leave me alone, you perv—"

And that's when the pigeons attacked.

CHAPTER NINE

I HADN'T NOTICED THEM IN THE CHURCH, WHICH MEANT they must have strolled in rather than flown. But all of a sudden, at least ten of them surrounded Gertie and started flapping and poking at the bottom of her habit. Gertie waved her arms, trying to shoo them away, but they weren't having any of it. Instead, they redoubled their efforts and started infiltrating the habit. Gertie yelled and started dancing around, flapping like the birds, and then set off sort of running for the exit. That's when I saw the trail of popcorn she was leaving behind.

Holy crap! No wonder the pigeons were on her like a free meal.

The other half of her pill obviously hadn't kicked in yet, because she was bouncing from one side of the aisle to the other, making the birds even more frantic to collect their lunch. Then one of the birds flew up into her face and she dropped the candle and grabbed on to a pew to keep from falling.

"She's on fire!" a woman on the other side of the church shrieked.

I stared in horror because the dropped candle had sent her cheap habit up in flames. Not a good look for a church or a nun. Not in any century. Gertie, apparently determined not to blow her cover, didn't bother to shed the flaming garment. Instead, she shoved herself off the pew and kept running.

Since setting herself on fire had Quentin and Tate's attention firmly locked on that spectacle, I took the opportunity to slip out of the far end of the pew and bolted for the door. I made it to the back of the church a second before Gertie, grabbed the bowl of holy water, and threw the entire thing on her as she ran past.

"Hey!"

I heard Tate shout, and I paused only long enough to make sure the flames were out before dashing into the gathering crowd. I hid behind a giant canvas of a woman and her poodle that had been abandoned by the artist and the model in favor of the Nun On Fire Show and peered around as Gertie stumbled out of the church, still smoldering.

The habit was burned halfway up and the sight of a nun wearing leopard-print bike shorts and Crocs with marijuana leaves had the phones coming out everywhere. I shook my head. I'd totally missed her slipping the Crocs back on. And why the heck didn't anyone render aid anymore? They'd rather film it in case they could be famous. And speaking of aid, Tate and Quentin burst out of the church and I wondered where the heck Ida Belle was.

Gertie glanced over and saw Tate and Quentin exit the church and took up her sideways run again. She barreled through the crowd of people, knocking some down as she went and ran right past my hiding place toward the side of the Square. The crowd locked in on Quentin and most shifted their attention from the sketchy nun to the senator.

I looked to see if Tate had spotted me, but he was still

scanning the crowd while his father dealt with the people gathering. I set off after Gertie but felt my heart drop when I glanced back and saw Tate's head bobbing in the crowd behind me. I didn't think he had seen me, so that meant he'd locked in on Gertie, which was even worse. No way she could outrun him, even if Nora's pill kicked in, and blending wasn't possible at that point either.

I kicked things up a notch and had almost caught up with Gertie when I reached the corner of the Square. I was just trying to figure out how to delay Tate without outright tackling him when someone shoved a laundry cart full of table linens right into Gertie's path. She flipped over into the cart and the person pushing it just kept going. One of her Crocs flew off and hit a young woman in the back of the head. Her boyfriend jumped up and gestured at a group of young men who'd been ogling her earlier, and the scuffle was on.

Ida Belle for the win!

I could barely control my grin as I ran across the street and dashed into a shop as Tate broke through the crowd at the corner of the Square. He scanned every direction, his clenched fists and set jaw telling me just how angry he was. But Gertie was well hidden in the laundry cart, and Ida Belle's back was to Tate and the shirt he'd seen her in earlier was covered with one of our emergency hoodies. And the scuffle had people scattering to either film it or get away from the fray. Either way, the chaos had sealed the deal. We'd gotten away.

I waited until Tate turned around and stalked back toward the church before leaving the shop and tailing him. My phone was still in the pew and hopefully, no one would snag it before I could retrieve it. As I walked, I said a silent prayer that Ida Belle managed to get away without being arrested for stealing those linens. And I didn't know if Gertie had broken any laws by impersonating a nun in a Catholic church, drawing a bunch of pigeons into the nave, or setting herself on fire, but I was pretty sure the cops wouldn't be impressed with any of it.

When I got back to the church, I paused behind the same canvas as before, but the artist and subject were back now, so I pretended to look at the work as I watched Tate speak quickly to his father in the Square, then stride off in the opposite direction. I gave the artist a thumbs-up, then hurried into the church.

There was a collection of people bent over in the center aisle and I wondered if there were scorch marks on the floor. I skirted the outside and entered the pew from the same end I'd exited from and sighed with relief when I saw my phone was still sitting on the songbook. I grabbed it up, then peered down the middle aisle and realized they were cleaning up what the pigeons left behind—feathers and, well, the other.

I slipped my phone in my pocket and hustled out of the church, pausing only a second at the exit to make sure Tate and his father were nowhere in sight. Then I jogged across the Square and paused again behind a horse carriage to scan the parking lot. I felt my shoulders relax when I saw Tate's car was gone, then hurried across the street and through the parking lot to Ida Belle's SUV. I was even more relieved when I saw them sitting inside.

"That was close," I said as I climbed in.

"That was awesome!" Gertie said, grinning as if she'd won the lottery.

"You were attacked by pigeons and set yourself on fire," Ida Belle said. "You're missing one of those ridiculous shoes that you weren't supposed to be wearing and the other is covered with pigeon poop. Since they've got big holes in them, we're not even going to discuss the sanitary side of things. You're definitely going to have to deep clean my SUV. How is any of that awesome?"

"We got away!" Gertie said.

"You really need to think about setting the bar higher," Ida Belle said.

My phone rang and I checked the display. Detective Casey. I answered. "Fortune's crisis."

Casey chuckled. "Just had a call go out—someone snapped a shot of Senator Rousseau and Tate while they were grieving in St. Louis Cathedral, then a nun got attacked by pigeons inside the church and set herself on fire. About the same time, some woman stole a linen cart, shoved a nun in it, and took off down the street. I don't suppose you guys are anywhere near Jackson Square."

"We won't be in about thirty seconds," I said and motioned for Ida Belle to head out.

"Jesus, Redding. I told you to be careful with the Rousseaus, and you've literally sent up smoke signals."

"Yeah, that part wasn't intended. And I'm not the one who snapped the picture, so at least when it hits the paper, they'll know who to blame. And I'm pretty sure Tate didn't recognize me."

"You're pretty sure—why would Tate even know what you look like?"

"Because I sort of interviewed him before we followed him to the church. But I went into the church in disguise, and he didn't get a good look at me before the nun caught on fire, so I think I'm in the clear."

Casey was silent for several seconds. Finally, she said, "You know what I'm going to do? When I get off work, I'm going to buy a nice bottle of scotch and send it to that deputy you're dating. Please tell me you got something, at least."

"I think I did, but I'm not sure exactly what."

"Let me know. This one still sits wrong with me."

She disconnected, and Gertie leaned forward between the seats.

"Lunch?"

"Fine by me," I said. "All that running made me hungry."

"Why did it take you so long to circle back this way?" Ida Belle asked as she directed the SUV toward our favorite po' boy restaurant. "I saw you when I clipped Gertie with the linen cart and figured you'd beat us back here."

"What did you do with that cart, by the way?" I asked.

"Pushed it behind a food delivery truck, dug Gertie out, and left it there. The company logo was printed on the side, so hopefully, someone will call and report it."

"And some poor restaurant will be breaking out the paper towels for lunch service," Gertie said. "You almost broke my hip with that thing."

"I could have let him catch you," Ida Belle said.

Gertie waved a hand in dismissal. "There wasn't anyone after me but those pigeons."

"You're wrong on that one," I said. "Tate ran after you."

"Really?" Gertie asked. "Do you think he recognized us?"

"I don't know if he recognized us or thought one of us took that picture, but either way, it would have been a bad outcome if he'd caught up to either one of us."

"What picture?" Ida Belle asked.

I explained what had set the whole church debacle off.

"That explains how it started, but what the heck was going on with those pigeons?" Ida Belle asked.

"They were following a trail of popcorn that was streaming from *somebody's* handbag," I said.

Ida Belle shook her head. "Popcorn? Really? And why was it falling out of your handbag?"

"I shot a hole in it last week when I was rearranging it to fit a taco salad in there," Gertie said.

"You're going to accidentally shoot more than your handbag one day," Ida Belle said. "If you're going to haul around half your pantry in your purse, then carry a gun with a safety and put it in a holster."

"You don't have time to deal with holsters and safeties when things are going down," Gertie said.

"The way you're doing things now, the only thing that's going to go down is one of us," Ida Belle said.

"Fine," Gertie said. "I'll put it in a holster and knit it a sweater. Will that do?"

"Perfect," Ida Belle said and looked over at me. "So back to why it took you so long to get to the car..."

I explained how I'd left my cell phone behind the pew and had to go back and retrieve it.

"Well, what are you waiting for!" Ida Belle exclaimed. "Fire it up."

I accessed my recordings, turned the volume all the way up, and hit Play. At first, there was just jostling noise from when I was putting the phone in place, then I heard low talking.

"What did you tell her?"

"I didn't tell her anything."

"You didn't kick her out or I would have heard about it, so you must have told her something."

"I didn't kick her out because I was hoping to find out what Athena was up to."

"You need to leave that sort of thing to me."

"Why? Because you don't think I can handle family business?"

"I'm not interested in having this discussion with you again. Not today and especially not here."

"Oh yeah, because today is all about the golden boy. Maybe you wish it was me you'd lit that candle for."

"Don't be ridiculous. Did you get this PI's name?"

"I might not be Beckett, but I'm not a moron. She left me her card."

"Interesting. Sounds like she might be legit."

"I'm more concerned with why Athena hired her. Despite all our efforts, she's walking around like she didn't do anything. Why does she need a PI?"

"Probably hoping she can collect the life insurance."

"You've got an election coming up. We can't afford for her to drag us through this all over again."

"Don't worry about that. I'll handle it."

"I can help."

"This is above your pay grade."

"But it wouldn't have been above Beckett's— You! You! Do I know you?"

"That's when Tate yelled at me after we heard that camera click," I said.

We listened to the rest but didn't hear Quentin or Tate again—just the general fray going on in the church. I stopped it when I was sure Quentin and Tate had made their move outside and frowned.

"So what do you think?" Ida Belle asked.

"I think Tate didn't like his brother much," I said, "which is interesting since he seemed angry when he talked about Athena being responsible for everything that had happened even if she wasn't the one who actually did the deed."

Gertie nodded. "You'd think he'd be shaking her hand for getting rid of the competition."

"Maybe he didn't like the taint she left on the family," Ida Belle said. "I mean, the death of a child is a sad thing, and murder is a tragedy, but murder by your wife is a scandal."

"That's possible," I said. "It also sounds like nothing's changed for Tate even though Beckett is gone. That's got to make him mad. Beckett gets to be the eternal number one and Athena is free and clear."

———

We polished off po' boys and left the case behind as we ate, choosing instead to debate the merits of Ida Belle purchasing a new bass boat, even though her old one was still in great shape. The restaurant was way too crowded to speak about sensitive issues, and we couldn't risk being overheard, especially using names like Athena, Tate, Beckett, and Quentin. Too many people would be happy to exchange information for favor with people like Senator Rousseau.

When we climbed back into the SUV, Ida Belle looked over at me. "You got anything else on the agenda for New Orleans or should I head back to Sinful?"

"I was wondering if we could find the girls who Athena used to live with. If so, we might be able to get some more backstory out of them," I said.

"Athena probably dumped them cold when she hooked up with Beckett," Gertie said.

"Which means they might be willing to lay out any dirt they have on her," Ida Belle said.

"Do you know where the hotel is that she worked at?" I asked.

Ida Belle started up the SUV. "On it."

The hotel was one of the nicer historic ones in the French Quarter. Ida Belle said she'd stayed there once for an investment conference and the mattresses were comfortable, the AC was good, and you didn't bang your elbows in the shower. That appeared to be the important things on her list for rating hotel rooms.

We managed to score street parking just a bit down from the entrance and headed inside. The lobby was dated but had been meticulously maintained. It had that old-world elegance and flair that brought people to New Orleans in the first place.

Ida Belle pointed to the right and I saw a sign indicating the bar was that direction. We didn't know the names of the women Athena had lived with, but the bar was usually the easiest place to get a conversation going, especially this time of the day, when it should be fairly empty.

I left them in the lobby and headed in first. My plan was to prompt the bartender or a server into talking and then have Ida Belle and Gertie on standby to follow if anyone stepped out for a phone call or went off to chat with another employee about my visit. The dividing-up ploy had gotten us information before, and I was hoping it worked again.

Only a few tables in the rear of the bar were occupied. A pair of men in suits sat at one, their laptops open, and they were engaged in what appeared to be a somewhat heated discussion over whatever the screens displayed. The other table was occupied by an elderly couple who probably went to bed by seven so were having their "evening" round of drinks and watching Court TV on the screen near their table.

I slipped onto a barstool at the empty counter, and a woman who'd been wiping down glasses made her way over. *Christi* was embroidered on her shirt, which sported the hotel logo.

Midtwenties. Five foot six. A hundred thirty pounds. Muscle tone most likely from standing and walking most of the day. Loose, dry skin indicating recent rapid weight loss and possible drinking problem. Threat level low.

"What can I get you," she asked, her tone as uninterested as her expression.

"Beer—whatever you have on tap that's good."

She nodded and walked off to get the beer, then put it in front of me on a napkin and placed a small bowl of mixed nuts next to it. "You want me to start a tab?"

"No. I won't be here long."

I pulled out one of my business cards and handed it to her. She glanced down at it. "A PI? That's cool."

She tried to give me the card back, but I shook my head. "You keep it."

"Why? You're not here to talk to me, are you?"

"I'm not sure if I am or not. How long have you worked here?"

She narrowed her eyes a bit, and I could see she was trying to figure out how answering that question would trap her. Since there was no way she could know where I was going with my line of questioning, she finally decided the truth was probably the best option.

"Almost eight years now," she said. "It's a decent gig. The manager isn't a butthole, and most people staying here tip well."

"Then you know Athena Durand."

She took an involuntary step back, like I'd just brandished a weapon. "Not really."

"She worked here though."

Christi shrugged. "She didn't work the bar. And there's not some rule that employees at the same place have to hang out."

"True enough, but I imagine that being a bartender you hear plenty and observe even more. Every bartender I've ever known was sharper than most detectives I've worked with."

I hoped the compliment would loosen her back up a little and apparently, it worked. She stared at me a couple seconds, then slowly nodded.

"I guess I'm more aware than most," she said. "But why do you want to know about Athena? All that went down a year ago. She'll be old enough for Social Security when she gets out."

"You didn't know? She's out."

She gasped. "What? When...how?"

"Her case was overturned a few days ago and they let her loose."

"Why didn't I hear anything about it?"

"Did she pose a threat to you in some way? That's really the only reason people are individually notified when inmates are released, except the victim's family, of course."

"Nothing like that. I just meant it was such a big deal. The Rousseaus—*they're* a big deal. Why wasn't this all over the news?"

I shrugged. "I'm guessing the DA isn't a fan of advertising his losses. And I imagine the Rousseaus aren't interested in reliving this just so the media can sell advertising space. It wouldn't bring Beckett back, and Athena can't be retried. Reporters aren't going to hear about it from any of them, although I'm sure it will make the rounds soon enough."

"Then who hired you, and why do you want information on Athena?"

"I'm not at liberty to say who hired me, but they're not interested in causing Ms. Durand any problems. They are simply looking for answers to some outstanding questions."

"Well, I can't help you. I didn't know Athena well and definitely didn't know Beckett Rousseau."

"My understanding was she met him while she was working a party here."

"Possibly. There are plenty of rich people who have events here, but I'm just here to fill glasses and collect tips."

"No interest in finding a husband with a fat bank account?"

She smirked. "Like you said, bartenders hear a lot and notice even more. Rich people have problems I'm not interested in taking on. I might not have a lot, but my rent is paid and I have a little extra. I'm not looking to trade peace of mind for money."

"You'd be one of the few."

"My grandma keeps saying people are getting dumber."

"Sounds like me and your grandma would get along. Do you know if anyone else here was friends with Athena? I was told she lived with a couple coworkers."

She shook her head. "Hotels have a lot of turnover. Hell, people move in and out of New Orleans like the tide. For an old city with deep history, it's got little permanence where some things are concerned. The hospitality business takes that to a whole different level."

"Yeah, I suppose it does. Well, if you think of anyone who might be able to help, give me a call. Or ask them to call me."

"Sure," she said, but I could tell she had zero interest in getting in the middle of whatever she assumed I was up to.

I looked over as Ida Belle and Gertie walked in—Gertie limping across the bar using the cane. I wasn't sure if the limp was an act or if the second half of Nora's pill had been a bust. At least she had on the skirt and sneakers. They sat at the opposite end of the bar, and Christi headed their direction, looking relieved.

"I want something strong and sweet," Gertie told her. "Do you have any hot men back there?"

"We seem to be out at the moment," Christi said, "but I'm sure I could come up with something that costs less and doesn't cheat."

"Setting the bar a little low, aren't you?" Ida Belle joked.

"Sometimes you have to in order to get over it. What about you?"

"Just water for me. I'm the designated driver and that's no picnic with this one. Drinks like a fish."

Christi smiled but she cast a nervous glance backward, and I knew she was checking to see if I was still there. She wasn't going to make a move with me still sitting there, so I tossed some money on the counter and headed out, figuring I'd wait in the SUV. I sent Ida Belle a text when I got there, letting her know where I was and to yell if they needed anything, then I settled back to ponder while I waited. I was certain the bartender was lying. She knew Athena, probably well, and she'd looked almost spooked when I'd told her Athena was out of prison. The question, of course, was why?

It only took a couple minutes before I got a text from Ida Belle.

Bartender leaving with cell phone out. Following.

Crap. I was hoping since the place was practically empty that if she decided to call someone, she'd just do it at the bar. I blew out a breath, trying to decide whether or not to go back inside. I trusted Ida Belle not to get into any trouble, but even Jesus couldn't keep Gertie from causing it. My question was answered when Christi walked out the front door of the hotel and sat on a bench right next to Ida Belle's SUV and lifted her cell phone.

Because our SUV activities sometimes consisted of things outside the normal fare—like the need to shoot and being shot at—Ida Belle had bulletproof glass installed on the windows, and the side glass had tint so dark no one could see inside. The window was lowered a crack but unless the bartender shouted, I was going to have to go with attempting to read her lips. Unfortunately, she had her head dipped down and I couldn't see her face.

"I said I needed some fresh air!" Gertie's voice filtered through the crack in the window, and I watched as she stomp-limped up the sidewalk and plopped down on the other end of the bench. Then she waved her hands at Ida Belle. "Just give me a minute. Go get the car or something. You're ruining my buzz."

Christi looked up when Gertie sat and lowered her phone. She cut her gaze to Ida Belle, who threw her hands in the air, then stalked off. Christi looked back over at Gertie, and I could see the indecision on her face. Gertie pulled a sample-size whiskey out of her bag and took a slug, then pulled out yarn and started knitting and singing the theme to *The Brady Bunch*.

Christi stared a couple seconds, and then apparently deciding Gertie was no threat to her conversation either because of the booze or the outright crazy, she lifted the phone and lowered her head again. It wasn't even a minute later when she jumped up and hurried back into the hotel. Ida Belle, who'd been lurking down the street, came back and got Gertie into the SUV. I remained in my seat just in case Christi exited again.

"Did you get anything?" I asked.

"She was talking to someone named Juno. I heard her say 'Athena' and 'PI' when I walked up. Then she said, 'Of course I didn't say anything.' And then, 'What if she finds out about the money?' Then she hung up and took off."

"What money do you think she was talking about?" Ida Belle asked. "And who is 'she,' you or Athena?"

"Good question, but I wonder if it has to do with the trial," I said. "According to the articles I read, none of her former friends were called to testify."

"But that shouldn't be a big surprise," Gertie asked. "Athena had been with Beckett for a couple years at that point. I'm sure she cut ties with those people as soon as she got a leg up."

"I agree," I said, "but with the case against her being so weak, I'm still surprised the girls she lived and worked with weren't called by one side or the other as character witnesses, depending on what they knew about her."

"Maybe they were afraid she did it, so if they had anything on her, they figured keeping their mouths shut was the best route to take," Ida Belle said. "I mean, if Athena could kill her own husband, then she wouldn't have any problem going after them or the means to do it."

"True, but where does the money Christi mentioned come in?" I asked. "This is what I think—I think either Athena paid them off to keep their mouths shut because they knew things about her that would hurt her defense or the Rousseaus paid them off to keep them from saying anything positive about her because it might help."

"But where would Athena have gotten the money?" Gertie asked. "She didn't have any of her own to speak of, and the Rousseaus would have made sure she had no access to anything they controlled."

"I'm sure Beckett supplied her with plenty of spending money," Ida Belle said. "Even with most everyone using credit cards, it's easy enough to buy a designer item and sell it online by consignment for the cash. Or even at a local resale shop."

I nodded. "And someone with huge trust issues like Athena would definitely want a nest egg in case things went south."

"That's true," Gertie said. "And it probably wouldn't take much money to get those girls to stay quiet. No one wants to be in the middle of a homicide trial."

"Christi looked awfully worried when she came over to take our orders," Ida Belle said.

"She was genuinely surprised when I told her Athena was out," I said.

Ida Belle frowned. "If Athena paid them to keep from airing her dirty laundry, then hiring you makes no sense. There's no prison term at stake anymore, but the Rousseaus aren't exactly a minor threat. So why not let her attorney chase down the insurance companies for the payout, then take the money, get a new identity, and leave the state? Go somewhere that the Rousseaus don't have any reach?"

"Maybe she really loved Beckett and wants to see his killer face justice," Gertie said.

"Given her history, the more likely scenario is that he was her ticket out of her old life," Ida Belle said.

Gertie rolled her eyes. "I don't know how you live with yourself being such a hopeless romantic."

I laughed. "I'm not winning any Hallmark awards either, and I know it doesn't make logical sense given what we know about her, but Athena's definitely got motives she isn't revealing to us. I've felt that way from the beginning."

"Well, we better figure out her angle before we get in too deep," Ida Belle said. "People around her seem to have longevity problems."

CHAPTER TEN

ON THE DRIVE BACK TO SINFUL, WE LET THE INVESTIGATION percolate for a while and talked about the upcoming Mardi Gras festival. Every year, based on a secret vote that occurred the year before, a new king and queen were revealed to the town before the start of the parade. The lead time gave the new queen time to get the elaborate gown ready. Last year, Ally and Deputy Breaux had won the honors and had made a great king and queen.

Voting was done at the General Store and since Ida Belle was one of the parade organizers and now married to the man collecting the votes, she always knew who had won before the festival reveal. She guarded that secret as strongly as her prime fishing spots, but Gertie and I didn't count. This year, she'd been beyond pleased with the choices.

Molly Broussard, who was famous for catering and cage fighting, had been chosen to be queen. She'd been a recent client of mine and was a woman I both liked and respected. She might also be the only person in town who could beat me at hand-to-hand combat. Given that most of the town was addicted to her crab dip, the vote was no surprise there.

But the elected king had been.

Ronald.

With his odd habits, questionable dress, and mostly intro-verted ways, I'd been momentarily surprised by the choice. But then I remembered all the money he pumped into the town with his charitable contributions and it made perfect sense. His gifts were supposed to be anonymous, but it was hard to keep big financial transactions secret in a small town. People in Sinful loved to gossip and they loved to gossip about big gestures almost as much as the trouble people got up to. Ronald might not have been born in Sinful, but he'd done more for the town than entire generations of people had.

When Molly had heard who her king would be, she'd immediately contacted Ronald and asked if he'd be interested in a wardrobe switch-up. So according to Ida Belle, Molly would be sporting a tuxedo with a purple sequined vest. Ronald was tight-lipped on his outfit, but he'd let slip that it was a custom design and was going to sparkle so much they'd see him in space. I definitely didn't occupy a seat on the fashion train, but this was one dress I couldn't wait to see.

"You keep thinking that hard, you're going to strain some-thing," Ida Belle said after a long bout of silence.

"Yeah," I said. "I guess I'm just trying to make sense of the case, but there's too much missing over too much ground covered."

"We're usually not investigating the client at the same time," Ida Belle said. "Not intentionally and specifically, anyway."

"Maybe we should be," Gertie said. "They all lie about something."

"True," Ida Belle agreed. "But it spreads us thinner."

"Have you made a decision on whether or not to continue the investigation?" Gertie asked. "I know we all agree that

Athena hasn't been forthcoming about everything, but I guess the bottom line is, do we think she killed Beckett?"

"Based on Casey's take, I'd say I'm leaning toward no," I said. "But I'm not completely ruling her out."

"So did you figure anything out with all that contemplation?" Ida Belle asked.

I sighed. "I wish. More like I added another item that doesn't add up to my list. Christi asked why she hadn't heard about Athena being out on the news. It's coming, I'm sure, but I figured the DA and the Rousseaus weren't going to offer it up because in their minds, they lost. And Athena's attorney wouldn't issue a press release unless she asked him to, which she won't."

"All reasonable," Ida Belle said.

"Perhaps," I said. "But if the Rousseaus really think Athena killed their son, and she's walking free, why let her get off easy? Why not crucify her in the press—make it impossible for her to stick around, dredging up their dead son?"

"Quentin probably thinks it would hurt his reelection to go after her publicly," Gertie said.

"Maybe," I said. "But then I think about that comment Tate made that sounded like Beckett might have been involved in shady financial stuff. If something like that got out, it could ruin the Rousseaus' business."

Ida Belle nodded. "I'm following you. If the Rousseaus start making noise about Athena's release and Beckett's murder, there would be public pressure on the cops to reopen the case. And things that weren't exposed the first round might be exposed the second."

"Not to mention, they'd need a new villain, because Athena is off the table," I said.

"Do you think they're covering for Tate?" Gertie asked. "Could he have done it?"

"Not personally because he's alibied," I said, "but I think he could have easily arranged it. He would have had the ability to track the boat, and he would only need access to Beckett's phone for a minute to make that transfer from his account."

"Paying for a hit man with the target's money is a new kind of low," Gertie said. "But do you really think Quentin and Lena would cover for Tate if they knew he had his brother killed?"

"They'd already lost one son," Ida Belle said. "Why lose another?"

"And everything else that would come with that level of scandal," I said. "But if neither side takes it to the next level, the cops won't be under pressure and all the secrets remain locked away. This is all speculation, of course."

"But it's darned good speculation," Ida Belle said.

"So if we roll with this theory—and I'm all for it—then where do we go from here?" Gertie asked.

"Everywhere," I said. "But more specifically, I want to stop by the motel on our way home."

"You going to do some spying on Athena?" Gertie asked.

"No," I said. "I'm going to get Shadow Chaser to do some spying."

Shadow Chaser was the main clerk at the motel and had harbored a very brief desire to be a PI. All it took was one life-threatening incident and seeing a grown man naked, and he'd changed his mind.

"I don't think he's interested in being a PI anymore," Ida Belle said. "Which isn't a bad thing since he's horrible at it."

"I'm not asking him to break into her room or anything," I said. "I'll leave the fun stuff for me. I just want him to tell me if anyone comes to see her."

"You thinking she's got a new man already?" Gertie asked.

"Or an old one."

Gertie sighed. "Dixon. God, I hope he's not foolish enough to get tangled up with her a second time."

"Who says he didn't already?" Ida Belle asked. "He's still got to explain what he was doing in New Orleans that got him punched by Beckett. Men with lots of assets don't generally go around punching other people without serious provocation. It leads to lawsuits."

"I plan on asking both of them about the incident," I said. "And Dixon outright lied about not having anything to do with Athena after they left Sinful."

Ida Belle took the exit for the motel, and I told her to pull in the back where she could park behind the dumpster, and I'd walk around the hedges to the office just in case Athena was in eyeshot.

"Looks like the hedges still haven't recovered from that explosion," Gertie said.

"Try not to add to their healing time," I said. "Just wait here. I won't be long."

I hopped out of the SUV and hurried behind what was left of the hedges toward the front of the motel. I peered around the corner and since I didn't see anyone in the parking lot, hotfooted it to the office. Shadow Chaser jumped up from his chair as I walked in and immediately started shaking his head.

"Whatever it is the answer is no," he said.

"What if it's something good?" I asked.

"Nothing good comes from the Angel of Death. Every time you come to the motel, someone dies or kills someone or something explodes or someone is naked—and never the people you'd like to see naked."

"So you're definitely not interested in the PI thing anymore?"

"No way. You people are insane. And coming from someone whose mother insists she was abducted by aliens, that's saying a lot. Besides, I've been promoted to manager, so I'm on a whole new career path."

"Congratulations. What happened to the other guy? Did he retire?"

"If you define 'retire' as not working, I'm pretty sure he retired long before he hired me. But the new owner fired him and promoted me. By text. You should have seen his face."

"Someone bought this place?"

"Hey, this place might be a dump, but it's a busy dump. With the infusion of cash I've been promised, I can double profit. And since part of my new pay structure includes profit sharing, I am all about keeping that dark cloud that follows you off the property."

"Who was the buyer?" I asked, wondering what corporation not only paid good money for this place but had promised to put more money into it.

"Shake Down Enterprises. It's one of those real estate holding companies with a lot of different interests. Great for me because it means the owners won't be standing here looking over my shoulder."

I'd started grinning as soon as he said the name and by the time he'd finished talking, I was laughing.

"No," I said. "They won't be looking over your shoulder. They pay other people to do that."

He frowned. "What do you mean?"

"Shake Down Enterprises? You really don't know?"

He shook his head.

"Shake Down Enterprises is owned by Big and Little Hebert. Shakedown...get it?"

He paled and dropped back into his chair. "Please tell me you're just saying that to scare me."

"I'm saying it because it's true. Scaring you is just a fun side effect. Have I mentioned that I'm a personal friend of the Heberts?"

He gave me a pained look. "Of course you are. You're right up their alley."

"So anyway, I'm sure they'd be happy for you to help me out. They're big supporters of my PI business."

He sighed, completely defeated. "Who are you after?"

"Not after. Just gathering information."

I pulled out my phone and showed him a picture of Athena. "She just got released from prison—the case was overturned."

His eyes widened and I knew she'd checked in. "What did she do? Or not do?"

"If you think they got it right when they overturned her case, then she didn't kill her husband."

He threw his hands in the air. "Every good-looking woman who comes in here—you included—is a serious risk to my health. How am I ever supposed to get a date?"

"Hasn't anyone told you not to crap where you eat?"

"Easy for you to say—you're not locked up in a ten-foot-square office most of your waking hours."

"No. I'm usually chasing down murderers. Trust me, the options in my dating pool are far worse."

"But you have a boyfriend."

"Our meeting was an occupational hazard. We're often going after the same bad guy."

"Hmmm. Maybe I should see about attending one of those educational conventions."

"Wouldn't hurt to ask. Bring it up to your new bosses."

"If I do this favor, I don't suppose you'd put in a good word for me."

"I don't see why not."

He perked up. "Okay, let me get the key."

I put up my hands. "I don't want to go into her room."

He stared. "Why not? She's the only person staying here right now that's worth seeing naked."

"Because I don't think she's hiding anything in there that will solve my case. I just want you to keep an eye out. If you see anyone come to visit her, call me. And get a picture if you can. If you can't, at least send me a description."

He eyed me suspiciously. "That's it?"

"That's it."

"Okay. That sounds too easy, but I'll roll with it."

"If we're lucky, all of the action on this one will take place somewhere else."

"I've never been lucky."

———

It was late afternoon by the time we got back to Sinful. We'd put a lot of miles in, but I didn't feel as though we'd gained enough for all that effort. We had some avenues to explore but nothing concrete.

"How do you want to handle questioning Athena and Dixon?" Ida Belle asked as we pulled into town.

"I've been thinking on that one," I said. "If they're involved, then neither one is going to talk straight. But I think I'd be able to tell if Dixon is lying. I think Athena is a pro who's been playing roles her entire life. She might be able to get past me."

Ida Belle nodded. "So we should talk to Dixon first. That way, if by any chance they're still in contact, he has no warning. You want to do it now?"

"Might as well. But what about the Sinful Ladies Cough Syrup? There's still a kitchen full of that stuff to bottle and label."

"I called in reinforcements," Ida Belle said. "The Sinful Ladies are handling the rest of it. Gertie and I will check in with them when we're done."

I looked back at Gertie and grinned. "If they get into that new batch, you might have an impromptu slumber party at your place."

"I hope not," she said. "Jeb is coming over tonight. We're reenacting scenes from movies. Tonight is *Dirty Dancing*."

"You can't walk five steps without a cane," Ida Belle said. "How the heck are you going to dance?"

"Good point. Maybe we'll do that pottery wheel thing from *Ghost*. They're sitting. At least, they start out sitting—"

"No!" Ida Belle said. "You are approaching that-which-shall-not-be-shared territory."

Gertie sighed. "I don't know how Walter stands being married to you. That huge romantic streak you have must be overwhelming."

"He doesn't have to worry about me taking out my joints or blowing myself up with my purse," Ida Belle said. "He appreciates the lower stress level."

"Carter doesn't have stress problems and he's with Fortune," Gertie argued.

I grinned. "I think he'd disagree. He just doesn't like wasting time, and asking me to change would be as successful as asking you to."

"Whatever," Gertie said. "I'm just trying to add some interest to your lives."

Ida Belle snorted. "If you add any more interest to our lives, we're going to be talking about it with our Maker."

The conversation ended because Ida Belle pulled up to the curb in front of Dixon's house and I spotted his truck in the driveway. As we headed up to the door, I thought about how to approach the conversation. But it had been a long day and I had a lot of stuff running around in my mind, so I figured the direct approach was probably the best to go with. Heck, who was I kidding? I didn't know any other approach.

Dixon looked a bit surprised when he opened the door, and I didn't blame him. Visiting for two days in a row was a lot, even for Sinful.

"We need to talk," I said to him.

CHAPTER ELEVEN

Dixon's eyes widened a little, but he just nodded and stood back so we could enter, then headed silently to the kitchen. He didn't offer us anything to drink this time, probably because he'd clued in by my tone that this was no polite social call.

"You lied to me yesterday," I said. "I asked you if you'd had any contact with Athena after you moved to New Orleans and you lied."

"I didn't lie," he argued. "I just said it was a big city and we didn't move in the same circles."

"Dixon Edwards!" Gertie said. "Don't you dare sit there pretending omission isn't a lie. It's a disservice to the woman who raised you."

He flushed, and I could tell he was a little embarrassed but also a little angry. "You realize you're saying that about a woman who omitted everything about my father to anyone who might have taken a closer look."

"Is that why you omitted the fight you had with Beckett?" I asked. "Afraid of a closer look?"

He sighed. "I guess I should have figured she'd tell. She

never had a problem throwing people under a bus if it suited her."

"Oddly enough, I didn't hear it from Athena, either, and I'll be addressing that with her later."

He looked a bit surprised and a tiny bit pleased, and it hit me that he still had feelings for her. After all this time and after everything she'd done. Some people were gluttons for punishment.

"So did you pick up your relationship with Athena in New Orleans?" I asked.

"No. I had no idea where she went when she left Sinful and I didn't go looking, I swear."

"Then how did you end up in a fight with her husband?"

"It wasn't much of a fight. He hit me with no warning and before I could even return the favor, a bunch of guys in tuxedos grabbed both of us. Then I got the heck out of there before the cops showed up. I'm sure the pretty boy went right back to sipping champagne."

"So tell me how it all went down."

He slumped back in his chair and shook his head. "It went down because I'm stupid. I'd been doing fine—my job was great, my mom was doing better, and living with my aunt was nice. She's a good woman. Reminds me a little of Miss Gertie. I wasn't looking for Athena, I swear. I knew that she'd left Sinful because one of the ladies from here filled my mom in on one of their gossip calls. But I didn't know where she'd gone."

"Then how did you come to be at a black-tie event, getting punched by her husband?"

"I was invited." He must have caught my unconvinced look because he hurried to explain. "I wasn't invited to the event. I never had that kind of money or clout and never will. But I got a letter from Athena, asking me to meet her in the bar of the hotel. She said she had some things she needed to say to me.

Said they were important. I didn't know there was going to be a fancy party going on and definitely didn't know her husband would be there. I sure as heck didn't know he was going to punch me."

I frowned. "Why would she invite you to an event to have what sounds like a private conversation?"

"If I knew, I'd tell you. I was a little surprised to walk in and see all those people in tuxedos, evening gowns, and jewelry dripping off them like raindrops, but I just headed past the ballroom and down the hall to the bar. It never occurred to me that Athena was at the event. I sat down at a table in the back and waited. I remember thinking I was a fool, going there to listen to the excuses from a woman I knew was a professional liar. Boy, I've never been more right about anything."

"So what happened?"

"Athena came into the bar talking on her phone. She stood there for a minute, then spotted me in the corner, ended her call, and came over. I stood up as she approached and she stopped in front of me and stared. Then she said, 'It's nice to see you.' Just like that—'nice.' Like I was an acquaintance—someone who never mattered."

"Maybe she was nervous," I suggested.

He snorted. "Athena Durand has never been nervous a day in her life. Even when they showed her going in and out of the courthouse, she looked confident. Hell, she looked shocked the day she was convicted. I was already questioning my sanity when she walked up, and that polite, dismissive tone was all it took to bring me to my senses. I jumped up and said this was all a mistake.

"So she put her hand on my chest and said to wait—there's something she wanted to say to me. And against my better judgment, I stood there. Then her husband walked in and saw her with her hand on my chest, and standing entirely too close to be acceptable, and he marched over and asked who the hell I am."

Ida Belle whistled. "There's a crap situation."

"No doubt," he said. "So what was I supposed to do—tell the man his wife asked me to meet her there? That sure didn't look like the best option to me. So I just said I was an old friend from Sinful and we'd run into each other in the bar."

"I take it he didn't buy it," I said.

"Hell no, he didn't buy it, and I wouldn't have either. The whole thing looked off. He looked at Athena and said, 'Is this the guy? The one from high school? The one you've been seeing behind my back?' And that's when I put my hands up and stepped back and said, 'Whoa, I don't know nothing about that.'"

"What did Athena say?" I asked.

"She was trying to tell him there wasn't anything going on, but he wouldn't listen. Then he said, 'High school is over,' and he punched me."

"Holy crap!" Gertie said.

"He caught me so off guard, I didn't even have time to deflect. Just took a right cross in the jaw and fell backward over a chair. Before I could get up, three of his buddies were on me and another three were hustling him out of the bar."

"What did Athena do?" I asked.

"She looked shocked and had the decency to apologize—which is all the credit I'll give her—then she ran out of the bar. The bartender told me to get out before the manager showed up because he didn't want to have to say who'd caused the damage to the chair. So that's exactly what I did."

"Did you ever hear from her again?" I asked.

"No, and since her husband was killed the next week, I figured I got off lucky."

"So what do you think she wanted?" I asked.

He shrugged. "I have absolutely no idea and the longer I thought about it, the less ideas I had."

"Where were you when Beckett was killed?" I asked.

He flushed, and I could tell the question made him mad. "I was welding a rig. Didn't even know about all that until I got back home the following week and my mom told me. Look, I've tried to put all that behind me because when I think about it, I just get mad all over again. And what good does getting mad do? The man who punched me is dead, and the woman who instigated it all is—or was—in prison. I don't know what kind of crap they had going on, but I wish I would have stayed home that day and watched talk shows with my mother and aunt."

"And now you've run into her again in Sinful," Gertie said. "That had to be a shock."

"You best believe it," he said. "And not one I'm interested in reliving. Is she sticking around here? Because if that's her plan, then I need to rethink my own."

"I don't know what her plans are," I said. "I don't think she knows either. Not yet."

"Well, if you're taking her on as a client, I can only suggest you watch your back. I didn't know what Athena was up to back when we were dating. I don't know what she was up to with that whole bar thing, and I darn sure don't know what she's up to now. But what I'm certain of is that it's no good."

———

GERTIE WAS SO STIFF BY THE TIME WE GOT DONE TALKING TO Dixon that I had to practically carry her into her house. Fortunately, the Sinful Ladies had cleared out and Jeb, who was already there and waiting patiently for their date night, jumped right in to help. I wasn't sure how long his back would hold out, but Gertie said she'd already sent Nora a text and she was going to drop off a few more of those pain pills—some she claimed should have longer-lasting effects. I just prayed all the effects went to her legs and not anywhere else—like her mind, or her mouth. She didn't need those relaxing any more than they already were.

Once Gertie was situated, Ida Belle dropped me off at home and headed for her own. It had been a really long day and I wanted to stand in a hot shower for an hour and then climb into my recliner with a beer and a sandwich. Carter had texted me earlier saying he was going to burn the midnight oil and try to clear out some of the paper in his office and he'd talk to me tomorrow, so the only male on my night's agenda was Merlin and he was easily bought off with tuna.

I hit the shower first, then fed Merlin so I didn't have to deal with hungry cat nonsense. I fixed myself a sandwich while Merlin did his nightly outdoor business, then I let him back in and headed for my recliner with my sandwich, an entire bag of potato chips, and two bottles of beer. That way, I didn't have to get up for a refill. I put on some reruns of *Kitchen Nightmares* —which I found entertaining because of all the yelling—and proceeded to eat and relax. I must have dozed off because my cell phone ringing startled me awake. It was pitch-dark outside and I glanced at my watch. Almost eleven. Phone calls at that hour were rarely a good thing. I checked the display and felt my pulse tick up a notch.

Shadow Chaser.

"I saw that woman arguing with a man in the parking lot just a few minutes ago," he said when I answered. "And why didn't you tell me she was Athena Durand?"

"You checked her in."

"No one uses their real name here! I thought she looked

familiar and then started Googling. Jesus H. Christ! She didn't just kill her husband. She killed a Rousseau."

"Her conviction was overturned. As far as the law is concerned, Athena is an innocent woman."

"And what about you—do you think she's innocent?"

"I'm withholding judgment at the moment."

"Oh God! Why does it always have to be my motel? Why can't they cough up the few extra bucks the others charge for cable television and take their drama somewhere else?"

"Maybe you could use that cash infusion to jack up the prices and clear out some of the riffraff. So what did the guy look like?"

"I couldn't see him well. They were at the end of the parking lot and away from the lights. He was taller than her by probably five or six inches and looked fairly lean, even in a jacket. He had a ball cap pulled down low and he was facing away from me most of the time, so I didn't really see much else. Even when he looked back this way, I still couldn't make out any facial features in the dark."

"But you're sure it was Athena?"

"No mistaking her body, even in silhouette."

"Why do you think they were arguing?"

"They were both standing all tense-like and throwing their hands in the air."

"Did you see his vehicle when he left?"

"No. He left through the woods at the far side of the property. He walked like a younger guy, though, if that makes sense."

"It does, and that's an excellent observation."

"Thanks." He sounded pleased. "I figure he must have parked on the service road or in the neighborhood behind the motel. I guess I could have driven around and seen if I spotted him but then I remembered it was Athena Durand and kept my butt right here in my chair."

"That's probably the best route. Thanks for calling, and let me know if you see anything else."

"If there's any way you can get her out of my motel before the Rousseaus go all tribal on her, I'd appreciate it. That cash infusion I'm hoping to get can't handle a large-scale attack—by them *or* you."

So dramatic, I thought as he disconnected. But then, he wasn't exactly incorrect. The motel was probably one incident with Gertie's purse away from being condemned. I leaned back on the couch and considered. The description he'd given me could match Dixon, but then, it was so vague, it could also match a thousand other guys in this area of the parish. Still, it wouldn't hurt to see if Dixon was at home. That way, I could eliminate him if he was and know that I was looking for another guy—a line of inquiry I had no idea where to start on.

Sighing, I pulled on my tennis shoes and headed out. No use taking my Jeep out for this when I could jog over there in a matter of minutes, and if he was the one at the motel, he wouldn't make it home before that. And if he *was* up to something, I didn't want him to catch sight of me cruising by.

I had my mental fingers crossed the entire way over, but a wave of frustration washed over me when I turned the corner to his block and saw that the driveway was empty. The lights were on inside, but I was pretty sure his truck didn't fit in the tiny one-car garage. I located a good hiding place behind a shrub in the yard of the house across the street and sat down to wait. It was a long, itchy fifteen minutes before I saw headlights round the block and approach, then I watched Dixon's truck pull into the driveway.

He jumped out, and I sighed again at the jacket and ball cap he was wearing. I couldn't be absolutely certain, because it was chilly and darn near every male in the state wore a ball cap, especially if it was cold out. But the timing was definitely suspect. I watched as he grabbed a sack of groceries from the back seat. I recognized the logo as one belonging to a larger chain store up the highway, not far from the motel. A chain that happened to be open twenty-four hours.

So was it just a coincidence that he was shopping for groceries while Athena was arguing with someone at the motel? Or was he simply making efficient use of his time and gas and creating a reason for being in the area by combining errands? Regardless, I had to talk to Athena first thing tomorrow about her relationship with Dixon.

I just hoped I could tell if she was lying.

I'd moved into a squat when Dixon pulled in—a habit from the days when I might need to make the transition from not moving at all to running—but I was waiting for the lights to go off at the front of Dixon's house before I gave up my hiding spot in case he had more groceries in the truck. The last thing I needed was for him to catch me spying on him. If he and Athena were up to something, I didn't want them knowing I was onto them. I was just about to give up on the living room light and sprint off when I heard a loud boom down the block.

In the direction of Gertie's house.

I yanked the hoodie over my head and jumped up just as the front door of the house whose yard I was hiding in flew open and the biggest Doberman I'd ever seen ran out.

"Get 'em, Sarge!" a man shouted.

CHAPTER TWELVE

I BOLTED OUT OF THE BUSH AND SPRINTED DOWN THE sidewalk. I knew I couldn't outrun the dog, but I didn't want him to nab me in front of Dixon's house or my cover was blown. As I neared Gertie's house, I saw a pizza delivery guy dashing across the yard of the house next door toward his car, which was still running. I veered to the left and dove through the open passenger window of his car just as the dog caught up with me. I barely got the window up before he jumped after me and slammed into the side of the car.

The pizza guy scrambled on the roof of his car and screamed for someone to save him. The dog tried to leap onto the hood of the car, miscalculated, and slid off. But he wasn't likely to miscalculate a second time.

More pizzas were in the back seat, so I grabbed one out of the heated sleeve, rolled the window down, and threw the whole thing like a Frisbee across the lawn. As it whizzed past the dog, he caught the scent and abandoned his pursuit of the pizza guy and went for dinner. I jumped into the driver's seat, yelled for the pizza guy to hold on, and took off down the block as fast as I dared to go given that he was clinging to the roof of the car.

I rounded the corner and pulled to a stop, then jumped out and was relieved to see he was still with us. I'd once seen a target have a heart attack while trying to escape assassination by jumping on the top of a freight train and we'd had to break his fingers to get the body off it. My day had been long enough without having to break fingers before I went to bed.

"You okay?" I asked.

"Are you crazy?" he yelled as he slid off the roof to stand in front of me. "Of course I'm not okay. Someone tried to shoot me. That dog was going to eat me. And I'm going to be fired. Do you know how expensive that pie was that you tossed across the lawn? People pay a premium for delivery out here."

"Would you have preferred I let the dog get you? Maybe 'thank you for saving me' would be a better choice of words."

"That dog was chasing you! You're the bad guy here. And you stole my car."

"I'm no bad guy. I was out jogging when that lunatic set that dog out the door. And who was shooting at you?"

"You didn't hear that gunshot?"

"I heard an explosion. I assume that's why the old man let Cujo loose. But that wasn't a gunshot."

"Someone trying to blow me up is no better."

A vehicle rounded the corner ahead of us and I put my hand up to block the oncoming headlights. I was hoping they would just pull past and keep going, but then I recognized the engine and sighed.

"Is there a problem here?" Carter asked as he pulled up next to us.

"Yes, there's a problem," Pizza Boy said. "Someone shot at me, and this woman stole my car."

"You're literally standing in the driver's door and the keys are in the ignition," I said.

"But you drove it away from where I parked it."

I threw my hands in the air. "Because you were on top of it and a killer Doberman was trying to eat you. Next time, I'll leave you to the dog."

He looked at Carter. "*And* she threw one of my delivery pizzas out the car window."

"Again—to save you from the *dog*!"

Carter frowned. "Who took a shot at you?"

Pizza Boy blew out a breath. "Everyone is so concerned about the shooting, and no one cares that this woman stole my car. What are you going to do about it?"

"Nothing," Carter said.

Pizza Boy blinked and stared. "What do you mean, nothing? Don't tell me you believe her ridiculous story about the random dog. She was probably robbing some poor soul and the dog was after her. She's probably the one who shot at me."

Carter shook his head.

"You actually believe her?" Pizza Boy asked.

"About this, yes. If she'd fired at you, you'd be dead. I'm not arresting her, because she's right, you're in possession of your car. And I'm not interested in ruining my weekend."

"How would that ruin your weekend?" he asked.

"Because this is my girlfriend."

"Fine, then! If your girlfriend is done using my vehicle as a getaway car, then I'd like to text in my notice and call my mom to tell her she can just get over my still living at home."

"Sounds like a plan," Carter said.

Pizza Boy huffed a few more times and lingered, as if either one of us were going to change our stories or our minds, then finally jumped into his car, slammed the door, and drove off.

"So this shooting..." Carter asked.

I shook my head. "It wasn't gunfire. Sounded more like an explosion."

"Don't tell me Gertie had another handbag incident."

"I don't know. I was out for a jog and then there was the explosion and some old dude let his angry dog out. Things went sideways with Pizza Boy, and here we are."

"Jogging? At eleven p.m.?"

"That's my story and I'm sticking to it."

"Uh-huh. Well, get in, because I still have an explosion to investigate, and from where I sit, it looks like guilty by association."

"This is date night," I said as I climbed in his truck. "What in the world could they be doing that caused an explosion?"

Then I remembered who we were discussing. "Never mind," I said.

Carter pulled up in front of Gertie's house and sure enough, I heard laughing in the backyard. At least they were alive and well enough to laugh. One less thing. But the second we climbed out of the truck, the angry dog came barreling across the lawn from the fence line. I dove back in the truck, but Carter had already closed his door and taken a couple steps away. He launched himself onto the hood and scrambled for the top.

I cracked the window. "Told you."

The dog proceeded to stand with two paws on the hood and bark as though he had found Bin Laden.

Carter pulled out his cell phone and dialed. "Wallace, your dog is terrorizing the neighborhood and impeding a police investigation. Get him inside, or you're going to be picking him up in a bag."

I heard incomprehensible yelling on the other end, but Carter could yell louder.

"If he's that important, you'll get him inside," Carter said.

"It's going toward midnight, I'm still on shift, and I wasn't even supposed to be working today. I don't even have one nerve or a single drop of patience left for this town's nonsense. Get that dog out of the street now!"

I saw the front door down the street open and Wallace stepped outside and whistled. The Doberman stopped his frantic barking and took off down the street and into the house.

"You're paying for the dents and scratches on my truck!" Carter yelled.

Wallace gave him the finger before slamming the front door. I hoped the old coot didn't get foolish and open the door again because I could tell by his tone that Carter had reached the end of his rope. I had a feeling that whatever Gertie had done wasn't likely to help matters.

I didn't hear laughing when we exited the truck this time, but I figured everyone within a block's radius had heard Carter yelling and had probably opted for silence. Since the laughing had come from the backyard earlier, I headed to the fence gate and called out as we entered.

"You guys back here?"

"Thank the Lord!" Gertie said. "Come help. We have a situation here."

I hurried to the corner of the house, then drew up short so fast that Carter ran into me.

"Are you guys dressed?" I asked before I stepped around into the backyard.

"Good. God," I heard Carter mutter behind me.

"All important things are covered," Gertie said.

That answer was as sketchy as the woman who'd given it, but I ventured around the corner anyway. Carter followed me and let out a strangled cry at the scene in front of us.

Gertie and Jeb stood in the backyard, looking as if they'd been in a mud fight.

A semi-naked mud fight.

They were dressed, but it was the minimum to qualify for the statement. And it was not enough to leave your house. Quite frankly, I wasn't convinced it was enough to be in a fenced backyard. Thank God the porch light was kinda weak, but I could still make out blue sequins peeking out of both their mud layers.

"What the heck happened?" I asked.

"Well, since my legs were shot, we rescheduled reenacting *Dirty Dancing* for next month and went with *Ghost* instead," Gertie said. "Did you know that pottery wheels can explode?"

Carter shook his head. "I didn't know that because it's not true."

"Well, it might have had a little help," Gertie said. "Good thing we were doing all this on the back porch."

Carter stared at them in dismay. "You were on your porch... dressed like that."

"More like undressed like that," I said.

"You're not helping," Carter said.

"Jeb cleaned up the kitchen after the Sinful Ladies left—mopped and everything," Gertie said. "I didn't want to mess up his hard work, so we moved our date outside. Since I've screened it, you can't really see in all that well. Besides, after we went through the romance building scenes, we were going to move back inside for the big—"

"Stop!" I said and held up my hand, because I knew she was about to say 'climax,' and Carter might shoot them both if she did.

Carter let out a strangled cry.

"I just want to hear about the explosion," I said.

"Do you have any idea how slick pottery mud is?" Gertie

asked. "I was doing good keeping it just on my hands, but then Jeb went for the reach-around and grabbed my chest instead of the vase. Not that I minded, but I was a little startled when he went off script and pushed too hard on the vase. It started slinging mud off everywhere, and when I tried to jump up, my legs were still wonky, so I pitched backward and knocked Jeb over. He tipped over onto the table, which broke, and a pipe bomb I'd been working on rolled under the pottery wheel and the whole thing went up."

Carter's jaw dropped. "Pipe...you were working...I just can't."

Gertie held up a garden hose. "I don't suppose you could give us a rinse? Our hands are too muddy to keep the nozzle depressed."

I was reaching for the hose when the sprinkler system cut on. The stream from one of the nearby heads hit Gertie and Jeb, and I got a quick lesson in just how easily pottery mud washed off skin.

"My legs are feeling better!" Gertie said and grabbed Jeb's hands.

They started dancing in the streams of water and every second revealed more of what the mud had been hiding.

"Done!" Carter said and stalked off.

"Get inside before you scare the locusts!" I yelled as I hurried after Carter.

I could still hear them laughing when I climbed into his truck.

———

DESPITE NOT MAKING IT INTO BED UNTIL WELL AFTER midnight, I woke early the next morning after a night full of jumbled dreaming. It always happened when I had a new case with multiple moving parts and too many things that didn't add up, and this one definitely fit that bill. I could only remember bits of the last dream and it involved Athena wearing a nun's habit and Gertie feeding popcorn to pigeons. The pigeons were wearing blue sequined thongs. Shadow Chaser was filming it and Carter was loading rounds into a magazine, which was the only part of it that made sense.

I headed downstairs for the coffee I desperately needed. I had just poured my first cup when I heard a knock at my front door. I frowned as I headed for the living room. It wasn't even 7:00 a.m. and anyone who had the nerve to come over that early had their own key. Except Ronald, but he would have come to the back door. I opened it to find a young girl I didn't recognize standing there holding a large folder.

"Delivery," she said and hurried away.

"Wait!" I called after her, but she jumped into the passenger side of a blue SUV and they took off. I made note of the license plate and make and model of the SUV when I got back to the kitchen, then sat down at the table and opened the file.

My eyes widened as I realized it was the police files from Beckett's murder investigation. This had to be from Casey. She had a daughter in college who sometimes helped her with things—on the sly, of course. She was probably the only person Casey would have trusted with something like this. I said a prayer Casey wouldn't get caught and dug into the file.

When I got to the autopsy report, I saw a sticky note. *I was never happy with this. It all struck me as odd. Won't say more. Want your cold take on it.*

I read through the report, scanning the list of noted injuries, and then the cause and manner of death. There was so little left of the body that some of it was mostly an educated guess, but ultimately, the coroner's conclusion was that

Beckett had sustained a blow to the back of the head and had likely drowned. What couldn't be determined was whether he'd received the blow before entering the water, as a function of falling into the water, or after he entered the water. Given the holes in the findings, it was clear this was where the political pressure had come down the pike and insisted on the homicide call, because this was a case for undetermined if I'd ever seen one.

I continued on to the verification, assuming I'd find DNA testing since the body couldn't be visibly identified. And that was the case, but I also found it somewhat odd. DNA comparison had been done using hair from a brush in Beckett's overnight bag on the boat. I checked the photo of the brush—silver-plated and engraved with his initials. A footnote claimed it was an anniversary present from Athena. Another note proclaimed gathering DNA from the penthouse was deemed unnecessary due to the validity of the hair sample and strong objection from the victim's family, who did not want Athena to have any part in the investigation.

Wow. So the Rousseaus had basically decided from the onset that the only role Athena was allowed was that of a suspect. Even the remains had been returned to his parents, and Athena hadn't even been arrested by then. The amount of pull the Rousseaus had was evident, but the note about sampling from the penthouse being unnecessary was clearly the coroner's attempt to cover his butt in case he was ever called into question.

I shook my head. Casey was right. The autopsy appeared to have been directed like a Hollywood movie. How the DA had managed to get a conviction when there wasn't any concrete proof of a homicide was beyond me. I had to wonder if there had been jury tampering as well as the obvious police and coroner tampering.

It took me an hour to finish up the rest of the file, making notes as I went. By that time, Ida Belle and Gertie turned up.

"You're walking much better today," I said as she came in.

Gertie grinned and grabbed coffee for her and Ida Belle. "Nora's trying a new mix on me. This one is a powder you put in your coffee."

I froze and stared at her. "This medicine you're getting from Nora is stuff she's mixing up herself?"

"Yeah. She's got a real knack for it."

Ida Belle shook her head. "If I were Catholic, this is where I'd do that whole sign of the cross thing."

"We've been mixing up our own brew for years," Gertie said.

"There's only so much damage that can be done with a shot of alcohol," Ida Belle said. "Even our new grape flavor can't compete against God only knows what that Nora has put together. The woman travels all over the world looking for new drugs."

Gertie nodded. "I know. She's definitely on the cutting edge."

Ida Belle threw her hands in the air. "I give up."

"Stop worrying," Gertie said. "It's not like I have to drug test at work next week or anything."

Ida Belle gave me a pointed look. "There's an idea."

"I'm sorta afraid to know what she's taking if it can get her from practically paralyzed to walking with a minimal limp overnight," I said. "Especially after that whole pipe bomb–pottery wheel explosion."

Ida Belle set her coffee down and stared. "You know what," she said finally. "I don't even want to know."

"Good, because we've got bigger fish to fry at the moment."

I told them about my special delivery that morning, and they both looked excited.

"Casey's taking a big risk doing that," Ida Belle said.

Gertie nodded. "This case must have really bothered her. So did you find any revelations?" Gertie asked.

"Not really. There wasn't a lot of actual investigation, but Casey had already told us as much. They did the bare minimum of questioning and didn't push on the interviews where I think they should have. There's a clear undercurrent with cops and witnesses of not wanting to tread on the Rousseaus. I have to wonder what might have come out if the cops hadn't just pursued evidence to fit the narrative they were writing on Athena."

"Did they interview Dixon about the fight?" Gertie asked.

"They did. He claimed he was headed for another bar but the only lot with availability was a couple blocks away. So he ducked into the hotel to use the restroom but when the bartender caught sight of him, he decided the appropriate thing to do was have at least one drink. Then he ran into Athena, and Beckett lost it."

"So he didn't tell them the same story he told us," Gertie said.

"I wouldn't have either," Ida Belle said. "Athena was under suspicion for murdering the man who'd punched him the week before. If Dixon had told them that he went to that hotel to meet her, they'd have been convinced the affair story was true and tried to fix him up as an accessory."

"Yeah," I agreed. "I'd have totally been liar-liar-pants-on-fire on that one too."

"True," Gertie said. "An investigation alone could have cost him his job, and who knows what it would have done to his mother's health."

I nodded. "So you think he told us the truth?"

Ida Belle shook her head. "At this point, I'm not betting on anything. We've already caught Dixon and Athena in multiple lies to multiple people—most importantly, us. Did the cops question Athena about the incident? What did she say?"

"She said she'd left the ballroom to make a phone call to a caterer about an event she and Beckett were hosting the following month, and when she saw Dixon, he'd already seen her so she thought the polite thing to do was to say hello. Then chaos ensued."

"And the cops didn't dig into them any deeper?" Ida Belle said.

"They questioned a couple of Dixon's friends and coworkers, but none of them had ever heard him mention Athena, and they weren't aware of him dating anyone. He'd dated a server in the bar they were regulars at for a couple months earlier that year, but she said he'd never mentioned Athena either, so they dropped that line of questioning after that."

"So anything else stand out?" Ida Belle asked.

"Yeah," I said and filled them in on the autopsy report.

"That's an even bigger mess than I thought it would be," Gertie said. "The Rousseaus really hate Athena. The number of strings they had to pull to push this through to a conviction is astounding."

Ida Belle shrugged. "If you have no conscience, I suppose it all falls under just another day's business. Manipulating people and situations to get what he wants is Quentin's daily norm. He'd always seen Athena as an anchor dragging the family down—this way he got rid of her for good."

I nodded. "But I can see why Casey isn't happy about it. The cops picked the perp—or to be more accurate, were told who the perp was—then set out to build a case around her instead of running an actual investigation. It's everything that's wrong with policing under political pressure."

"So how do you want to move forward?" Ida Belle asked. "Do you want to talk to Athena this morning?"

"Definitely, but there's something else." I told them about the call from Shadow Chaser the night before and my subsequent jog to his house, leaving out the pizza and pottery portion of the evening.

"Oh no!" Gertie said when I finished. "I thought you came with Carter on the police call last night. I didn't realize you were out working."

"Police call?" Ida Belle asked.

"There was a *fluke* at Gertie's house involving a pottery wheel and an explosion," I said before Gertie could venture into disallowed territory.

"That one really was a fluke," Gertie said. "I mean, how often can I have a pipe bomb and a pottery wheel on my porch?"

Ida Belle stared at her in dismay, but wisely said nothing.

"Back to what Shadow Chaser saw," Gertie said. "I really don't want Dixon to be involved with anything Athena related."

"None of us do," Ida Belle said. "But it's looking more and more like he is, so that conversation with Athena is a priority. What else is on the agenda?"

"Well, if Ronald manages to get invitations to Veronique Vidal's event, then I guess I'm going shopping. There's no way he'll want to leave it for tomorrow."

"You look like someone said they're going to shoot the cat," Gertie said. "It's just shopping. How bad could it be?"

"The last time I went evening gown shopping, the shop owner got into a fight with Celia in the middle of the street, and you took out a display of something called 'Valentino' with feathers that cost more than my house."

"Oh yeah. Maybe don't shop at that store again."

"I have a feeling I'll be shopping wherever Ronald tells me to."

Ida Belle rose from the table. "Before the feather snatching and street fighting can commence Round 2, let's head over to the motel and have a chat with Athena."

CHAPTER THIRTEEN

WE HEADED OUT AND I SENT ATHENA A TEXT ON THE WAY, asking if I could drop by and have her clear up a couple things for me. It took a while for her to respond, and given that it was barely 8:00 a.m., I figured she'd still been asleep. We grabbed some coffees at a local gas station before heading to the motel. If she was only half awake, the caffeine might get her brain working and mouth going.

Athena looked tired, and I could see from the bags under her eyes and the condition of her skin that she wasn't hydrated or sleeping well. It surprised me for a minute. I guess I assumed that if a person got released from prison and there was no chance of going back, they'd probably do some of the best sleeping they had in a while. But clearly freedom wasn't the only thing that weighed on her.

"We brought coffee," I said and held up a huge cup. "I wasn't sure how you took it, so there's a bag of creamer and a choice of sweeteners."

"You're a lifesaver," she said. "Coffee is usually the first thing I reach for when I get up, but this motel doesn't have coffee makers in the room. I think I'm going to buy one. They're cheap and portable enough."

"You wouldn't catch me living without one," Ida Belle said. "Back in my youthful camping days, people used to make fun of me because I brought a thermos of coffee with me to heat up. Just for that, I wouldn't share. Then I figured out how to rig a pot to work on batteries. They were all singing a different tune then."

Athena laughed and waved at the room. "Have a seat. There's only a couple chairs but you're welcome to sit on the bed or the dresser."

Ida Belle and I took the chairs and Gertie claimed the foot of the bed. Athena pulled the luggage stand out of the closet and perched on it with a poise and balance that was noteworthy. Even her ragged appearance didn't detract from her overall looks. Athena was a naturally beautiful woman with a graceful way about her, even when sitting. I could see why men were drawn to her.

"I've been doing some digging and I have questions," I said.

"Shoot," she said.

"Why didn't you tell me that Beckett punched Dixon the week before he was killed?"

She stared at me for several seconds, then sighed. "Because it didn't mean anything."

"But that's not for you to decide. To do my job properly, I need to know *all* the facts and then *I* get to decide whether it's important or not. Deliberate omission is lying. So why did you do it?"

She shrugged. "I guess I didn't want to get him in trouble."

"You either want me to find suspects or you don't, but it's not your place to decide who makes the cut. So I'm going to ask you straight out—were you cheating on Beckett? Was Dixon the other man?"

"No! I swear I was surprised to see Dixon at that hotel. But when I realized he'd seen me, too, I felt odd about just pretending I hadn't seen him and walking off. So I went over and said hello and asked him how he'd been. He said he still loved me. That he had a good job now and could take care of me if I'd just give him another chance. I told him I was happily married and that what he'd said was inappropriate, but when I started to walk away, he grabbed my wrist. I guess I looked startled because when Beckett came into the bar, he thought Dixon was harassing me."

"So he punched him? Just like that?"

"Well, first he accused Dixon of having an affair with me, which I denied, of course."

"Did Beckett know Dixon was someone you'd dated?"

"Yes. I told him everything about that time in my life. Like I said, he was easy to talk to and actually listened. But I also told him I never loved Dixon. I was still a kid and all about making bad decisions. The irony, right? That I thought I was an adult now and finally doing better."

"I guess your denial of an affair wasn't accepted?"

She shook her head. "But there was no reasoning with him when he was like that."

"Was Beckett always so short on temper?"

"He wasn't long on it, but he'd had a row with his father just before the party kicked off and he still had a mad on. He'd just finished chiding me about some catering detail for our upcoming event. The entire reason I left the party and walked into the bar was to make a phone call about it and get him off my back."

"What happened after Beckett punched Dixon?"

"A couple of Beckett's buddies rushed in and grabbed

Dixon before he could retaliate, and a couple more hustled Beckett out of the bar. If Quentin had found out that Beckett had punched someone in the bar, he would have been livid, and he was already on a tirade."

"What was he on a tirade about?"

"I don't know exactly. Something to do with investments that didn't turn out well."

"But that's how the stock market goes," Ida Belle said. "You can't win all the time. It's a long game."

Athena shrugged. "I don't begin to understand it all, but it seemed to me that Beckett and his father had different opinions on investments all the time. Not that it mattered. The buck stopped with Quentin. It was his company and the majority of the clients were people he'd brought in. Beckett was expected to toe the line, not question it."

"Did the police question you about the fight during the investigation into Beckett's death?" I studied her closely because I already knew the answer to the next couple questions and wanted to see if what she told me lined up.

"Yes," she said.

"Did you tell them what Dixon said?"

"No. I just told them that Beckett had a jealous streak and had misconstrued what was going on. He knew that Dixon was the only other guy I'd ever dated for any length of time, and he knew Dixon hadn't wanted the relationship to end."

"Why didn't you tell them the truth?"

"Because even though I didn't love Dixon, I didn't want to cause him problems. I'd already hurt him enough when I was young and too selfish to think about anyone but myself."

"So you never considered that Dixon might have killed Beckett?"

"No. The police said he was at work at the time, so I already knew it couldn't have been him. Besides, they were never looking at Dixon for the actual murder. They were just trying to link him to me to make their case against me stronger."

"But Dixon is a marine welder, so if he was at work, that means he was in the Gulf. You said Beckett used to anchor around rigs because the fishing was better. The police may have ruled him out, but I haven't."

A flicker of uncertainty passed over her face, but she quickly put the mask back in place. "I don't think he's capable," she said. "And besides, what would it get him? Dixon is a great guy. He was the first person who ever actually cared about me, but I didn't love him. Even if Beckett hadn't been in the picture, I still wouldn't have gone back to him."

"So you never saw Dixon after you left Sinful?"

"Not until that day. That's the first and only time I saw him."

"Were you having an affair with someone else?"

She sighed and shook her head. "The Rousseaus wanted everyone to believe that so they could get rid of me. But there was never anyone else. Not from the first day I met Beckett and not even today."

She looked me straight in the eyes. "I loved my husband—flaws and nasty family and all. He might be the only person I ever *did* love."

————

"Do you believe her?" Gertie asked as we drove away from the motel.

"About which part?" I asked.

"All of it."

I shook my head. "I don't know. If it went down the way

she described it, then Dixon is lying. If it went down the way Dixon described it, then Athena is lying."

"Maybe the truth is somewhere in the middle," Gertie said.

"What middle?" Ida Belle asked. "I think that's usually the right take, but the bottom line on this one is somehow they were both in the same place at the same time. And I don't think for a second it was coincidence."

"I agree," I said.

"But there's only two options then," Gertie said. "Either Athena asked Dixon to meet her there or he went there knowing she'd be there, hoping to force a meeting."

"But how would he know where to find her?" I asked.

"Because society people post that kind of thing all over social media," Gertie said.

I sighed. "Maybe they're both lying."

"But were or are they involved?" Ida Belle asked. "That's the question. And when you consider it in light of the motel clerk seeing someone who matched Dixon's description arguing with her last night and then you seeing him return home shortly after that, dressed the way the clerk described, I have to say, it looks really bad."

Gertie sighed. "I hate thinking Dixon is involved with her again."

"I don't like it either," Ida Belle said, "but he's a grown man and is responsible for his own choices."

"The most fascinating thing to me is the one thing I'm certain she was telling the truth about," I said.

"What's that?" Gertie asked.

"I think she loved Beckett."

Ida Belle raised her eyebrows. "Really? Well, that puts an interesting kink into things, don't you think?"

"Only if you think Athena killed Beckett," Gertie said.

Ida Belle nodded. "So where to now? You heard anything from Ronald?"

"Not yet," I said. "Hopefully we'll hear this morning, so we have time to get me something Ronald deems suitable to wear. I had another stop in mind, though. I'd like to talk to Big and Little. They have ears to the ground in finance and political circles. If anyone has dirt on the Rousseaus, it would be them. Let me send a text and see if they can talk to us."

Ten minutes later, we pulled up in front of the main building of a warehouse that served as both offices and living quarters for the Heberts and their right-hand man Mannie. I knew Big owned other homes—like the apartment in NOLA he'd graciously lent us for Mardi Gras the year before—but he spent most of his time in this highly secure facility tucked away from the main roads.

Mannie greeted us at the door with a huge smile.

"The Heberts were excited to get your call," he said as we headed upstairs. "They assume you're working on a case and are eager to help. It's been a little slow around here lately."

"No legs to break and money to collect?" I joked.

"Not so far, but it's only Tuesday. Big has been making some business changes, but it's not my place to tell you about them. Let's just say they've led to quieter days."

"I heard he bought the motel up the highway. Given all the things that go down there, I'm not sure that's going to help his quiet quest."

"That motel will never be the Ritz, but hopefully, in time, the clientele will improve."

"You're assuming improved clientele exists out here."

He grinned. "You moved here."

"Touché."

He knocked on the door to Big's office and then opened it and stepped back to his spot in the corner. Big was in his usual place behind the desk and Little stood at the bar, ready to serve everyone.

"Coffee? Tea? Something stronger?" Little asked as we took seats in front of the desk.

After Little had poured us all rounds of coffee, he perched on a stool next to Big, and we got through the usual pleasantries of how good it was to see each other and how well we were all doing.

"I hear congratulations are in order—I think," I said. "You've taken on the Bayou Inn motel."

"Ah yes," Big said. "Not the most reputable of places but it turns a decent profit, even now."

"I know the guy you just promoted to manager," I said.

"Really?" Big said. "He doesn't seem like the type of person you'd hang out with."

"He's helped me with a few cases."

Big raised one eyebrow.

"I probably shouldn't tell you more than that," I said. "But I just wanted you to know that he's a good guy and really wants the motel to improve."

"He's lucky to have your endorsement," Big said. "So now that we've exchanged the appropriate pleasantries, let's get to the interesting part of the conversation. I take it you have a new case that you might need my assistance with?"

He looked so eager I had to hold in a smile. For a mob boss, Big Hebert was one of the nicest people I'd ever met. And the nosiest, which had come in handy for me time and time again.

"I do and I think you're going to find it an interesting one," I said. "My client is Athena Durand."

Little's eyes widened and even Big looked suitably impressed.

"That *is* an interesting client," Big said. "So why has she hired you?"

"She claims she didn't kill her husband."

He nodded. "I heard her case had been overturned, but what does she want you to accomplish? She can't be retried. She's a free woman."

"Free from prison, yes. But she's not free from public opinion."

"I see. A somewhat understandable pursuit but perhaps also a futile one. Even if you could find evidence that pointed to another killer, it likely wouldn't be enough to prove anything. And honestly, without a video of his death, I'm afraid most people are going to believe what they want to believe."

"And those dependent on the Rousseaus in some form or fashion are going to believe what the Rousseaus tell them to," Little said.

"Very true," Big agreed. "So what is it I can help you with?"

"I've got some information on the original investigation, and talked to a couple of people, and I was hoping you might be able to shed some light on some things that seem off."

"I can certainly try."

"First up, I talked to Tate Rousseau."

"Really?" Big asked. "I'm surprised he agreed to that."

"I lied to get in, but I found it surprising that he talked to me after I told him who I was and what I was doing there."

I recounted my conversation with Tate and our speculation over his comment about Beckett's trouble, then told him about the conversation I'd recorded in the church. I left out the whole nun-pigeon fiasco.

Big was nodding as I finished. "Tate let his emotions override his discretion during your chat, which is interesting in itself. He must have strong feelings, still, about his brother for them to preempt his father's commands. And rest assured, those boys weren't raised, they were ordered like soldiers. Tate still is, as you heard from the conversation in the church."

"So do you know anything about a mess Beckett caused?"

"There was talk—all hushed up by Quentin, of course—about some unapproved investments that Beckett made with client money."

"Unapproved by the clients?"

"Unapproved by Quentin. His clients give him complete control over their funds when they agree to use his firm, but it won't surprise you to know that Quentin doesn't trust anyone —not even his sons—to handle large investments. They're only allowed to touch the small, low- to moderate-risk items like bonds, historically stable companies, and established REITs that they have been doing business with for years and that have proven up. But the riskier stuff was all Quentin's call."

"So Quentin's on the line for it but also gets all the glory."

Little nodded. "And I'm going to hazard a guess that when Quentin *does* make perceived risky moves, he's actually operating on insider information. His success rate is simply outside of the range of an investor who has only legally acquired information. Not so much that he's been investigated for it, but there are rumors that he's been given the side-eye by authorities more than once."

"Which is why he has no interest in his sons making risky investments," Big said. "They're not operating with the same information and Quentin has to fly below radar with the Feds. Being a senator will only buy him so much leeway."

"So Beckett went behind his father's back and made bad investments," I asked.

"That's what I heard," Big said. "But to make matters worse, 'they' also say Beckett took money from other client accounts to cover his mistakes."

I frowned. "But that makes no sense. Even someone who doesn't check their account often eventually looks at a statement. How does using one client's funds to cover for another work out in the long run?"

"It doesn't unless you can cover the loss quickly and have a viable lie to deal out," Little said. "But Beckett was a known gambler. He ran up a tab at the local casino until his father let them know he wouldn't be paying it off again. Before that, he was jetting off to Vegas once a month. He liked women of questionable virtue as well—another form of gambling, I suppose."

Big nodded. "We see it all the time with our own clients. My guess is Beckett thought the next investment would hit and he'd pay the money back and his father would cover for him. Those with gambling addictions always think they're going to win the next time."

"Then why wasn't there an outcry over the money after Beckett died?"

"My guess is because Quentin made everyone whole, and sympathy for the man who'd just lost his son kept them from pressing the issue."

"But you're talking what—hundreds of thousands of dollars?"

"More likely millions."

Ida Belle whistled.

"I know the Rousseaus have money, but do they have that kind of money?" I asked.

"Yes, although it wouldn't be liquid," Big said. "But Quentin didn't have to dig into his own pockets for the money. His firm had Beckett insured for five million."

"What?"

"You're kidding me!"

"That's a lot of cash!"

Ida Belle, Gertie, and I all piped up at once.

"Why would they have him insured for such a large amount?" I asked.

"It's normal for the top executives at a corporation to be heavily insured," Big said. "The theory being that replacing their level of expertise would be costly and would be an immediate requirement, so the offering has to be sweet to pull the right people over."

"I know it's speaking ill of the dead," I said, "but based on what you're telling me, it doesn't sound like Beckett was all that hard to replace."

"In this case, I think it was more of Quentin playing the odds. Given his all-or-nothing personality, Beckett was destined for either greatness or death. I've known too many like him."

"That's harsh," Gertie said.

"But realistic," Ida Belle said.

"By all accounts, Beckett was a very flawed, very troubled young man," Big said. "But he was also an extremely charming one. I interacted with him once and more importantly, had the chance to watch him interact with others on a handful of occasions. He had the ability to make women feel as if they were the most beautiful and interesting creature on earth, and men feel they were the most intelligent and successful. If he'd lived, and Quentin could have impressed upon him some propriety, he would have made a superb politician."

"The whole family sounds like a nightmare to me," Gertie said.

"Which leads me to my next topic," I said and passed him the autopsy report.

He read the document silently, nodding as he went. "So the homicide ruling was complete speculation, bordering on fiction. A lot of money, threats, or favors must have exchanged hands to get Athena charged, much less convicted."

"Probably all three," Little said as he reviewed the document. "I'm not surprised it was overturned."

"There's something else I find troubling," I said and described Casey's story about informing the family of Beckett's death.

"I know the Rousseaus never thought Athena good enough," I said when I finished. "So their treatment of her doesn't surprise me. But their own reaction—or lack thereof—kinda does. I mean, I get that he was a handful, but this was their son, their first in line to the Rousseau throne, and my friend said they looked more put out by the whole thing than anything else. There's cold and then there's whatever the heck that is."

Big's eyebrows lifted as I spoke and then he looked at me and smiled. "Just as I suspected..."

"You suspected what?" I asked. "That they were going to cut him off, so he saved them the trouble?"

"I'm certain Beckett would have reached Quentin's breaking point if he'd maintained his destructive path. But what I always suspected was that Beckett wasn't the Rousseaus' biological son."

I stared. My train of thought had never once gone in that direction, but now that he'd said it, things shifted to a whole other perspective.

"Holy crap!" Gertie said. "There's the big reveal."

"You're pretty certain?" Ida Belle asked.

"Yes," Big said. "When Lena announced her pregnancy, it was a big deal. The Rousseaus firstborn and the heir apparent, and it was a boy. A friend of mine worked at the Rousseau estate back then as a private chef. She said cooking for Lena had been difficult because she'd been so ill. Then one day, she showed up for work and was told that Lena would be living in California until delivery, where she could be seen regularly by one of the finest doctors in the country for high-risk pregnancies."

"That sounds like the norm for people with their level of wealth," Ida Belle said.

"I agree," Big said. "And I wouldn't have given it another thought if I hadn't seen her in Miami two weeks later wearing a bikini—definitely not pregnant—and she should have been close to her due date at the time. Two weeks after that, she returned to New Orleans with her bundle of joy."

"That's not enough time to push an adoption through, is it?" I asked.

"They probably bought a baby," Ida Belle said.

Big nodded.

"I wonder if she was ever pregnant at all," Gertie said.

"My chef friend thinks so," Big said. "She said Lena experienced morning sickness during the normal stages for that sort of thing and my friend, who had two children of her own, noticed the common changes in Lena's body over time."

"She must have miscarried at some point," Gertie said. "That's sad."

"And Quentin fixed it for her," I said. "And him. He got his son. I wonder if Tate is theirs?"

"He is," Big said. "Lena remained in residence the entire duration of her pregnancy with Tate, and my friend was discussing the week's menu with her when her water broke and she went into labor."

"I wonder if Tate knows," I said.

"That's an important question," Big said. "If he does, it would go deeper into explaining his animosity toward Beckett. After all, Beckett wasn't even a 'real' Rousseau, yet he held the favored position of first son and primary heir."

I stared at Big.

"Do you think Tate had Beckett killed? It solved everything, right? The person who'd made the bad investments was dead, Quentin collected the funds and reimbursed his clients, Athena was booted out of the family, and Tate was the sole living heir to the Rousseau throne."

Big put his hands up. "If you're asking me if Tate is capable, I'd say without a doubt. But unlike Beckett, Tate is not a gambler. Beckett's death drew a lot of the wrong kind of attention to the family. I'm not certain that's a risk Tate would have taken."

"But Quentin made sure all the negative attention quickly shifted to Athena," I said.

"That's true," Big said. "If Tate was reasonably certain that's the way things would go, then he might have considered it a risk worthwhile. So given all the information you have, and after assessing her firsthand, do you think Ms. Durand killed her husband?"

"No. But I do think she's still hiding things from me."

"A common problem in your line of work, I'd imagine," Little said. "The question is always, are they lying about something relevant to your investigation?"

"I wish I knew."

"Tread lightly on this one," Big said. "I know your capabilities better than most, but you tend to fight more on the side of fair than not. The Rousseaus don't have the same compulsion."

CHAPTER FOURTEEN

RONALD STARTED BLOWING UP MY PHONE WITH TEXTS AS soon as we climbed into Ida Belle's SUV. I felt my pulse spike when I read that he'd managed to score two invitations to Veronique's event, which was instantly replaced with that slight feeling of dread I got when I had to go shopping for girlie things.

"He's going to make me buy new shoes and do my hair and makeup," I said and sighed. "But I'm not wearing a push-up bra."

Ida Belle nodded. "It's always good to know where your line in the sand is."

"The two of you are hopeless," Gertie said. "I know we can't go to the party, but at least we can go shopping with you."

"What?" Ida Belle gave her a quick glance. "Why do we have to go shopping?"

"We don't *have* to go," Gertie said. "But we *should* go to offer our support, and to protect Ronald. You know how he gets about these things, and Fortune's always armed."

"*You* might defend Ronald," Ida Belle said. "But I'm more likely to side with Fortune, and she doesn't need any help."

"I'm buying lunch," I said.

Ida Belle perked up. "Antoine's?"

"You play taxi, I'll pay for gas, and food is your choice."

"Definitely Antoine's," Ida Belle said. "And I'm having appetizer and dessert."

"So am I," I grumbled. "I probably won't be able to eat a single grape once I'm shoehorned into that dress tomorrow."

"And won't be able to breathe until Thursday," Ida Belle said.

"You're not helping," I said.

Ida Belle grinned. "I'm just glad it's not me."

"Good Lord, the two of you talk like it's a walk down the plank," Gertie said. "It's a party that's bound to have the most expensive food and drinks you can get in the state. You get to buy a fabulous dress—as a business expense, I might add—and you might find a clue to our increasingly complex case. Where is the downside in all of that?"

"I'm guessing the dress and all the other people circling the expensive food and drinks," Ida Belle said.

I nodded and sent Ronald a text letting him know we were on our way and would pick him up in a few minutes. He was waiting on his front porch and hurried up as soon as we pulled into the driveway. He stopped at my window and looked into the SUV, then shook his head. "That sports bra won't do at all."

"I'm not wearing a push-up anything."

"Fine," he said and climbed inside. "Since this isn't about getting extra votes from the Swamp Bar crowd, we can go with no bra at all. You're not old enough for gravity to be an issue yet, anyway."

Ida Belle grinned and I shot her a dirty look.

I was more than a little concerned when Ronald insisted we shop at Enchanted Evening. After our last disastrous shopping visit there, I figured if Daphne, the owner, didn't lay eyes on us anytime in the next century, it would be too soon. But Ronald swore that Daphne was a total fan of mine, especially since I'd been crowned New Year's queen—wearing a dress purchased from Daphne—and beaten out Celia and her classless entry.

Besides, Ronald insisted that Daphne would know what everyone who mattered was wearing and for some reason unknown to me, that was important. I didn't ask why. I just planned on buying the cheapest dress I could get away with and donating it after, assuming it made it through the night. Me wearing a fancy dress tended to attract trouble.

Daphne surprised me with a welcoming hug and a quick assessment. "You've lost a couple pounds."

"Maybe," I said and shrugged. "I don't own a scale."

Daphne looked over at Ronald. "Can we just take a moment to reflect on how much I hate her?"

"It's probably going to take more than a moment," Ronald said.

They exchanged a knowing nod, then Daphne motioned us to the fitting room. "So Veronique is wearing a Vidal original she designed herself, of course, and the usual crowd is going with couture, but plenty are going off-rack. I know because there's been more spandex through my shop than a gym and more wire than you'd find at AT&T. If it can be lifted or tucked, it has been."

"I'll bet all *those* women own a scale," Ronald said.

"You know that's right," Daphne said. "I've sold at least thirty dresses for tonight's event, so I know the lay of the land. After Ronald called, I set aside several dresses that I think work for the event and will look fabulous on you. More importantly, I'm only carrying one each of those, *and* I checked with my brand sales reps and no other shops locally are carrying those designs. So unless someone shopped out of town, you're not likely to face the dreaded twinsie issue."

"Is it really that big a catastrophe if two women are wearing the same dress?" I asked.

"If you look better in it than the one with the clout and money, it's worse than Hurricane Katrina," Daphne said. "And trust me, you'll look better—spandex and wire, remember? Now, let's get you into these dresses. Start with the pale pink, I think."

The plus side was that Daphne had narrowed things down to only five dresses before we got there, and apparently, Ronald had texted her about my bra stipulation because all had plunging fronts or backs, or both, so no bra possible. It took every ounce of patience I could muster, but I managed to put the gowns on one at a time and parade out into the dressing area for the critiques, which were as expected. Ida Belle frowned at everything. Daphne and Ronald were only okay with everything, and Gertie wanted me to buy everything.

Then I got to the last one—a sapphire-blue silk with sequined trim across the bottom. It was simple, but the little band of sequins and the plunging back took it all up a notch. When I walked out, everyone nodded as if choreographed.

"That's it," Ronald said. "We should just always start with blue. It's her color."

Daphne nodded. "I agree. That turquoise number she wore for the New Year's parade was simply gorgeous on her. This sapphire is perfect as well. And since you're going to outshine most there, even in a far less expensive gown, I suggest going simple with hair and makeup."

"Since all I can manage with my hair is dried or a ponytail and I only own flavored ChapStick, that will be no problem," I said.

Ronald patted Daphne's hand. "If anyone gets sideways, I'll tell them she's had work done."

"Good idea," Daphne agreed and sighed. "It's such a shame —all that potential wasted on someone who'd rather spend her days in yoga pants and chasing criminals. What I wouldn't give for those cheekbones and legs."

Ronald held one hand up in the air. "Preach!"

"I'm pretty sure my chasing criminals is doing more for society than wearing makeup and having fancy hair would accomplish," I said.

Daphne whimpered and Ronald patted her arm again.

"I know, honey," he said. "Her practicality totally ruins the vision. But you can't save them all. And as much as it pains me to say, she does provide an irreplaceable service to the citizens by taking down the bad guys."

"You guys should probably cut yourself some slack," Ida Belle said. "The CIA couldn't break her, so you never really stood a chance."

Daphne waved a hand in dismissal. "Pffft. The CIA."

"So Daphne, you know everyone important in the city, right?" I asked.

"Socially, I'd say that's true, although the word *know* should be taken in varying degrees."

"Then tell us about Beckett Rousseau and Veronique Vidal."

Her eyes widened. "Oh Lord! This is about a case. You're going to this event because you're working. Please don't tell me you're investigating Veronique. I might not be able to sell you a dress if that's the case. Good Lord, if word gets out that I'm aiding and abetting an investigation of the princess of NOLA—"

"No," I interrupted. "I'm trying to figure out who murdered Beckett."

Daphne sucked in a breath. "Athena? Are you working for Athena Durand? I'd heard rumors, of course, that they turned her loose. Gossip filters through my store faster than confession on Ash Wednesday, but hiring an investigator is a move I never saw coming from her."

"I'm neither confirming nor denying who my client is, but I do need you to keep this all to yourself. I've been told by a lot of people that I'm treading on delicate toes here."

Daphne let out a single laugh. "You're treading on *bare* toes while wearing stilettos. So trust me, I will *not* be jumping on that gossip train. I've got to work in this town."

"So did gossip about Beckett and Veronique filter through your store?" I asked.

"A little. What I heard was that Beckett and Veronique had been dating for months but it was all very below radar."

"Why do you think that was?" I asked. "After all, they were both single and both families have money and status."

Daphne gave me a pitying look and patted my hand. "Oh, honey, old money—old, *earned* money—hates nouveau riche. And Lord, politicians might as well be pimps. Old money finds them useful to have on their secret payroll, but they only pretend they want them sitting at their dinner table. And Quentin Rousseau is one of the most unpleasant men to hold office. The real Quentin, of course. Not the one he plays when the cameras are rolling."

"So you think they kept things quiet because Veronique's family would have had a problem with her dating Beckett," I said.

"A classic Romeo and Juliet," Gertie said.

Ida Belle snorted. "Except in this version, Romeo ran off with the help. The only thing those two stories have in common is that someone ended up dead."

"So tragically true," Daphne agreed. "Anyway, the gossip

was that Veronique was expecting an engagement offer, but instead, she found out Beckett had been seeing Athena. I heard that she sent him a certified letter informing him to lose her number and never try to contact her again."

"I guess texting is for commoners," I said. "So is that it? She didn't break something in a fit of rage, or at least yell where the servants could hear her?"

Daphne shook her head. "She simply treated it like a business deal gone wrong and shut the door. Cold as ice, that one. Rumor is that one time a coworker tried to steal a design of hers and she had his entire family deported back to France, grandparents, cousins...everyone. In high school, she caught a supposed friend of hers flirting with her boyfriend and got her acceptance to Yale pulled."

"Sounds like she's a good suspect for killing Beckett then," Gertie said.

Daphne gave me a worried look. "I know you're probably going to this event to see what you can see, and there's nothing I could do to talk you out of it, but add me to the list of people who are cautioning you. Veronique is not someone to be toyed with. She's smart and vicious. The Vidals don't have a reputation for shady stuff like the Rousseaus. Those two stories I told you are the only ones I've ever heard about her."

"But that's a good thing, right?" I asked, somewhat confused.

Daphne shook her head, her expression grave. "No. It just means they're so much better at covering things up that you never hear about it. You thought only the CIA could bury things. Be careful, Fortune. I like you, and I'd like to sell you another dress the next time you're forced to wear one. I just don't want it to be the one they lower you into the ground in."

Since Daphne had issued the edict on simple hair, Ronald couldn't force me to the salon, but I didn't win the fight over shoes. I showed him a ton of pictures on Instagram of teens wearing evening gowns and high-top tennis shoes but apparently, you're not allowed that level of comfort and whimsy once you've graduated from high school.

The shoe search took a painful two hours, mostly because I refused to wear anything I couldn't run in, but we finally found a pair of low silver heels that Ronald deemed 'acceptable in the barest of ways' and we headed for home. It had been a long day and I was supposed to have dinner with Carter, assuming he didn't get hung up with work again.

Ida Belle and Gertie needed to check in on the Sinful Ladies and see how the syrup packaging was going, and I was desperate to get away from Ronald before he told me about some mud mask for the eightieth time. I asked Ida Belle to drop me off at the General Store. The battery in my Jeep had finally given up its last start and Walter had ordered me one and it was in. I figured if I picked it up now, I could put it in first thing tomorrow morning and be ready to roll again.

Since I was on foot, Walter insisted on having Scooter drop the battery off on my front porch, so I paid the bill and headed over to Ally's bakery. It was close to closing time, and I hoped we'd get a chance to chat. She'd been so busy preparing for the Mardi Gras festival that we'd skipped our Monday girls' night of wine, cookies, and complaining.

There was only one customer at the counter when I went in and Ally gave me a smile and a wave. The display was almost empty and only three cookies remained after Ally ushered the woman out the door and locked it behind her.

"We can split those last three cookies," she said. "What do you want to drink?"

"Whatever's easy."

She collected the cookies and a couple sodas and yelled into the back. "Lillie Mae, I've locked the front. Wrap it up and get out of here."

She headed over to the table I'd taken a seat at, deposited the cookies and sodas, then plopped down in a chair across from me.

"Long day?" I asked.

"You know it. Between the regular bakery stuff, the goods I'm supplying for other businesses, and the festival coming up, I don't think I've slept more than four hours a night. And I'm not done tonight either."

"You need some more help."

"I keep telling her that." Lillie Mae, Ally's right-hand baker and cousin to Francine, walked behind the counter and gave me a wave.

"I know, I know," Ally said. "But it's so hard to find good help. They're not all as talented as Lillie Mae. The two I've tried out didn't last a day. They think they just get to stand there and smile and eat cookies all day. When they're bent over the table in the back, developing arm cramps from stirring, and sweating like a prizefighter with all those ovens going, reality sets in."

"I'd offer to help, but I'd probably just create more work."

Ally laughed. "You would, but I appreciate the genuine desire to make my life easier. Lillie Mae, I put a box of chocolate peanut butter cookies under the counter for you and Scooter."

Lillie Mae reached down and came up with the box, beaming. "Thanks! These are Scooter's favorites."

I perked up. "You and Scooter...?"

Lillie Mae blushed a bit. "We've gone out a few times now. He's a nice guy and funny. Francine said I could trust him, so that's a big deal."

"You can definitely trust him," Ally said and I nodded. "Scooter is honest and reliable."

"And he's cute," Lillie Mae said and giggled. "Anyway, thanks for the cookies."

"I guess Scooter got his baker after all," I said after she left. "That's nice."

Ally laughed. Everyone in Sinful knew Scooter had carried a torch for Ally for a long time, but she'd never felt the same way. When she started dating Mannie, he'd extinguished that flame, so I was glad to see that he'd found someone he could pursue.

"You've been hanging around Gertie too long," Allie said. "Getting all excited over a new romance."

"It takes a lot more than that to move me to excited, but I'd go with pleased. Scooter's a good guy, and Lillie Mae doesn't strike me as the kind of girl who would jerk him around."

Ally gave me a curious look. "No, she's not. But that statement doesn't sound at all like things you contemplate. Why'd you even go there?"

"Probably because of my new client."

Ally nodded. "A convicted murderer can't just stroll down Main Street without getting gums flapping. And Old Lady Fontenot told me she saw Athena going into your house on Sunday. So following that chain of events, you were thinking about Athena and Dixon."

I straightened up in my chair. "I'm an idiot. You must have known them both from school."

"Dixon and I are the same age. I did kindergarten through high school graduation with him. Athena was a year behind, but I was still living in Sinful when she came. Hard not to know people in a place this small."

"So what is your take on her?"

"I always got the impression she could have given my cousin Pansy a run for her money if she'd wanted to."

"Really?"

Pansy was Celia's daughter, who had a penchant for black-mail, and had finally paid the ultimate price for her poor choices. She'd stolen several of Ally's boyfriends in high school by flashing her wares and had been generally nasty, so there had been no love lost between the two. So for sweet, polite Ally to compare someone to Pansy definitely wasn't a good thing.

Ally looked a tiny bit remorseful. "I know, it's a horrible thing to say, and maybe I'm wrong. It's probably just my teen angst resurfacing. I always felt less than when Athena was in the same room as me, but that being said, Athena never did anything nasty to me or any other girl that I'm aware of. The only person she really did a number on was Dixon."

"Then why did she elicit such strong emotions in you?"

Ally frowned, considering. "She was beautiful, probably still is. And she was charming. But I never felt like anything with her went deeper than the expression on her face, and even I could tell everything about her was practiced. Now that I'm older and have heard some of the gossip about her awful family, I understand that playing a role was how she got by, but younger and immature me didn't see the trauma. I was too busy being intimidated by her confidence and jealous of her perfect skin and curves in all the right places."

"So how did Pansy feel about her?"

"She hated her on sight, but instead of taking the bait when Pansy got catty with her, Athena just pretended she didn't exist. In hindsight, I get that it just pissed Pansy off even more."

"So do you think she killed her husband?"

"Well...wow. I followed the case—pretty much everyone

from Sinful did, I'm sure. But I have to say that I thought the evidence was flimsy. Honestly, I was surprised when the guilty verdict was announced."

"I agree that the evidence doesn't support a conviction, which is why it was overturned, but what about personally? You knew her and saw more of her than the jurors. Do you have a gut feeling about her innocence or guilt?"

"If you'd asked me two years ago, I would have said probably not. But I have to admit that since I've seen the dark side of some people I thought were good, I don't count anybody out for anything these days. I will say there was something almost mercenary about her, which is probably what reminded me of Pansy. Did she hire you to prove she didn't do it?"

"Not exactly. And I haven't agreed to officially take the case because for one, I wanted to see if there was enough to pursue and honestly, I wanted to figure her out a bit more before I dove into the deep end."

"So you think she's sketchy."

"Yes, but I was CIA. We pretty much think everyone we don't see in our bathroom mirror is sketchy."

"Good to know I'm still on the sketchy list."

"I've taken some people off—you, Emmaline, Walter."

"What about Ida Belle and Gertie?"

"They're the definition of sketchy, but at least they're using their powers for good."

Ally laughed, then sobered. "I bet the Rousseaus are mad enough to spit right now. It was clear from interviews during the trial coverage that they thought she was a gold digger who would ruin the family name."

"I get that, but you'd think they'd be more concerned with who actually murdered their son. I don't get putting money and power over justice."

She smiled. "That's because you care about people more than money. You just don't like to let on."

"I care about right and wrong and *some* people more than money. Others I'd pay to get rid of. So what about Dixon? You think he's capable of carrying a torch for Athena all these years?"

"Carrying a torch, maybe. He was pretty hung up on her. But taking it all the way to murder, I can't see. What good would it do? It wasn't like Athena was going to shrug off her widow's clothes and go running back to Dixon. He still doesn't have the money and clout she's looking for and isn't likely to ever have it."

"Yeah, you're probably right."

"But something about it is bothering you?"

I nodded. "I've caught both of them lying about things that have to do with each other. That doesn't make them murderers, but it makes it hard to stop giving them the side-eye. Especially Athena. How am I supposed to help someone who's not telling me the truth?"

Ally shook her head. "I don't envy you one bit. Maybe you should take a pass on this case. After all this time and with the lack of evidence or people who are willing to speak up and risk the wrath of the Rousseaus, you're facing a steep uphill battle."

"I know, but a man was murdered. And even though he didn't sound like someone I'd like very much, he still deserves justice. So do his family and his wife."

"But what if one of them is the killer?"

I smiled. "Don't worry about me. Middle Eastern arms dealers make the Rousseaus look like amateurs. I'll be fine. Did you hear that Celia got to spend part of Sunday in jail?"

Ally shook her head. She knew I was changing the subject, but she was going to go along with it anyway, especially since it meant talking smack about her aunt.

"She marched into the bakery yesterday morning and stood in the middle of the room, running her mouth about the upcoming election and how people needed to think hard about who they were voting for if Carter thought putting God-fearing citizens in jail was the way to run the town."

"Good Lord. How did that go over with the customers?"

"One of them told her he was considering changing his vote away from Carter because he'd let her out."

I laughed.

"Everyone else did exactly what you're doing," Ally said. "Then Celia stomped up to the counter, demanded a dozen fruit tarts *and* a family discount, then stomped out."

"The woman is a menace, but at least it's of the annoying variety. I can handle annoying. It's evil I can't live with."

"She wasn't always this bad. Or maybe I was a kid and didn't know any better. But I swear, as time goes by, she just keeps turning up the dial."

"I would suggest she's having a beyond-midlife crisis, but Gertie has assured me that demons don't die. So what about you and Mannie? How are things going there?"

Ally blushed a little and I took that as a sign that the romance was still going strong. "It's going great. He's such a smart man and so respectful and sometimes sweet."

I smiled as I tried to picture a sweet Mannie.

"And I have to admit that it's super sexy being with a guy that treats you like a lady but could dispatch a bad guy before I pulled my Mace out," she said. "Before Mannie, I only felt that safe around you, and you're hot, but you're not my type."

I laughed. "He's definitely an alpha male. How are you feeling about his work? Have you talked at all?"

"A little. He brought it up, actually. Some of the local gossip has gotten back to him and he's concerned about me and my business. I told him that the people who use my dating him as a reason not to give my bakery a try are the people who wouldn't have come in here anyway."

"That's probably true, but what about the bigger accounts you're trying to score—high-end events and that sort of thing?"

She frowned a little. "I suppose if I'm being honest, it could hurt me a bit on that side of things. But I've decided it doesn't matter. Even with putting thirty percent of the profit back into improvements to the bakery, I'm making more here than I was at the café. My house and car are paid for, and I still have some of the insurance money left over. I never wanted or needed the high life. What I have here is closer to perfect than I ever thought I'd get."

I smiled. "Yeah, I feel the same way."

Ally reached over and squeezed my hand. "I'm so glad you came here, Fortune. It changed both our lives for the better."

―――――

CARTER MANAGED TO GET OFF WORK BY SEVEN THAT NIGHT and swung by my house for dinner. I'd picked up steaks from the butcher a couple days before and already had the baked potatoes going with plenty of butter, cheese, and sour cream ready to fix them up. I added a side salad because Ida Belle was always on me about greens, and since the bottle of wine I'd purchased could constitute fruit, I figured we had all the important food groups covered.

He'd had another rough day of it, with calls for everything from a fight over a fishing pole to neighbors stealing chicken eggs. He was still light years behind on his paperwork but had decided he couldn't concentrate any longer without some time off and a good night's sleep. After dinner, he'd relaxed for a bit, then headed home to spend some quality time with Tiny and his recliner. He was so exhausted, I figured he'd probably never make it out of the recliner and into bed.

I wished he had more help, but I knew he wasn't about to ask the state police. One, he didn't want them in his business, and two, he didn't think it would be a good reflection on his ability as acting sheriff, even though he was running everything one man short. I locked the door after he left and sank onto my couch, shaking my head at all the BS that surrounded government jobs. I knew exactly what Carter was dealing with and it was the main reason I was now sitting in a house in Sinful instead of a condo in DC.

And yet. I needed to get my mind back into that game if I wanted to move this case forward.

My cell phone rang and I figured it was Ida Belle or Gertie checking in but I tensed when I saw Shadow Chaser's number on the display.

CHAPTER FIFTEEN

"There was a guy here earlier asking for Athena," Shadow Chaser said. "Claimed he was her cousin but I didn't buy that for a second. I told him I had never seen her before. He didn't look convinced, but he drove off."

"When was that?"

"Couple hours ago. I was going to call you then, but a pipe burst in one of the upstairs rooms and I've been trying to get that customer and the one staying below situated. But that's not even the important part. I saw him again. After I handled the whole pipe fiasco, I drove over to the convenience store to pick up some energy drinks as my night person called off and I've got to pull a double. That guy was there in the parking lot."

"Maybe he lives nearby."

"Then why was he parked at the end of the lot and drinking coffee in his car? That convenience store has stale coffee and lacks a fabulous view."

"Good point," I said as I pulled on my tennis shoes. "How long ago did you see him at the store?"

"Five minutes ago. I came straight back here and called you."

"Is Athena in her room?"

"I didn't see her car in the lot. I wanted to check before I called because I figured you'd ask."

"Great work. I'm on my way now. Call back if Athena returns or you see that guy at the motel. But don't leave the office."

"Heck no!"

I started to grab my keys and head out but remembered the battery on my front porch and sighed before calling Ida Belle. It was only 10:00 p.m. but Ida Belle was sometimes a stickler for her sleep, and now that she'd married Walter, there was always the possibility that he'd tell Carter when we took off for a late-night jaunt.

She answered on the first ring and didn't sound as though she'd been asleep, so I quickly filled her in. I could hear her grab her keys as I was explaining. She disconnected and I headed outside to wait. Five minutes later, she sped around the corner and into my drive.

Gertie was in the back seat, looking a little less alert than Ida Belle.

"Are you wearing the Flash pajamas?" I asked her.

Ida Belle snorted. "She loves the irony."

Gertie gave her the finger. "They're comfortable and warm. You get me out of the house after bedtime, this is what you get."

"Who are you kidding?" Ida Belle asked. "We get that in the morning too."

"If you two didn't insist on being awake at indecent hours, you wouldn't have any idea what I sleep in. And you're lucky Jeb wasn't over because then I sleep in nothing."

Ida Belle glanced back in dismay. "If you ever stroll out of your house naked, I will keep driving right to the hospital to book you a room."

I nodded. "And cases of beer for everyone who witnessed it."

"You two are hilarious," Gertie said. "You should start your own YouTube channel. Call it Shame and Fortune."

"That's not bad, actually," Ida Belle said.

"Anyway, Ida Belle said we're going to the motel, so I figured it doesn't matter what I'm wearing. Not like that place is fashion-forward. Just having on clothes puts me ahead of the game for the most part."

"Unfortunately true," I said. "Was Walter sleeping already?"

"No. We were watching this war movie. I was taking notes but he was about to nod off."

"Then what did you tell him when you were leaving?"

"Nothing. I'm sure he heard your voice on the phone, and he darn well knows better than to ask questions he won't like the answer to."

"Smart man."

"He married Ida Belle," Gertie pointed out.

Ida Belle grinned. "Like she said..."

We were almost to the exit for the motel when my phone rang again. Shadow Chaser.

"That guy pulled into the parking lot a couple minutes ago. He's sitting in his car in the middle of the parking lot."

"Where he can see all the rooms."

"Yeah. I don't like it."

"Neither do I. We're almost there."

"Well drive faster or something—holy crap—she's back! Athena just pulled into the parking lot. Get over here before someone dies!"

Ida Belle pressed down the accelerator and we flew off the highway and onto the exit. I grabbed my door handle as she took the turn back under the highway and heard Gertie yell as she went tumbling across the back seat.

"Seat belts!" Ida Belle yelled. "How many times do I have to tell you?"

"Shadow," I said once I'd freed up my hands. "What's going on?"

"I had to leave the office to see. I'm behind the vending machine. She's getting out of her car and going into her room... She's inside now. Oh. My. God. He's getting out of his car and heading right to her room. He's going to kill her, right? I don't even have a gun. Why haven't I bought a gun?"

"Because you'd end up shooting yourself," I said.

"Hurtful, but probably true. Where *are* you—there's screaming. Oh my God! There's screaming!"

Ida Belle flew into the parking lot, the dip at the entrance jolting the entire SUV up. Shadow Chaser popped out from behind the vending machine and motioned to the end of the parking lot. We spotted Athena's car and Ida Belle slammed to a stop right behind it. I was out of the SUV, gun ready, before the SUV had stopped rocking.

I could hear yelling inside and what sounded like a scuffle. The door was partially open, and I bolted inside and took a half second to assess the scene in front of me.

Late thirties. Six foot two. A hundred eighty pounds of lean body mass. Strapped with two guns that I could see. Threat level high. Whoever this guy was, he was dangerous.

He stood next to an overturned chair and had a pink travel bag in one of his gloved hands. Athena had hold of one strap, trying to get it back. He backhanded her with his right hand, and I leveled my gun at him.

"Stop right there and drop the bag!" I commanded.

He looked over in surprise because he'd never noticed me come in. Then he smiled at me before bolting into the bathroom and slamming the door shut behind him. I heard the sound of glass breaking and ran out of the room.

"He's going out the back window!" I yelled as I ran past Ida Belle.

I was halfway to the corner of the building when the explosion happened.

I glanced back as I rounded the corner in time to see a car in the middle of the parking lot go up in flames. Ida Belle's SUV fired up as I ran, and I figured Ida Belle was coming behind me, but I didn't have time to wait. I hit the back parking lot just as the man disappeared into the woods behind the motel. I turned up the juice and sprinted after him, but when I hit the tree line, gunfire echoed through the woods and a bullet whizzed right past my head. I jumped behind a tree and listened. When I heard footsteps pounding away from me, I set off again.

I paused on the other side of the tree line and peered out. If he was lurking somewhere in the neighborhood behind the motel, I'd be easy to pick off if I left my cover. Then a motion light came on in a driveway down the street and I saw him jump onto a motorcycle. I prayed the key wasn't in it as I ran toward a car parked on the street, but my hopes were dashed when the bike fired up and he pushed himself backward, away from the house.

He grabbed a handful of throttle leaving the driveway and almost lost control. The front door to the house flew open and a man wearing nothing but boxers came out firing. I dove behind the parked car as a spray of bullets hit the street and ricocheted around me, but the engine on the motorcycle wound up again and headed away. I heard cursing and peered around the car to see the man standing in his front yard, still clutching the pistol.

"I saw you out there!" he yelled, slurring his words. "You

best come out or I'll fill you with the lead I intended for your thieving friend."

Good. God. He thought I was with the motorcycle thief.

Just what I needed. A drunk man with a gun who thought I was a criminal.

I quickly weighed my options. The tree line was too far to make a run for it, even though he wasn't a very good shot. Even a bad shot landed one sometimes. But there were no buildings, trees, or shrubs close enough to change positions and work my way into better coverage. I could always shoot him, but I was really trying to avoid killing people, especially if they weren't the bad guys.

Then I heard Ida Belle's SUV as it roared around the end of the block. The drunken shooter turned to look and got an eye full of headlights. I used his temporary blindness to jump up and wave and hoped that Ida Belle could see me. I heard the engine rev as she sped up and then slid to a stop next to the car I was hiding behind. I rushed into the back seat, and she took off before I'd even gotten the door closed. I heard gunfire again and a couple rounds hit the side of the SUV.

Ida Belle sighed. "That's probably not going to buff out."

I shook my head, marveling at her calm demeanor. "You know, we really could have used you in Iraq."

"Gertie would have been a quicker solution, but the cleanup would have been massive."

"I almost hate to ask, but what was that explosion?"

She gave me a pointed look.

"Never mind," I said. "Let's just hope she wasn't near it went it went up."

I could see the smoke from the blast rising above the roof of the motel before we even reached the entry to the parking lot. When we pulled in, I saw the burned-out car in the middle of the lot and prayed it belonged to the bad guy. Fortunately, the motel didn't have a ton of customers at the moment, but I was pretty sure every one of them was standing outside.

I spotted Gertie and Shadow Chaser at the end of the building with Athena and let out a breath of relief. At least the paramedics were the worst-case scenario and not the coroner. Ida Belle pulled up in front of Athena's room and we jumped out. Athena was already developing a nasty bruise on her face where the guy had struck her, and I knew that was going to be tender for a while.

Gertie looked as if she'd been standing in a fireplace with a blower on the bottom. Her hair was stuck straight up as though she'd put gel and ashes in it and dried it that way. The Flash emblem on her pajama top was barely outlined under the layer of grime.

"Are you all right?" I asked.

"Of course I'm all right," she said gleefully. "And I disabled his car."

Shadow Chaser's jaw dropped and he stared at her as if she'd lost her mind.

"You blew that car apart," Shadow Chaser said. "You shouldn't even be allowed to carry matches, much less whatever the heck that was."

I had a sneaky suspicion that despite the pottery wheel fiasco, Gertie had still been tinkering with pipe bombs and made a mental note to start checking her purse again before I got into a vehicle with her.

Gertie shrugged. "I only had a small charge. He must have had some explosives in the car. You know how the bad guys are."

"Really?" Shadow Chaser said. "That's what you're going with? I can't wait to see what the cops make of that."

"Me either," Ida Belle grumbled.

I looked over at Shadow Chaser. "Can you grab some ice

and a soft rag for Athena? She needs to put something on that shiner."

I looked at Athena, who'd been sitting on the window ledge completely silent the entire time. "Do you have any other injuries?" I asked.

She shook her head.

"Did you know that guy?"

"I've never seen him before in my life."

"He came into the motel earlier today asking for you."

She looked up at me, her eyes wide. "How do you know that? Why are you even here right now?"

"Because the manager is a friend of mine. I asked him to keep an eye out. He called me after the guy showed up asking for you and then again when he spotted him at the convenience store around the corner. It was clear he was hanging around and you were the only reason we figured that was the case."

"The manager told that guy I was here?"

"No. He said he'd never seen you before, but obviously that guy didn't believe him."

She gave me a pointed look. "So was the manager spying *for* me or *on* me? You know what, it doesn't matter. I should be thanking you, because who knows what would have happened if you hadn't asked the manager to look out. So thank you."

I nodded. "I know your reasons for wanting this investigation to happen, but I don't think you've considered all the consequences of hiring me. Whoever killed Beckett thought they got away with it when you were convicted."

She blew out a breath. "So you're saying if I'd come out of prison and disappeared, then everyone would have just kept going as before. But since I hired you, I put a target on my back. Both our backs, I guess."

"That's exactly what I'm saying. Look, I have no problem

with it—this is what I do—but this is not what you're trained for. I want you to rethink all of this, because I might not be able to get the answers you're looking for, and you're risking a hell of a lot for a slim maybe."

She opened her mouth to reply when Carter's truck turned into the parking lot. I held in a sigh. He was looking at another long night.

He pulled up behind Ida Belle's SUV and stopped. When he got out of the truck, he looked over at the smoldering car, then headed over toward us. Shadow Chaser ran up with the ice and rag and handed it to Athena and she put it on her face.

"I brought a key for the room next door," he said. "I figure your current one is a crime scene. I know how that goes. Jeez. The fact that I even know that is troubling."

"Was anyone hurt in that blast?" Carter asked as he approached.

"No," Gertie said. "I have a little dirt on me, but that's it. He must have been carrying some unstable explosives in there."

Carter glared at her. "Probably a pipe bomb. I hear they can be tricky to manage."

"I've heard that too," Gertie agreed.

"So who wants to tell me what happened here? I've got calls for an assault, an explosion, gunfire, and a stolen motorcycle, all happening in a one-block radius."

"The whole thing starts with the assault," I said, trying to pass him off so I could think about my story. "You'll want to talk to Athena."

"Uh-huh. So Athena assaulted herself, blew up a car, stole a motorcycle, and was firing a pistol? That's a big night for one individual who isn't Gertie."

"Fine. So maybe we can just go into Athena's new room and give our statements since we have an audience," I said and waved a hand at all the people standing around the motel parking lot and balcony. "Shadow Chaser—you too."

"Oh, man!" he complained. "Every time you come on the property it's like this. You're not the Angel of Death because people don't always die, but is there an Angel of Chaos?"

"No," Gertie said. "But if you take interpretations from the Old Testament, you could go with plague for one of them."

"Not helping," I said.

"Everyone in the room," Carter said, then yelled at all the onlookers. "The rest of you get back in your rooms! Show's over!"

We all shuffled in and perched somewhere except Gertie and Carter, who elected to stand.

"Who wants to start?" Carter asked.

I gave him a rundown of the events leading up to our arrival and my movements afterward and he took notes, frowning the entire time.

"Did anyone recognize the attacker?" he asked.

We all shook our heads.

"Is that burned-out car in the parking lot his?"

"Yes," Shadow Chaser said.

Carter made a note, and I knew he would run the plates and track the guy down. Unfortunately, I also knew there was no way he was going to divulge that information, so I was going to have to find our mystery man another way.

"Okay," Carter said. "Unless the rest of you have anything to add, I need you to wait outside while I finish up with Ms. Durand."

"*Now* you want us to leave?" I asked. "She's just going to tell us everything afterward."

"Yes, but I can't get in trouble for what she does when I'm not here in an official capacity."

Shadow Chaser raised his hand as if he were back in school. "Sir, is it okay if I go back to my office?"

"Sure. But no one goes near that car. And I have a clear view of it from that window."

We all trailed out.

"This having to keep everything aboveboard is highly inefficient," Gertie grumbled as we exited.

"If there's not some other awful situation you want to thrust me into," Shadow Chaser said, "I'm going to go lock myself in my office with a bottle of scotch."

"Hey," I said as he started to turn away. "Thank you. Athena could have been seriously hurt—maybe even killed—if you hadn't been paying attention."

He perked up a bit and nodded. "Yeah. I guess that's true? I suppose saving someone's life outweighs a car explosion, right? Especially since the car belonged to the bad guy and it was the only thing destroyed in the blast. Do you think the Heberts are going to be upset?"

"Not with you," I said. "And I put in a good word when I visited with them this morning. They know what I'm working on, so this won't be a problem."

"Really?" He looked more excited than I'd ever seen him short of when bullets were flying. "You put in a word for me? That's awesome. Thanks!"

"You made his day," Ida Belle said as he skipped away.

"He deserves it," I said. "I wasn't lying about his contribution. I don't know what that guy wanted, but you can bet it was nothing good."

Gertie limped over to the window and leaned back against it, her torso all rigid.

"Why are you moving so weird?" Ida Belle asked. "Did you hurt your back in that explosion? Why don't you sit down?

Carter won't care if you get in the SUV. He's got a clear view of it."

Gertie shook her head and brushed some ashes off her arm. "I'm fine, and you don't want to have to clean all this mess off your seats. Once he finishes with Athena, I'll grab my spare clothes from our emergency stash and try to wash some of this off before we leave."

I glanced over at Ida Belle, who shrugged. Gertie had been acting strange ever since Ida Belle and I had gotten back. Maybe the explosion had affected her more than she was admitting.

It was only a couple minutes later that Carter came out of the room, Athena trailing behind. "I'm done with all of you for now."

"Can I get my stuff from the other room?" Athena asked.

Carter nodded and opened the door to allow her in. He stood in the doorway while she tossed everything into a laundry bag and then locked the room up when she was done.

"The team will be here shortly to work the room," he said. "I'll tell the manager on the way out. Not that I expect them to find anything since he was wearing gloves. But I'll get the information off that car and for the stolen motorcycle, and maybe I can run this guy down."

"Sorry about your sleeping plans," I said.

"Yeah, me too."

He headed for the smoldering car, I grabbed Gertie's emergency clothes, and we all went into Athena's new room.

"What happened?" I asked as soon as we closed the door.

"I got back to the motel and came into my room," she said. "I was rinsing my face and this guy was just there—right behind me. I spun around and screamed, and he grabbed me and put one hand over my mouth, then he said, 'Where is it?'"

"What did he want?" I asked.

"I have no idea. I thought he was there to rape me. He shoved me into the wall and took my bag from the closet, then I grabbed the handle to keep him from taking it."

"What was in the bag?"

"My clothes, some paperwork from my lawyer, cash, and a bracelet. I know it was stupid, but I just reacted. The bracelet was something Beckett gave me."

"Was it valuable?" I asked.

Her eyes misted up and she swiped at the unshed tears. "It was a cheap plastic one that he won for me at the state fair. He spent over a hundred dollars to win it, but it's not worth anything to anyone but me."

"You had a small purse on the nightstand," I said. "He didn't make a move for that?"

"No."

"That makes no sense," Ida Belle said.

"Unless you're looking for something too large for her purse," I said. "And you're sure you have no idea what he wanted?"

Athena shook her head, and I could tell she was as confused as the rest of us.

I heard Carter's truck start up and looked out the window as he drove off.

"Thank God!" Gertie said as she limped over to the window to pull the shades. "I have been dying to sit but couldn't bend."

She reached under her pajama top and pulled out a license plate, then tossed it on the dresser and plopped into a chair.

"Give me a minute and I'll clean up and change clothes," she said.

Athena stared at the plate, her eyes wide. "You stole that off his car?"

"Well, we have to identify him, right?" Gertie said.

"You could have just taken a picture," Ida Belle said.

"You want to get to this guy before Carter does, don't you?"

"He can still trace the VIN on the car," Ida Belle said.

"He can if he can read it, but he's got to send a forensic team down here to handle it. That gives us the jump on him."

Ida Belle threw her hands in the air. "And you're going to stroll into the DMV tomorrow and ask for a search on that plate?"

"No," Gertie said. "But I figure we have a friend who would be interested in helping."

She meant Detective Casey, and she probably wasn't wrong. But Casey had already stuck her neck out. Still, it wasn't the worst idea Gertie had ever had, so I took a picture of the license plate and headed outside.

"Give me a minute," I said.

"I'll go change while you're doing that," Gertie said as I left the room.

I dialed Casey, praying I wasn't interrupting her sleep, but she answered on the first ring.

"I know if you're calling this late, I need to ask about bail."

"No. You're still not on that task, but I'm glad to know you're open to it. I do have a situation, though, and you can say no. In fact, I would be more surprised if you didn't."

"What's up?" she asked, now completely serious.

I explained what had happened. "I have a license plate."

"And you'd like to get on this guy before your sexy sheriff has a go at him. I don't know that I give your relationship good odds, but you and those assistants of yours are resourceful as hell. Give me a couple minutes. I have someone on dispatch who owes me and can lie like a politician."

She disconnected and I laughed, not sure what to think of a police dispatcher who was also a professional liar. In the meantime, I headed over to the car and did a walk-around.

Gertie's pipe bomb had really done a number on it. This was one hobby I was going to insist that she curtail. If the bomb that had taken out her pottery wheel had been the same strength as the one she'd stuck under this car, Ida Belle and I would be planning a funeral.

I was on my way back to the room when the phone rang. Casey.

"I've got to say this for you, Redding. When you step in it, you do it with both feet and in the biggest, smelliest pile you can find."

"I take it you got a name."

"Oh, I got a name all right. Burkhead Security."

I cursed.

Burkhead Security was an international security firm that catered to high-profile clientele and employed former military —mostly Special Forces—and the rumor mill was they only hired the less ethical among them.

"So who do you think has the money, clout, and desire to hire a mercenary to beat up on a tiny woman?" Casey asked.

I blew out a breath. "I get it. But what the heck are they after?"

"You don't think Athena knows?"

"She's as confused as I am. Of that much, I'm sure."

"Well, you best start going over all her possessions. Because if those who shall not be named on a cell phone call have stuck their necks and wallets out far enough to hire Burkhead, and they find whatever it is before you do, this avenue of investigation will be lost forever. And it might just be the thing that blows it wide open."

CHAPTER SIXTEEN

I thanked Detective Casey, then headed back into the motel room, more confused than ever about what was going on. When I walked back inside, everyone gave me an expectant look.

"Is there anything you have that is worth hiring private security to retrieve?" I asked Athena.

Her eyes widened. "What? No. I sold everything that was worth anything."

"What about things that don't have monetary value?"

"Like what?"

"Did Beckett keep a journal, a laptop, iPad—anything he might have kept notes on?"

She shook her head. "Not that I can think of. I mean, he had a laptop, but the cops took it and I never got it back. I figure his dad claimed it was company property or something. And they already had his cell phone from the boat."

"Did he have a home office with binders, a notepad—anything that might contain accounts or passwords or something else that people would be looking for?"

"He had a home office and a bunch of books. Maybe there

was something in them, but I never looked. The Rousseaus owned the penthouse and most everything in it, remember? After my attorney sold off everything of mine with any value, he put what was left in storage for me. If there was something the Rousseaus wanted, they would already have it. Why would they be looking for something a year later?"

"I don't know. But someone has hired a very expensive security firm to obtain something from you. Can you think of anyone besides the Rousseaus who would want anything you have?"

Athena threw her hands up in frustration. "No, but I can't think of anything the Rousseaus would want from me, either. They've already taken everything. They had access to my entire life. *They* deemed what was my personal property and marital share. I was behind bars. It makes absolutely no sense that they'd be after me for something now when they are the ones who decided what I got to keep in the first place."

"Was the key to your storage unit in the bag that guy took?"

"Yes."

"What about a card or paperwork that identified where it was?"

"There was a tag on the key with the unit number and the gate code, but—"

"Let's go!" I said to Ida Belle and Gertie. "Text me the location of that storage facility and the unit number."

"Okay, but—"

I ran out the door and hopped in the SUV, Ida Belle and Gertie right behind me.

"You think he's headed for the storage unit?" Ida Belle asked as she pulled away.

"He's looking for something specific, and unless Athena lied about what was in that bag he stole—and I don't think she did—then he still doesn't have it. And since he's been seen and had to leave his car behind, he has to hit the storage place tonight before Carter tracks that car back to Burkhead Security."

Ida Belle whistled. "Burkhead. That's a serious investment."

"What do you think he's after?" Gertie asked.

"I don't know—a list of foreign accounts and passwords, maybe? Maybe Beckett didn't lose as often as Athena thought."

"But then why didn't they go after the information before now?" Gertie asked. "Like Athena said, the Rousseaus already had access to everything. And if someone else hired them, Burkhead could have broken into the attorney's office and found out where Athena's personal belongings were."

I frowned. She was right. The timing was important and something that needed to be explained.

"Maybe they're afraid Beckett hid something and they overlooked it when they let the movers pack Athena's things."

"Sure, that might be what they're looking for," Gertie said, "but it still doesn't answer my question, which is, why now?"

"Because Athena's case was overturned," I said as it hit me. "As long as Athena was behind bars, then anything that might have been overlooked was safely tucked away in a box and a storage unit to rot until it no longer mattered. Her release was a game changer."

Ida Belle nodded. "So you're thinking information that could hurt someone, not secret account numbers."

"That would explain the timing," I said.

A text came through and I looked at my phone.

"All Saints Storage. Off the highway just before we get to NOLA."

Ida Belle wheeled around the corner and onto the access road. By the time we hit the highway, we'd passed a hundred miles per hour, and I was praying the state police weren't looking to increase their speeding ticket revenue tonight.

"He's got a big lead on us," Gertie said.

"Probably not as much as you'd think," I said. "He had to stop and dig through the bag, find the key, and get the location of the storage unit. All that took more than a couple minutes."

Ida Belle nodded. "That motorcycle he stole wasn't the fastest thing on two wheels, and he didn't look like he was riding it all that well, either."

"He probably ditched it and called for backup," I said.

Gertie clapped her hands. "So we have a shot at catching him!"

"A really good one."

———

IDA BELLE MADE THE DRIVE TO THE STORAGE UNIT IN twenty minutes flat, which might have been a new land speed record. When she exited the highway and slowed to a pace that wouldn't get us thrown under the jail, it felt as if we were idling. I had the storage facility on satellite view and was trying to figure out the best approach.

"Take a right on the road before the red light," I said. "That road runs through a neighborhood that shares a back fence line with our target."

"How high is the fence?" Ida Belle asked.

"Probably eight feet but I won't have any problem getting over it."

"I have a stick of dynamite," Gertie said. "I can blow up a section and then we can all go through," Gertie said.

"It's supposed to be a surprise attack," Ida Belle said. "I'm pretty sure explosions ruin the element of surprise, especially since you already blew up his car."

"Hey, I have a signature move," Gertie said. "I need to think about how to market that."

Ida Belle took the turn and shut down her headlights as we slowly made our way down the road. Her hopped-up engine was great for high-speed chases and for when we needed to get somewhere quickly, but it wasn't the quietest on approach. When we reached the back wall of the facility, Gertie handed me a ski mask and gloves and I jumped out. Storage facilities had notoriously good security systems and lighting, and I couldn't rely on the Burkhead guys disabling it since they were in a time crunch.

I stopped at the driver's door to give instructions. "Head around front. Park a bit down the street and text me if you spot anyone. Do. Not. Engage. I cannot stress this enough. Burkhead field guys have a reputation and none of it good. Seriously. Promise me you're not going to engage."

Apparently, my tone and expression must have gotten across the gravity of my words because they both gave me somber nods.

"You be careful too," Gertie said. "If he called for backup then there's at least two of them."

I grinned. "I was CIA. They don't call us spooks for nothing."

I took a couple steps to the wall, gave a single leap up, grabbed the top and pulled myself on top of the wall. I checked the ground and eased myself over, landing between two boats. I scanned the numbers to my left and right. I was looking for unit 24, and it looked as though the numbers decreased on the right side as you went toward the front of the facility.

I hurried to the end of the center building and peered around. I didn't see any vehicles or movement, but that didn't mean I was in the clear. I listened for several seconds and could make out the faint sound of movement but it wasn't close by. I pulled out my pistol, slipped silently around the corner, and hurried down the aisle, staying as close to the building as I could. The lights were pointed out from the building just a little, so I had pockets of darkness that I could disappear into.

When I reached the end of the building, I stopped again and the sound I'd heard earlier was more pronounced. Unfortunately, her unit was inside the building, so I had no way of determining how many of them there were. What I *did* know is that one of them had not hesitated to fire at me.

My cell phone buzzed and I pulled it out.

Black SUV parked up front. Guy is working to disable gates. They must not have code.

So that meant at least two minimum, maybe more. I considered my options, but none of them were good. I couldn't sneak up on the target when he had the advantage of being inside and without knowing how many were there. And even if I knew those things, I couldn't dispatch people just for breaking into the storage unit. I didn't own the facility and it wasn't even my belongings. Even if they fired first, my defense would be übersketchy at best. It looked as though my only option was to get them out of the facility before they found what they were looking for.

Mind made up, I sent Ida Belle a text.

Call cops and report men breaking into the storage facility and shots fired. Remind them this is a residential neighborhood.

I shoved my phone back into my pocket and ran across the aisle to a dumpster in the corner. I positioned myself behind it and pointed my pistol at the metal entrance door of the storage building. I squeezed off five rounds, then ducked behind the dumpster again, praying my ploy sent them scrambling to leave rather than look for the shooter.

I heard an engine rev and a couple seconds later, a huge crash and the sound of metal dragging on the ground. A black SUV wheeled around the corner, the front end smashed, and slammed to a stop right in front of the door I'd just put rounds into. Two men ran out of the building, and I recognized one as the guy who'd attacked Athena. They tossed two boxes in the SUV and took off.

Crap! I hoped whatever we were looking for wasn't in those boxes.

I heard police sirens approaching, so as soon as the SUV was out of sight, I ran inside the building and located Athena's unit. The door was up and boxes were torn open, the contents strewn everywhere. If the cops saw this, it would become a crime scene and we wouldn't have access until they released it.

I pulled the door down and clicked the lock into place, then I hurried out of the building. The police sirens were right around the corner, so I made a dash for the concrete wall and vaulted over it, landing in a thick set of shrubs. I hurried down the line of bushes to the street and spotted Ida Belle's SUV parked a short distance away. I could see the swirling lights from the police car behind the wall of the storage facility, so I sprinted for the SUV and jumped in.

"Back up slowly around the corner and head for that diner at the access road," I said.

I pulled out my phone and texted Athena, asking her to meet us at the diner as soon as possible.

As soon as I put my phone away, they both started firing questions at me.

"Did they shoot at you?"

"Did you see them?"

"What was in the storage unit?"

"Why did you let them get away?"

"Because this isn't the Middle East and I don't have a get-out-of-jail-free card to shoot the bad guys anymore," I said in reply to the last question, which had naturally come from Gertie.

"Oh yeah," she said, looking somewhat disappointed.

I filled them in on what had gone down. "I just texted Athena and told her to meet us at the diner."

Ida Belle nodded as she pulled into the parking lot. "So you put rounds in the door to scare them out before the cops got there."

"I didn't think the locals would fare well against Burkhead and didn't want it on my conscience. The sirens were all I needed."

"Good call. And since you closed the unit back up, the cops will think they didn't have time to steal anything. Smart."

"I hope so," I said. "Gertie, stuff that crazy hair of yours into a ball cap and let's go in here and grab some coffee while we're waiting on Athena. Hopefully, the cops will be gone by the time she gets here."

We headed inside and secured a table in the back corner and ordered a round of coffees.

"You don't think the cops will stick around since the gate is torn off?" Gertie asked once the server had dropped off the drinks and gone back into the kitchen.

"Doubt it," Ida Belle said. "They'll assume it was low-rent thieves hoping to ransack some units for things they could hock. It's fairly common. The facility manager might show up, but he's not going to refuse access to someone who has a legit reason for being there. And the sign on the gate said 24/7 access. The bad guys just didn't have the code."

"The fact that they took the gate off the hinges works to our advantage," I said. "It looks like an amateur hit by incompetent thieves."

"What about Carter?" Gertie asked. "Are you going to tell him about this?"

I shook my head. "I don't want Carter in the middle of this. Burkhead can't cause me problems but they have the political connections to make life impossible for him."

"I agree," Ida Belle said. "He's going to hack enough people off when he identifies the car owner and questions them."

"They'll claim it was stolen," I said.

"Ah," Ida Belle said. "I should have thought of that. That's good, though. It gets Carter out of the loop."

"Ha. It only gets Carter out of the loop if he lets that explanation ride, and there's no way that's happening."

"Maybe you could suggest he let it ride," Gertie said.

"I would, but since Carter is never going to give me information about an ongoing investigation, and I only know who that car belongs to because you stole the license plate, I can't say anything."

Gertie sighed. "Oh yeah. I suppose you could give him the plate and tell him that we found it in the bushes."

"And the forensics team missed it?" Ida Belle asked. "And it's completely unscathed from the blast?"

"Weird things just happen," Gertie argued.

"More like *Gertie* things just happen," Ida Belle said.

"Don't worry about it, guys," I said. "I'll figure out something. Right now, Carter is spread so thin, he doesn't have the bandwidth to focus on just one thing. That works to our advantage—well, and his. He just doesn't know it."

We sipped our coffee and waited for Athena to show up. I was a bit surprised when she walked through the door thirty minutes later.

"She must have taken driving tips from you," Gertie said to Ida Belle.

Athena slipped into the chair across from me, an anxious

look on her face. The bruise on her cheek was darker than before, and I could easily see the swelling. The waitress popped over and asked if she wanted anything and didn't so much as blink an eye at Athena's appearance. She came back a minute later with the ginger ale Athena had ordered and a ziplock bag of ice.

"You hold that to your face, sweetie," the older woman said. "And you get the hell away from the man who did that. Don't end up like me."

She walked off and Athena put the bag of ice on her cheek and shook her head. "I forgot how nice people are outside of the city."

"I'm sure there are plenty of nice people in the city too," Gertie said.

"I'm not," Ida Belle grumbled.

Athena laughed. "I'm not either, but it's a different culture there. People are so busy, you know? Everything is about the hustle to move up or just make the rent. I think there's more survival mode—more tunnel vision. You stop noticing what's going on around you because you're too wrapped up in your own crap."

"Small towns are too wrapped up in everyone else's crap," Gertie said. "But it does lend itself to more helping hands."

She nodded. "I packed up my stuff—what was left of it—and brought it with me. I don't feel safe staying at that motel any longer."

"I agree," I said. "We'll find you something when we're done at your storage unit."

"So that guy went there?"

"Yes. And I'll tell you what went down, but I need you to promise me that you will not share any of this with the police, especially not Carter."

"I don't understand."

"If this tracks back to the Rousseaus or anyone else with political pull, they can make a lot of trouble for Carter. Enough trouble to cost him his job. Without that job, he'd have to leave Sinful. Selfishly, I like it there and am not looking to relocate because shady people are trying to cover their butts."

Her expression cleared in understanding, and she nodded. "I get it and you're right. People like the Rousseaus wouldn't hesitate to ruin his life just to avoid an issue in their own."

I filled her in on the storage events and she shook her head as I talked.

"I thought you were crazy when you fixated on this," she said. "And I still don't claim to understand it."

"I don't either. But I need you to take a look at everything there and tell me what's still there and what's missing. Then we're going to go through everything that's left with a fine-tooth comb. Maybe there's a flash drive hidden somewhere or a piece of paper tucked away. The bottom line is somebody wants something badly enough to pay top dollar for its recovery."

She blew out a breath. "I don't have another key."

"Don't worry about it," Ida Belle said. "We carry bolt cutters."

Athena smiled. "Of course you do."

CHAPTER SEVENTEEN

AN OLDER GENTLEMAN APPROACHED OUR SUV AS WE DROVE through the broken gate of the storage unit. Athena showed him ID and gave her unit number and he checked a list on his clipboard.

"Coming in kinda late, aren't you?" he asked.

"Yeah—some friends have been helping me move," Athena said. "This is the last of it."

"Was there an accident?" I asked, pointing to the gate.

"Attempted robbery," the man said.

We all put on our best shocked and anxious faces.

"Did the police catch them?" Gertie asked.

"I'm afraid not."

"Did you get them on camera at least?" I asked.

"No. One of them sprayed the cameras up front with paint. After that, all we could make out was two people moving—well, and another one driving through the gate so they could get away."

"That's scary," Athena said.

"I don't want you ladies to worry, though," he said. "I walked the whole place with the cops and no units were open, so I guess they didn't have time to do anything. But you check your stuff carefully and let me know if there's anything missing. I've got to call everyone who's renting and tell them about this. You've saved me one call."

Ida Belle parked in front of the building where Athena's storage unit was housed, and I checked to make sure the manager wasn't lurking before I grabbed the bolt cutters from the back of the SUV and hurried inside. I made quick work of the lock, pushed up the door, and Athena let out a gasp.

I had to admit, it did look bad. Clothes were strewn everywhere and broken glass covered the floor. Boxes were ripped open and pieces of tape and cardboard dangled from the tops. Athena bent over and picked up a smashed picture frame and turned it over, letting out a strangled cry at the photo of her and Beckett with a rip through it.

"I left the pictures in storage because I didn't have a permanent place," she said. "I thought they'd be safe."

Gertie put an arm around her shoulder and squeezed. "It's going to be okay. Young people have all that stuff on the cloud, right? So we'll get you another copy and an even prettier frame. I'll help you pick one out, even."

Athena sniffed and nodded. "I just don't understand this. Why smash everything?"

"Could be they were looking for something small and breaking is usually faster than taking apart," I said. "Could be they're just buttholes."

"I'm voting for the last one until you prove me otherwise," Ida Belle said as she held up a sweater that had been ripped in two. "This is the third one I've found this way."

"The first guy was probably mad over how things went down at the motel," I said. "Then they couldn't get through the gate."

"It wasn't working right when I came the other day either," Athena said.

"So they pitched a toddler fit," Gertie said. "Just what we needed—highly trained bad guys with anger issues."

"It's a good thing it was on the fritz," I said. "Or they'd have just tossed all these boxes in their SUV and searched them at their leisure somewhere else. But they did get away with two. First thing up is figuring out what was in those boxes. Do you know what you had in all of them?"

Athena nodded. "I opened them when I was here the other day. And they were all labeled. There were only ten total—sad, right? My entire life fit in ten storage boxes. Four had clothes, two had linens, one was books, and the other three were pictures and decor."

"But nothing valuable?"

"No. Everything that could bring money was sold a long time ago."

I nodded and we started sorting the boxes, trying to identify the missing ones. As we went, we thoroughly searched each item to make sure nothing could be contained inside. When we'd gone through what was left in the boxes, we combined like stuff in the boxes that were sound enough to be taped back together and managed to cobble two empty ones together, one for stuff that could be saved but needed cleaning or repair, and one for stuff that had to be thrown away.

"Looks like we're missing one box of clothes," I said.

"And the books," Ida Belle said.

"Crap," I said. "I was really hoping the books would be here. People always hide stuff in books."

"But they weren't Beckett's books," Athena said. "They were mine—our wedding album, a couple of signed hardbacks from authors I like, and the rest were cookbooks. I took the wedding album and the hardbacks with me when I got some of my clothes. I had them stashed in the nightstand. Right after you ran out of the motel, I thought about what you said and went through every page of them, just in case there was a note somewhere, but there's nothing."

"The rest were cookbooks?" Gertie asked.

Athena nodded. "I always liked to cook. When I was a server, I'd fill in sometimes in the kitchen for prep if people called off at the last minute. If I hadn't met Beckett, I probably would have asked them to give me a shot at it full time."

"Good for you," Gertie said.

"How often did you get into the cookbooks?" I asked.

"All the time," Athena said. "Probably every day or at least every other. After putting on a show all day long for the clients, Beckett preferred to eat dinner at home. But you can't eat NOLA takeout every day without packing on the pounds."

"Truth," Gertie said.

"So I cooked probably five dinners a week, at least," Athena said. "I was always looking for ways to make something that we liked a little healthier so we could keep eating it without negative side effects."

I slumped against the wall and blew out a breath. If Athena was in the books almost every day, then it wouldn't have been a good place for Beckett to stash anything. "And there's nothing else? Nothing you forgot?"

Athena shook her head, looking as miserable as I felt. "The stuff in this unit and the bit I have at the motel are it. That's everything I..."

Her voice trailed off and she frowned.

"What?" I asked. "You thought of something."

"Yeah, but I don't see how..."

"Let me decide if it's important."

"I have a sweater," she said. "It was Beckett's. A Vidal Limited edition. But I was always wearing it. It was soft as tissue paper and big and roomy. I don't recall seeing it in the pictures my attorney had, but it's possible they missed it. I was shocked when I saw it in my stuff, but I figured it was probably in my closet and the Rousseaus didn't look close enough to know what it was."

"How much would something like that be worth?" I asked.

"Several thousand, at least," she said. "But I wouldn't part with it."

I sighed. "And I assume that sweater was in the missing box of clothes?"

"No. Like I said, I was shocked to find it here when I came after I got out of prison to get some clothes. It smelled musty so I took it to a specialty cleaner in New Orleans. It's not the kind of thing you can take care of at a laundromat."

"Even if the sweater was worth thousands," I said, "it isn't worth what Burkhead charges."

"But there were three sweaters ripped in two," Ida Belle said. "Are you sure it isn't worth more?"

Athena shook her head. "No. I checked some online shops but couldn't bring myself to part with it."

And then a thought occurred to me. "What if it had sentimental value to someone else besides you? Where did Beckett get the sweater?"

Athena shrugged and looked at the ground. "I'm not sure. I guess he bought it."

I raised one eyebrow and waited until she was looking at me again. "No one would ever accuse me of being a fashionista, but my neighbor Ronald is always going on and on about that culture. So I happen to know that a limited edition anything from an exclusive designer like the Vidals are usually for existing, long-term clients, family, besties, and to garner favors. Did Veronique Vidal give Beckett that sweater?"

Athena looked down again. "Yes."

"And you were well aware that they had been dating for a while when he asked you out?"

She sighed. "Yeah, I knew."

"But you went out with him anyway, then you married him shortly after that. When I asked you if you had enemies, you insisted that it must be Quentin's political or financial rivals. And that the only enemies you had were the Rousseaus. Did you forget Veronique?"

"No," she said quietly.

"I have it on good authority that the Vidals are NOLA royalty, and that Veronique is smart and vicious and has a zero tolerance policy on being screwed. You stole her boyfriend right under her nose and didn't think that painted a target on your back? Have you never heard the expression 'a woman scorned'?"

She threw her hands up in the air. "I know, but Beckett said they were just friends."

Gertie snorted. "That's what they all say."

I shook my head. "Even I have enough estrogen to know that's a bullshit line."

Athena sighed. "I can't change what happened."

"No, but you can stop pretending it didn't," I said. "Did Veronique ever ask Beckett to return that sweater?"

"Not that I'm aware of," Athena said, then frowned. "We saw her once in the French Quarter. It was chilly and I'd grabbed the sweater on our way out in case I needed another layer. She was polite when Beckett spoke to her, but she never acknowledged I was standing there. She gave me a dirty look when she walked off."

"You were wearing the sweater?"

She nodded.

I pointed my finger at her, beyond frustrated. "I told you I needed to know everything, even if you don't think it's important and most especially if you think it will make you look bad. People don't murder for no reason, and all your attempts to hide things only make it impossible for me to protect you. You could have been killed tonight, and if I'd had any idea the threat was that great, I'd have made different arrangements for you with regard to where you were staying."

At least she had the decency to look contrite. "I get that. And if you don't want to continue with the investigation, I understand."

I stared at her for a long time. "A man is dead. I'll stick for a while longer because of that. But now that you have an opportunity to restart your life, you need to give some serious thought to how you live it, or you're going to find yourself at odds with people until you die."

Frustrated, I grabbed a box and headed out of the unit. "Let's load this stuff up and go find a hotel."

———

We emptied the unit completely, pulling some clothes out to replace those that were stolen, and I told Athena I'd store the boxes for her at my house until she had a place to take them. Emptying the unit and getting her settled at a new hotel took us another hour, so it was well into the next day when we finally got home. What few hours of sleep I managed weren't good and I shuffled into the kitchen for coffee before sunup. I was pouring my first cup when I heard Carter call out from my front door. He didn't look as though he'd had any more sleep than me and he clutched the coffee I handed him as if I'd just passed off the winning touchdown in the Super Bowl.

"Will you marry me?" he asked after his first sip.

"You're a really cheap score," I said. "But I can appreciate the sentiment."

"You *look* like the sentiment. What time did you get in?"

"After three. It took us a while to get Athena settled, but I can't blame her for being upset."

"She had to know the risks."

"You know, I don't think she did. Not really. For someone who's had major trauma in her life from a young age, she sometimes strikes me as a little naive."

"Really? Maybe she's just skilled at ignoring reality if it furthers her agenda."

Considering the things Athena had conveniently left out of the information she'd provided me, he had a point.

"Regardless," he continued, "stirring up the Rousseaus isn't a smart move. She should have expected trouble."

"We don't know that the trouble last night came from the Rousseaus."

He huffed in his coffee—a sure sign that he knew something he wasn't going to share—and I figured he'd traced the car back to Burkhead and had leaped to the same assumption that I originally had about the Burkhead hourly billing rate, and the connections needed to even get them to take the job.

But then, Carter didn't know about that stupid sweater and Veronique Vidal.

"If the Rousseaus are behind it, I don't get why," I said. "Athena swears she doesn't have anything worth taking. The Rousseaus owned the penthouse she lived in with Beckett and darn near everything in it. They supervised her attorney packing up her stuff and he sold off anything of value to pay his fees and put the rest in her bank account. She literally only has what they agreed to give her."

He considered that for a moment. "Maybe they're trying to scare her. You know, convince her that she has something the bad guys want and since she doesn't have anything to give them, she'll leave town. You know that's what they want."

"I'm sure it is."

And it wasn't a bad theory given the information he had.

"So how's Athena feeling about the investigation after last night?" he asked.

"She says she wants me to continue."

"And what do you think? Is there anything to find?"

"There's always something to find."

"But are you investigating your client or someone else?"

"I don't think she did it."

He studied me for a moment, then nodded. "Then she probably didn't. I better run. I've got a bunch of extra things to take care of this morning—courtesy of last night—before I get around to the stuff I was *supposed* to be doing this morning."

"Remember I have that thing tonight with Ronald."

I'd told Carter about the Vidal event the night before, but I'd presented it as an opportunity to overhear some gossip about the Rousseaus. He wasn't thrilled with the idea but when he heard Ida Belle and Gertie weren't invited, he'd relaxed a little.

Carter grinned. "I was going to stop by and get a picture of you in your fancy dress. It's like an astronomical event—doesn't happen a lot."

"You'll have to settle for a picture from Ronald. I booked us rooms at the hotel hosting the event. I'm not interested in an hour-long drive each way in a dress I can't breathe in. And since they're sure to be serving the kind of champagne I can't afford, I have no desire to curb my drinking."

"Can't say that I blame you on that one. Be careful with those people. They love to talk but none of it means anything.

If you go in there asking real questions and expecting real answers, they'll show you the door."

"Don't worry. I have Ronald to jab me in the ribs if I get off script."

He rose from his chair and leaned over to kiss me.

"Text me before you go to bed."

I smiled because I knew that was his way of saying he would worry until he heard from me. "I will. See you tomorrow."

I didn't tell him that Ida Belle and Gertie were booked into the hotel hosting the event, same as me and Ronald. No way they were going to stay home, and they'd be on hand in case I needed backup. With any luck, Walter wouldn't mention to Carter that Ida Belle would be out of town, because it wouldn't take a detective to put that one together.

He hadn't been gone for ten minutes when Ida Belle and Gertie made their way into the kitchen. They both looked as exhausted as me but then, we'd had a long, tiring night.

"Why aren't we all still in bed?" Gertie asked. "Something's wrong with us."

"You've finally said something I don't need to argue with," Ida Belle said as she poured us all a round of coffee. "How many pots have you had this morning?"

"That's my second," I said. "But in my defense, Carter dropped by and consumed a good part of the first one."

"He might be the only person in Sinful getting less sleep than us," Gertie said. "Did he say anything about last night?"

"Not much. But I could tell by what he said and didn't say that he's identified Burkhead as the owner of the car. He went with the same train of thought we did at first and made a comment about maybe the Rousseaus were trying to scare Athena into leaving and there's not really anything they're looking for."

"That's actually a good thought," Ida Belle said. "Unless you know that they ransacked her storage unit and stole some boxes. That's a lot of length to go to and risk to take just to scare someone."

"I agree," I said. "I'm still betting they're looking for something."

"So now that you've had some time to sleep on it—albeit very little time—what are your thoughts on our client?" Ida Belle asked. "I noticed you still haven't asked her who she was arguing with in the motel parking lot night before last."

I nodded. "I wanted to see if she'd offer up that information."

"But she didn't," Ida Belle said. "Which means she's still hiding stuff."

"Maybe it *was* Dixon," Gertie said. "Maybe she's hiding this for the same reasons she did his fight with Beckett. She definitely treated Dixon badly, but she was still a kid. Maybe now that she's older, she really does feel guilty and doesn't want to cause him any more trouble."

"That's possible," I said. "But if that was Dixon in the parking lot with her and Athena is protecting him, then you realize that means Dixon is lying to us, right? And that he's probably still in love with her. Why else would he keep turning up in her orbit?"

Gertie frowned. "I don't want Dixon to get in any trouble over her."

"None of us do," Ida Belle said. "But he's a grown man now and needs to make better decisions. Trying to get involved with Athena is about the worst one he could go with, but can't any of us keep him from doing it."

"Why are men so stupid when it comes to women?" Gertie asked.

"If you figure that one out, you'll have solved a lot of the world's problems," Ida Belle said. "So what's on the agenda today?"

My back door swung open and Ronald burst in and stared at me. "Good Lord, you have bags under your eyes that we could move a family of four in, and I swear all the moisture went out of your skin and hair overnight."

"Probably because I was out chasing bad guys for most of it instead of sleeping," I said.

He waved a hand in dismissal. "You can sleep while they work on you."

"While who works on me?"

"The team is already assembled and will be at the hotel in an hour and a half—hair, nails, makeup, and massage. And don't even think about trying to escape. When they're done, it's straight into that dress, and chase the bad guys in style."

He hurried to the table, snatched my cup of coffee right out of my hands and dumped it in the sink. Then he grabbed a bottle of water from the fridge and shoved it in my hands before running back out the door.

"We leave in fifteen minutes."

Kill me now.

CHAPTER EIGHTEEN

At 7:00 p.m. I stood in my hotel room feeling like someone I didn't know. My hair had been trimmed and conditioned so that it felt and looked like shiny silk. My face had been subjected to some sort of mask that Gertie said made my skin look like I had a filter on it because it was so flawless. I had silver chrome effect polish on my nails and toes but had drawn the line at nail extensions. Anything that interfered with the possible need to take people out was a solid no. At first, I was leery of the massage, but it was this hot stone thing that actually felt nice. I might even consider it again.

Gertie had opted for a massage and facial as well while the crew was there. Ida Belle had not-so-politely declined, then sat in a chair in our room, drinking copious amounts of caffeine—which I wasn't allowed—and altogether enjoyed my discomfort.

Ronald practically wept when I opened the door.

"It's perfect!" he raved. "Everything is absolutely perfect. I am so glad I insisted on that trim. Your ends were splitting but now, your hair just glows. And Daphne was right—that bitch always is—the simple hairstyle and light makeup is just fabulous. You'll be the most gorgeous woman in the room, but don't you dare tell anyone I said that. These people pay a lot of money to not look nearly as good. Are you ready?"

"As ready as I'm getting."

He sighed at my unenthusiastic response. "Come on, then. Let's go find some gossip before you revolt and end up back in your room in yoga pants and a ponytail."

"Wait!" Gertie yelled. "I need a pic. She hasn't stood still long enough for me to get one."

I paused in the hallway next to a weird sculpture on an antique table and Gertie got her picture, then Ronald and I headed downstairs. The doorman guarding entry to the ballroom checked Ronald's invitation and gave him a nod.

"Let the show begin," he said. "Remember everything I told you this afternoon and you'll be fine."

During the hostile beauty takeover, Ronald had taken advantage of my inability to flee and fed me information on expected behavior and the people who would be attending. I didn't have the heart to tell him that the CIA had sent me to extensive courses on proper etiquette for different situations because then he'd be appalled that I was electing not to use any of it rather than being simply ignorant about the requirements. I was happy to get a rundown on the guests, though. That gave me an idea about which ones were more likely to gossip and which ones not to waste time on.

"Ronald!"

I heard someone off to our side call his name as soon as we walked inside and turned to make my first assessment.

Midforties. Six feet tall. A hundred eighty pounds. Looked like nice muscle tone under his tuxedo and a smooth walk, so no lower limb encumbrances. The fact that he was wearing a pink tuxedo and was excited to see Ronald had me placing him in the 'no threat' category.

They exchanged air kisses and then the man gave me a

once-over. "Who is this delightful vision and where did you find her?"

"This is my friend and neighbor, Fortune," Ronald said. "Fortune, this is Broderick Cameron Bartholomew III."

"They made three of you walk around with that name?" I asked, smiling. This was one of the people Ronald had labeled a huge gossip but a well-known one, which meant people didn't tell him anything good because they knew it would be repeated. That meant I didn't have to cater to him because he wouldn't have anything useful.

Broderick laughed. "Oh my God, she's clever and charming as well. You can call me Brody. All my friends do and trust me, everyone who sees you will want you as a friend. So tell me—"

"Have you seen the items up for auction?" Ronald asked as he took two glasses of champagne from a server who was working the room.

I knew he'd interrupted because he could tell Brody was about to start pumping me for personal information. We'd agreed that the basics—I was Ronald's neighbor and friend—were fine, but sharing information about my profession, current or past, wouldn't work in my favor. If either of us found ourselves in a conversation we couldn't redirect, then we were going for the old tried and true inheritance avenue. Ronald said it was something the entire room would accept as half of them were in the same boat.

"I just came from viewing them," Brody said. "The Vidals have gone all out with this one. Handbags, sunglasses, dresses, shoes...and Oh. My. God. there's a Dolphin at Sunset bag for sale. They only made ten of them, you know. You should bid on it. It would look exquisite with Fortune's dress."

Ronald laughed. "I'd have to liquidate my entire life to afford it."

"It's for charity."

"If I bought that purse, I'd be asking for charity next week."

Brody sighed. "Oh, I know. But it's still fun to dream about walking through Paris with a half-million-dollar handbag."

I had just taken a sip of the extremely excellent champagne and almost choked. Some of it definitely went up my nose.

"Half a million for a purse?" I asked.

"Most people consider them investments, really," Brody said. "They usually appreciate in value—like fine art."

"If you stroll around Paris with a half-million-dollar handbag, you'll need armed guards," I said. "Maybe a tank."

Brody laughed again. "Charming and clever. And you're not wrong. People never actually carry a bag of that importance unless it's a significant event and you need it to prove you're worthy of attending."

"Like what? Colonizing the moon? Dinner with Jesus?"

"No. More like a presidential inauguration."

I tried not to smile. I'd attended a presidential inauguration and didn't even own a purse at the time. But I didn't figure Brody would benefit from knowing that if you could kill a man a hundred different ways without breaking a sweat, you got to sit up front.

"Oh look!" Brody said, his voice going up several octaves. "Veronique just walked in and her dress is breathtaking. That woman is going to sit on top of the fashion world one day."

Ronald nodded in agreement.

I stepped to the side to get my first look at Veronique Vidal and had to admit, it was impressive. The dress was white but looked like the inside of an oyster shell. It had delicate gold straps and gold stitching that made the whole thing look like a very expensive piece of jewelry, which I assumed was what she was going for. The woman wearing the dress was tall and thin, with dark straight hair that fell halfway down her back, long black eyelashes, and minimal makeup.

"See," I said to Ronald. "Our host opted for very little makeup as well."

They both chuckled and Brody shook his head. "She spent at least two hours on that. It's far easier to do the glam look than make it look like you're wearing very little. Surely you know that. Your makeup is stunning."

Ronald rolled his eyes. "That's actually her own skin."

Brody's eyes widened. "Don't tell anyone that. They might make you leave."

"I heard the stitching on that dress is twenty-four-karat gold," Ronald said, changing the subject. "It's a prototype that Veronique designed, but they're thinking of putting it into production—minus the real gold, of course. You could probably buy a Rolls with the thread on that dress."

Brody turned his gaze away from Veronique and let out a gasp. "Tate Rousseau is here. Lord, after the news tonight, I didn't expect to see any of that family here."

"What news?" I asked.

"You didn't see?" Brody asked. "There was a breaking news article online from the local paper that said Athena Durand's case had been overturned, and she'd been released from prison."

"Really?" Ronald feigned shock.

"Who's Athena Durand?" I asked, trying to sound casual even though I felt anything but, given what he'd told us. I'd really been hoping for a couple more days of radio silence from the press on Athena's release.

Brody took a deep breath and then did the speediest whispering recap I'd ever heard on Athena, Beckett, and the trial.

"Anyway," he continued, "I can't even imagine what the Rousseaus are feeling right now."

I nodded. "That has to be hard. I think I remember some ladies at church talking about that case. The woman lived in Sinful for a bit, right? And wasn't Beckett dating Veronique when he met Athena?"

Brody's eyes widened. He put one finger over his lips and glanced nervously around. "Mentioning those three in the same sentence is the equivalent of summoning the societal hellhounds."

"But if the families have beef between them, then why invite Tate?" I asked.

"Because the Rousseaus want to make up for the way things went down. That means they'll spend top dollar to try to get back in good graces."

"So it wasn't about inviting him as much as it was inviting his credit card."

"Now you're getting it."

I shook my head. "Arms dealers are a lot less complicated than this."

Brody stared at me. "Huh?"

"She said she's armed herself for a deal tonight," Ronald said. "We should go take a look at the auction items. Let's get together soon for tea."

Then he took my arm and practically pulled me away before Brody could protest.

"Thanks for the save," I said. "The snobbery and the finery are throwing me off."

"It floors me that when you're halfway around the world to place a bullet through a supposed impossible target, you can keep your composure. But you put on a dress and it's like you've forgotten everything you know."

"Playing dress-up is what ultimately got me into trouble at the CIA."

"*Now* you tell me these things."

"If I could have everyone's attention, please."

A woman's voice boomed over the loudspeakers that had previously been blasting soft classical music, and everyone turned to look toward the stage in the corner of the room. An elegant woman, probably in her fifties, stood there with a microphone, waiting until all the attention was on her.

"Mrs. Vidal," Ronald whispered.

"I'd like to welcome everyone to our annual event," she said. "Your generosity is what enables our charities to continue the wonderful work they do around our great city. My designers have put together an impressive number of items for you to bid on. For the winners, we have two associates set up at a table in the back of the room to take your payments. And if you don't win, we're still thrilled and humbled to accept your donations."

"I'll just bet," I mumbled.

"I also have a special announcement tonight," she said. "Normally, I would have called a press conference for this sort of thing, but the decisions were finalized just this afternoon, and I'm too excited to wait. So here, in front of our closest friends and clients, I wanted to announce that this summer Vidal Enterprises is opening a new studio, manufacturing plant, and exclusive boutique in Paris, France. The Vidals are returning to our roots."

Excited talking began among the crowd and some clapped.

"Even more exciting," she continued, "my beautiful and talented daughter Veronique will be heading up this new division. Please, everyone, take a moment tonight to congratulate Veronique on this much-deserved honor."

Mrs. Vidal stepped off the platform and the cheering began in earnest, then came the calls for Veronique to speak. She finally took her mother's vacated spot and thanked everyone for coming. Her voice sounded as smooth and delightful as the champagne.

"There have been many among you who've been friend, business associate, and inspiration during my career, and I want to thank each of you for your constant support," Veronique said. "I have been given an opportunity that most designers can only dream of, and I intend to make the most of it. I expect you all to hold my brother Matisse to standards here with the New Orleans division after I abandon him."

Everyone laughed and Veronique flashed the crowd a brilliant smile.

"Thank you again for coming," she said and left the stage.

I stepped away from the crowd so I'd have a better overview of the room and shook my head. Ronald, who'd followed me as if glued, looked over.

"What's wrong?" he asked.

"I don't understand why Beckett would pick Athena over Veronique. Don't get me wrong, Athena is beautiful, but Veronique is straight off a magazine cover. And she's got absolutely everything going for her."

Ronald nodded. "And Athena came with baggage. I'm sure it's the question that was on everyone's lips back then, but even blatant speculation couldn't come up with anything that made sense."

"What do *you* think?"

He frowned. "I think it would take a strong man to be Veronique's romantic partner, as it does to be your romantic partner. Athena presented challenges in some areas but she was ready and willing to worship him."

I sighed. "I guess you could be right."

As Veronique left the stage, I got that prickling feeling that I was being watched. I scanned the crowd and my eyes locked on the one person I was hoping wouldn't see me.

Tate Rousseau.

"Oh no," I said. Ronald followed my gaze as Tate headed our way, a determined look on his face.

"Please don't shoot him," Ronald begged. "Blood won't wash out of anything in this room."

I stared at him. "For a minute there, I thought you were more concerned about me being arrested."

He waved a hand in dismissal. "You're like a cat with nine lives. At least promise me that if you *have* to shoot him, you won't tell anyone you came with me."

"I think that secret is out of the bag given that you told your friend Gossip Central as soon as we walked in."

"Oh no, you're right!" Ronald grabbed two glasses of champagne off a tray as a server walked past and downed one of them. "How did I let you talk me into this?"

"All I did was ask," I said.

He downed the second glass.

"You're following me," Tate said as he stepped in front of us. "I should call the cops and have you arrested."

"Hmmm. Well, getting this dressed up isn't my norm but I hardly think it's a criminal act," I said. "And it *is* for charity, after all."

"I don't believe for a minute that you were invited. You don't have the class or the money to be welcome at this event."

"The money, perhaps not," Ronald said and elbowed me before I could laugh. "But her class is a lot higher than yours at the moment. This young lady is my guest."

"I don't buy that and neither will Veronique when I tell her you're working for Athena Durand." He stepped closer to me. "You've got a ton of nerve coming to her event given who you're working for. But then, following me into a church shows just how low you'll go. You think you're clever but you're nothing. Do the smart thing and drop this investigation while you still have options."

"Is that a threat?"

"Hell yes. So I suggest you and your 'date' leave now, or I'll inform Veronique exactly who you are and what you're doing here."

"He goosed me!" a woman yelled just off to my right.

We all turned to look just as she backhanded the man behind her. "You pervert! I'll have words with your wife next time she's in the country."

The man stared at her, startled, then his face flushed. "Have you lost your mind? I would never lower myself to put my hands on your butt. And it would take a claw crane to get a pinch of your back end."

She flung her glass of champagne at him, but he ducked, and it splashed onto a couple standing behind him.

Ronald gasped. "Not the Valentino."

Suddenly, someone shoved the champagne-wearing husband into the back of the accused gooser, and he lurched forward, lost his balance, and planted his face smack in the middle of the irate woman's chest. They both fell backward into the dessert bar and whipped cream flew everywhere. The hotel staff scrambled for a cleanup and cell phones came out everywhere to film.

"This isn't nearly as sexy as it sounds on paper," Ronald said.

Tate grabbed my arm. "You're coming with me."

"Quentin?" I heard a familiar voice yell, and looked over to see Gertie coming toward me.

All of a sudden, I had a clear idea who was doing the goosing and shoving, and I wasn't sure if I should laugh, cry, or simply flee.

Gertie wore a bright pink evening gown and a fake leopard coat. She had a Cleopatra wig on and the makeup to match, so no way Tate was going to recognize her. She had a purple-and-yellow feather boa wrapped around her neck, and her feet were clad in neon-green high-top tennis shoes. At least she'd accounted for the possibility of fleeing, although I wasn't sure how quickly she could run since her dress was tapered at the bottom.

That...and she was using a walker.

Tate stared at her, his expression a mixture of frustration and horror.

"Yep, it's Quentin," Gertie said as she stepped in front of us. "I'd recognize that nose anywhere. Had some work done, haven't you? All that grousing about growing old gracefully—well you weren't complaining about our age when we hit the sauce and the mattress in that hotel in Cabo."

Several people around us snickered and Tate's face turned beet red.

"I've never seen you before in my life," Tate said.

"That's ole Gina," Gertie said smugly. "So mind-blowing you actually forget."

The laughing intensified and Tate clenched his hands

"Pardon me, sir," the doorman said as he hurried up. "I can take care of this. Mrs. Vidal would like everyone to continue with their evening."

Tate shot me a death stare and stalked toward the exit.

"Ma'am, I need to see your invitation," the man said. "This is a private event."

Gertie waved a hand at him. "Do you know who I am?"

"No, ma'am, which is the point."

Ida Belle hurried up and frowned at Gertie. "I'm so sorry about this," she said. "Mother has these spells and then there's no changing her mind about things."

Gertie gave Ida Belle a dirty look that made me glad she didn't have her purse tucked in there anywhere.

"I can't even go to the bathroom for five minutes," Ida Belle said, "and she's off wandering the hotel. Why just last week when we were in New York, I told her to stick close and what does she do? Climbs a tree in Central Park and then watches while I run around in a panic looking for her."

The doorman stared at Ida Belle, uncertain what to do given that the events of the evening so far were not the norm for this type of thing. Then he realized Gertie had wandered off again while Ida Belle was going on about trees in Central Park.

"Where is she?" he asked, looking a bit panicked.

"Hey! There's an old lady with her head under the champagne fountain," someone called out.

"That's my cue!" Ida Belle said and headed off.

The doorman stared after her in dismay, then gave us a dismissive nod and hurried off to his post.

"Do we need to get her out of the fountain?" Ronald asked, looking as though he needed a Xanax and a vacation.

"Ma'am!" a lady yelled. "Ma'am, your mother has absconded with a tray of crème brûlée under her fake fur and there's a tablecloth hooked on her walker!"

Ronald groaned. "Cancel that. I need to go stand in that champagne fountain."

———

GERTIE'S PLAY WORKED AND TATE NEVER RETURNED. Although I was happy to be able to mingle again—well, maybe not happy but satisfied to be able to continue with my job— the rest of the evening was mostly a bore. After the goosing and shoving mishap, everyone seemed more controlled and less inclined to chat. I heard the general mumblings about Athena being out and how bad the Rousseaus must feel, but a surprising number said they were more shocked she'd ever been convicted and wondered what had actually happened.

So at least there was that.

If I never got anything concrete enough to let loose into the general public, at least Athena could walk away with the knowledge that even among high society, the opinions on her guilt were mixed. She'd likely find even more support among the working class.

Ronald ended up winning a bid on what looked like a basic blue scarf, but you'd have thought he'd been knighted by the king. He'd thrilled the other attendees by insisting on putting it on right then. It was pretty, but it had cost as much as a really good used car. I put in a bid on a couple of things but knew I'd never make it to the win. I didn't have the deep pockets that Ronald did. But because it was all for charity, I made a donation before we left. I'd researched the Vidals' foundation and they did a lot of good work for the city.

So the dress wasn't horribly uncomfortable since I wasn't wearing metal anywhere—except my gun, of course—and the food and champagne were stellar, as promised. But the whispers of the attendees hadn't really led my investigation anywhere except to firm up what I already knew—that the Rousseaus didn't like rules and would pay to avoid them, and people mostly stayed off their radar because of that.

I figured I wouldn't be able to sleep, and I was right. Gertie dropped off as though she'd fallen into a coma, but then after drinking half a champagne fountain and consuming an entire tray of crème brûlée, that was no surprise. Ida Belle, who was as structured with her sleep as everything else, changed into her pajamas, brushed her teeth, put on noise-canceling headphones, lay flat back on the bed like a corpse, and was asleep almost as quickly as Gertie. I prayed I managed that much self-control at some point. Since I was left with nothing but late-night TV and snoring, I fluffed up pillows on my bed and leaned back to think. I was about an hour into solving absolutely nothing when I heard a faint tap on my door.

I frowned. We had a connecting door with Ronald, but this was coming from the hallway.

I didn't know a single other person here besides the ones snoring and Ronald, so I grabbed my pistol and headed for the door. I didn't bother to keep the chain on it when I opened, because let's face it, those things didn't actually prevent anyone from entering. Instead, I eased the door open with my left hand, and kept my pistol clutched behind my back in the right.

My jaw actually dropped when I saw Veronique Vidal standing there.

CHAPTER NINETEEN

"Can we talk?" Veronique asked. "I have a suite."

I glanced back in and saw Ida Belle, already sitting on the side of the bed, clutching her own pistol, which was impressive given that she'd been dead asleep and wearing noise-canceling headphones. That woman had some sort of sixth sense, I was convinced. I inclined my head toward the door and she gave me a nod, letting me know that if I wasn't back in a reasonable amount of time, she was coming to find me. Not that I was worried. People with means like Veronique Vidal didn't commit murder.

I tucked my pistol in the waistband of my shorts and, not even bothering with shoes, followed her to the elevator. It stopped on the penthouse level—of course—and opened to a massive and expensively decorated suite that was probably more square footage than my entire house. She motioned me to a sitting area with a fireplace going and offered me a drink. I accepted a bottled water, because while I wasn't afraid, I also wasn't a fool, and took a seat in a chair in front of the fire that offered a clear view of the elevator and the door to what I presumed was the bedroom. Veronique poured herself a splash of what I knew was ridiculously expensive whiskey and took a seat opposite of me.

"I want to talk to you about Beckett Rousseau," she said. "I heard about Tate accosting you at the party and did some checking. You're a PI from Sinful, and I assume based on Tate's accusation that you've been hired by Athena Durand."

"What if Ronald really *is* my friend and he didn't want to come alone?"

She smiled. "If he hadn't been attending these events alone for years now, I might buy that. I do, however, believe that you're friends. Ronald would never risk his society status unless it was for someone he cared about. And I'm afraid your reputation for hating all things girlie, pompous, and filled with people precedes you. Yet you were here tonight, wearing a beautiful gown and shoes, hair and makeup done, instead of lounging at home with your sexy sheriff. And since I know Athena lived in Sinful for a while, I figure she still has connections there which is how she learned about your exploits."

I shook my head. "My exploits are all classified and in the past."

She nodded. "CIA. Impressive. I imagine you were excellent at your job."

"What makes you say that?"

"I'm very good at assessing people. When you have assets and power, you have to be or you're constantly taken advantage of. But since I imagine you possess the same skill set, I have to wonder why you would work for someone like Athena Durand."

"Someone like...what?"

"Conniving, lying, always grasping for more on the back of others, a user who plays the perpetual victim."

I shrugged. "Do you think she killed Beckett?"

Obviously, Veronique hadn't expected the question because

she opened her mouth to respond, then frowned. She considered for several seconds, then sighed. "I don't know. The case against her was weak, and to be honest, I imagine Beckett was worth more to her alive than dead as there wouldn't have been enough insurance to carry her for very long in the lifestyle she'd become accustomed to."

She tapped one long nail on her glass, and I remained silent because she still hadn't answered my question. Not really.

"Athena was never accepted by his family and never would have been," she finally continued. "And since I don't rate stupidity among Athena's many flaws, I have to think she would have expected a move to separate her from the family immediately upon Beckett's death. Perhaps a murder conviction was something she couldn't have predicted, but a complete severing of financial ties for certain. And since money is what Athena cares about most...I guess ultimately, my answer is no."

I nodded. "So you see my dilemma? My personal opinions about Athena's character aside, a man is still dead, and I'd like to know why."

Veronique pursed her lips. "I hadn't considered that about you. That your real interest was solving the puzzle. It's illuminating and more importantly, I respect it. Do you know why the Vidals are so successful?"

"Because you're good at what you do?"

"Because we *love* and *care* about what we do. Like recognizes like. So since your quest is for the truth, and as you said, a man is dead, I'm going to do something that I'm certain my family and attorneys would advise strongly against—I'm going to answer any questions you have. Because if Beckett was indeed murdered, then I want you to find the person responsible."

I was somewhat surprised at the turn this had taken, but

then, I'd been somewhat surprised since I'd opened the door to my room and seen Veronique standing there.

"Okay, then first up is your relationship with Beckett," I said, figuring I might as well hit her with the hardest stuff first. If she made it through their relationship fallout without kicking me out of the room, everything else was lagniappe.

"Beckett and I were friends."

"Just friends? Because the rumor is you were engaged to be engaged. Apparently that's a thing in your realm."

She laughed and I couldn't help but be charmed by the sound. Veronique Vidal had that 'thing' that everyone talks about. That thing that made people flock to her. It went beyond looks and wealth and power. It was something deep in the DNA that could be experienced but wasn't easily described.

"My realm," she said. "If only I were queen...but alas, I am but an American commoner with money but no title."

"Seems like you're titled enough in New Orleans."

"I suppose in fashion circles there's some truth to that. But to reiterate, Beckett and I *were* just friends. For the briefest of moments, I thought there could be more, but I came back to my senses long before things moved even a step in that direction."

"So the rumors..."

"When a single man and woman, especially in our circles, spend time alone, then tongues wag. The 'two heirs' and all that."

"Why didn't you correct them?"

"Because honestly, it gave us both a break from the awkward setups and constant pushing from our parents to 'find the right one' and 'build an empire.' There are some things about society families that still linger back in the dark ages. A proper marriage is one of them, although I'll admit that my family wasn't thrilled with the pairing. They find Quentin vulgar and lacking the finesse he should have given the station he's attempting to occupy."

"You said you came to your senses. What did you mean?"

She sighed. "Beckett was attractive and charming and a lot of fun to be around. He was a good listener and that's nothing to sneeze at when it comes to men."

"But?"

"But he wasn't a happy person. No one is all the time, of course, but Beckett was miserable. He put on a good front for his clients and in public because it was expected, but he wanted nothing more than to leave it all behind."

"Why didn't he?"

She rubbed her fingers together. "Crass, I know, but the reality is, Quentin owned Beckett, and he'd made it clear that if his son didn't toe the line, then he'd be out with nothing."

"That's harsh."

"That's Quentin. I don't think he's as interested in being a father as he is in being a dictator. My own father was hard on me, but I never once doubted that he loved me and wanted the best for me. I never got that feeling from Quentin, and I daresay Beckett didn't either."

"There's some loose talk—very loose and very old—that Beckett might have been adopted. Did you ever hear anything like that?"

She raised her eyebrows. "No. As far as I know, Lena gave birth to Beckett, and no one has ever even implied differently. Who told you that?"

"I can't divulge my sources. I'm just trying to verify the information. But if it's true, then maybe it explains why Quentin treated Beckett so poorly."

"He treats Tate just as badly, so I don't think birthright has anything to do with it. And that's assuming that rumor is even true, which I highly doubt. It's really hard to keep that sort of thing a secret."

"Even with the money to hide it?"

She blew out a breath. "I'm not saying it couldn't happen, but why would it? There's no crime in adopting a child—" She stopped speaking and narrowed her eyes at me. "You think it might not have been aboveboard. Is that it?"

"I don't know. I don't even know if it's true. I just thought if it was, and since Beckett was so miserable with his family, that he might have alluded to the fact that they weren't actually related—perhaps to explain where he thought the conflict originated."

"He used to joke and say he wished he were adopted. Then he'd have a reason to dislike them all so much. But he never suggested it was actually the case."

"So you didn't consider a romantic relationship with Beckett because all that bitterness was something you didn't want to make part of your everyday life."

"That was certainly part of it. But when I finally understood just how unhappy Beckett was and that his foremost goal in life was to get away from his father, I realized he saw me as that golden ticket."

"How so?"

"That announcement that my mother made tonight—about expanding our business to Paris—I told Beckett it was in the works and that I would be asked to head it up."

"And if you and Beckett were a couple, then it would be the perfect way to get out from under his father's grasp with his blessing while ensuring no slippage in his lifestyle. In fact, it would have been a big step up."

She nodded. "I will admit that when I realized what was actually going on, it stung some. Even though I didn't have strong feelings for him at that point, I think that in time I could have. And it angered me that I'd been led down that path by someone I had considered a friend."

"You thought he was using you."

"I think he absolutely would have given the opportunity."

"That sucks."

"Professional and personal hazard, I'm afraid. So now you know the unfortunate truth—the rumors of our relationship were greatly exaggerated, but neither of us did anything to correct them because it was convenient. My reported anger at being cheated on was, in fact, real anger, but mostly at myself and not for that reason."

"You were angry that he was trying to play you."

"Yes."

"But you still gave him a very expensive sweater—an exclusive, I believe?"

"That was before I figured out his ulterior motive, and I don't regret it. Regret is a wasted emotion. Beckett had a golf meeting to attend with a potential client. It was the biggest one he'd ever had a shot at, and he was hoping to score points with his father by signing him. I was acquainted with the gentleman he was meeting and knew he'd be impressed with the sweater."

"Because it denoted a relationship, on some level, with the Vidals."

"Exactly. And the client signed with them. But it didn't change anything for Beckett. To be honest, I don't think anything he did ever would have. Just like I don't think there's anything Tate can do to measure up."

"Why didn't you ask for it back when you got his number?"

She gave me a disdainful look. "Because I have class. The sweater was part of my personal allotment. It didn't cost me anything, and honestly, I was happy to help him, even though it didn't ultimately help."

"Even with the way things turned out between the two of you?"

"Someone else's bad behavior doesn't change my own."

"When we first started talking, you were less than complimentary about what kind of person Athena was. But if you and Beckett were never really an item, why do you hold those opinions?"

She raised one eyebrow. "Because *Athena* didn't know the truth. When she met Beckett, she was under the same impression as all the other gossips—that Beckett and I were a couple who were moving toward an engagement. Yet she went out with him anyway. Her motives have never been a mystery."

I nodded. It was a valid point.

"Okay. Well, since you knew Beckett better than most, I have to ask—why would he pick Athena? She certainly doesn't fit the lifesaver model. In fact, she's the exact opposite of you. Not just no money and no name, but no money and a huge black mark on her family name."

She shrugged. "She's beautiful, and that's never to be discounted when you're discussing men and their choices in a mate. And she *did* understand how to move in society because she'd been raised in it. But sometimes, I think he chose her because he knew that it would make Quentin mad."

"So why didn't Quentin cut him off for marrying her?"

"I suppose he could have, but that wouldn't have looked good in the public eye, would it? The evil father standing in the way of true love. You know the press would have gone wild with it. Quentin's entire political platform is based on him being for the common man. The family man. It would have been a hard sell if he'd cut off his son for marrying Athena, especially as the press saw her marriage to Beckett as a Cinderella story, with *her* father being the bad guy."

"So what did he say to you when he took up with Athena?"

"Just that he'd met someone he thought he had a real future with and that meant our charade was over. Then he apologized for the tongue-wagging that was bound to ensue."

"Did he tell you who he was dating?"

"No. And I didn't ask because ultimately, it didn't matter."

"Were you surprised when you found out who it was?"

"Shocked, really, especially when they married so soon. I always wished I could have been a fly on the wall when Beckett told his father that he had run off and married Gerard Durand's daughter. Several of the people who Gerard took for millions were clients of Quentin's."

I shook my head. "That doesn't sound like a smart move if Beckett wanted his father to give him more freedom."

"No. It never made sense to me, but perhaps it was as simple as infatuation. Like I said, Athena is a beautiful woman, and I'm certain there was no end to her charms if she thought it would get her what she wanted. It would have been interesting to see if it lasted. I have my doubts."

I nodded. "So if we assume that Beckett's death wasn't an accident and that Athena didn't kill him, who wanted him dead?"

"I wish I knew."

CHAPTER TWENTY

I WOKE UP EARLY THE NEXT MORNING, MOMENTARILY confused about where I was. Then I remembered the hotel and the event and my conversation with Veronique and relaxed. Ida Belle had remained up until I returned and by then, Gertie had stirred and realized I was gone, so they'd both been sipping sodas and eating pretzels when I'd walked in. I'd told them about the exchange, but was still mulling the whole thing over along with a few other things and wasn't ready to commit to an opinion on any of it.

But now that I'd slept and had finished a cup of coffee, things were starting to fall in line—which made the holes in the case so much clearer.

Ida Belle and Gertie awakened a little while after me and grabbed a cup of coffee, and we all sat propped up in our beds.

Ida Belle studied me for a minute. "You figure out anything about that conversation with Veronique last night?"

"Maybe."

"Do you believe her?"

"About which part?"

"All of it."

"I don't know. She's very convincing but there's also something about her that makes everything sound too perfect. And no matter what I asked, I couldn't make her falter. It's like she's wrapped in that same clear shield you have on your SUV."

"Nothing sticks to her," Ida Belle said. "That's an interesting description, but I can see how it fits."

"She didn't strike me as a woman scorned, though," I said. "But then, I suppose she's been polished to perfection by everyone around her since birth. She didn't strike me as remotely concerned about the sweater, but she can't stand Athena."

"It's a blow to the ego to be tossed aside for another girl," Gertie said, "even if you don't want the guy. I'm still shocked that she spoke to you at all."

"Maybe she did it to throw us off the scent," Ida Belle said. "Not like we were ever going to have grounds to question her. So offer up information and you look like you have nothing to hide."

"Certainly a smarter play than lying to us, like our client has been doing," I agreed. "But I'm inclined to believe Veronique was being truthful, which makes me wonder if Carter wasn't on the right track in thinking that the Rousseaus hired Burkhead to scare Athena off."

"No word from her yesterday?" Ida Belle asked.

"She's probably afraid you're going to fire her as a client after thinking about it all," Gertie said.

"I got a text last night saying she needed to talk to me today when I had time," I said.

"Probably because the news picked up on her release," Ida Belle said.

"Could be," I agreed. "I want to have that conversation first thing this morning. So I'm going to arrange for a premium car service to take Ronald home, and we're going to head over to Athena's hotel as soon as we check out."

We hadn't carried much with us, so it didn't take long to pack it all up and get the SUV loaded, and Ronald was thrilled with the Escalade I'd arranged for his ride home. I think Ida Belle's driving terrified him just a little bit. We all had an excellent breakfast downstairs, then Ida Belle, Gertie, and I took off. It was barely 8:00 a.m. when I called Athena and told her we were in NOLA and needed to stop by and chat. She sounded alert but somewhat anxious and I wondered why.

She was dressed and looked ready for a day out when she opened the door and waved us in. This room was a big upgrade over the motel, but then, it was also double the price. It had a mini fridge stocked with water and a cute little seating area with a tiny couch and a recliner. I dragged the office chair over from the desk, Athena served us all up a bottle of water, and as we all sat, she looked at my hands and frowned.

"Are you wearing chrome nail polish?" she asked.

"Long story," I said. "I assume you know that the media got wind of your release late yesterday?"

She nodded. "It was on the news this morning. There's probably no one left in southwest Louisiana who doesn't know at this point."

"Any problems yet?"

"No. But I haven't left my hotel room since then either. I know I can't stay locked in here forever but it's seemed like a good idea so far."

"Is that what you wanted to talk about?"

"No. But before we get started, I want to thank you for helping me the other night."

"Part of the job," I said. "And your boxes can stay in my garage until you're ready for them."

She gave me a small smile. "I guess no one is foolish enough to break into your house."

"Oh, there've been a few attempts, but people don't usually live to talk about it."

Athena gave Ida Belle and Gertie a worried glance. "Is she joking?"

Gertie patted her arm. "She doesn't joke about shooting people."

Athena looked at me nervously, then nodded. "Anyway, if you hadn't been anticipating something bad happening, I might not be sitting here right now. I know you clued in from the beginning that you couldn't take my story as the gospel."

"She wouldn't take a story from Jesus as the gospel," Gertie said. "That's why she's the best at what she does."

I studied her for a moment. She wasn't wrong about anything she'd said, but if she thought she was going to pacify me with compliments and thanks then she still had no idea who I was. She'd been holding out from the beginning, and I had a feeling those missing pieces were crucial to moving forward. I was done playing her game.

I leaned forward and looked her straight in the eyes. "Athena, I don't know your reasons for lying to me and to be honest, I don't care anymore. But it all stops now. Either you tell me everything—and I do mean absolutely everything—or this conversation is the last billable hour I work for you."

Ida Belle and Gertie stared at me, and I could tell they were surprised with the shift in conversation, but Athena just looked guilty.

"So we'll start with a simple question first," I said. "Who were you arguing with two nights ago in the motel parking lot?"

"I guess the manager saw that too," she said. "I was arguing with Dixon."

I sighed. I'd figured as much but was hoping it wasn't the case.

"Did you arrange to meet him?"

"No! He said word was out that I met with you. He figured I'd hired you and was staying in the area, so he checked at the motel."

"What did he want?"

"He wanted to know if there was any chance that we could try again."

"And you said?"

"I said that a relationship was the last thing on my mind. Definitely now, maybe forever. Then I apologized for the way I'd treated him in high school and told him he needed to move on to someone better and stop wasting his life thinking of me. That no matter what I did, there was a dark cloud above me, and he deserved better than standing in the storm with me."

"I take it he didn't agree."

"He said it didn't matter to him," she said and sighed. "I tried to make it about me...to save his feelings this time. But he wasn't going to accept that, so I finally told him the truth— that I didn't love him and never had. I *did* care about him a lot at one time, but the only man I have ever loved was Beckett Rousseau."

"How did he take it?" I asked.

"How do you think? He called me a couple of unpleasant but probably earned names, then said he would be counting the days until I left town. Then he stalked off."

"Have you seen or heard from him since?"

"No. And I don't expect to. I think I finally said enough to shift him over to hating me."

"Why didn't you tell me about it when it happened?"

"Because you showed up the next morning asking about that fight between Dixon and Beckett, and I was afraid it would make things look worse for him. I was shocked when he said he still had feelings for me. I already felt guilty about how I'd treated him years ago, and about that situation in the hotel with Beckett, and then I hurt him all over again by telling him the raw truth. I couldn't toss him into the middle of my mess. He didn't deserve that. He didn't do anything wrong."

"So you still don't think there's any way that Dixon did it?"

She shook her head.

"Good. Because I don't either."

She stared at me, somewhat surprised. "You don't? But you said before that he was in the Gulf at the time. That it was possible."

"And that still holds, but even if what you said in the parking lot finally got through to him, and he was the maddest person in the world, Dixon doesn't have the money or the knowledge to hire someone like Burkhead. And to be honest, they probably wouldn't take him as a client."

"Oh. So that's good, right?"

"Since I like Dixon, I think it's good," I said.

"Well, I had a run-in with someone yesterday that you probably wouldn't like," Athena said. "Tate Rousseau."

"Is that what your text was about? And you didn't think you should tell me that immediately?"

"You said you'd be busy yesterday and I knew you weren't happy with me, so I guess since I wasn't in any danger, I figured it could wait. But God knows I've been wrong about almost everything so far, so I should have called."

"What happened?"

"He was waiting in the lobby of my attorney's office building. I had walked down with my attorney, and the building has a doorman and a security guard, so I was safe enough. I asked him if he was there to finish the job that his hired goons had mangled."

"And how did he react to that?"

"He completely ignored the statement and said he was there to offer me twenty thousand to drop the investigation and leave town. My attorney asked him if he'd lost his mind and Tate asked what law he was breaking. I told him I wasn't interested in their money, so he upped it to fifty thousand and a first-class plane ticket to anywhere I wanted to go."

"Nice," Gertie said. "Another five minutes and you could have owned the farm the way Tate negotiates."

"What did you say?" I asked.

"I told him that no amount of money could get me to leave until I knew who'd murdered Beckett and I didn't understand why he didn't want to know as well."

"And how did he take that?"

"He said he already knew who was to blame for Beckett's death, and whether I'd paid someone else to do it or just drove him to get drunk and have a fatal accident, it didn't matter. It still all came down to it being my fault that his brother was dead and there was nothing I could do to change that. I told him he could blame me all he wanted but that all of Beckett's stress came from his family, not from me. And they all needed to take some responsibility for the way they treated him."

She took a breath, then continued. "Then he said I was nothing but a money-grubbing whore and I said if that was true, I'd take his money. He said his family had been through enough and if I had any decency, I'd leave. Then he stalked off. My attorney sent the security guard to make sure he left, and then he personally walked me to my car."

"At least he didn't threaten you," Gertie said.

"Because her attorney was standing there," I said. "So since the Rousseaus couldn't scare you away with Burkhead, they decided to go with the ole tried and true—paying people off."

"You really think it was them who hired Burkhead, don't you?" Athena asked. "What about Veronique and the sweater?"

I shook my head. "Last night, I was at an event hosted by the Vidals, and I had an interesting conversation with Veronique after it was over."

Athena's eyes widened. "Veronique talked to you?"

"Yes. And she said she and Beckett were never a couple—they just let the rumors stand to keep their families from forcing awkward setups. And she gave him the sweater out of her personal allotment to wear to a golf game with a high-profile client Beckett was hoping to score for the firm."

"And you think she was telling the truth?" Athena asked.

"I think I do."

"So that only leaves the Rousseaus, right?"

"Of the three we were initially considering, yes."

She took a drink of water, and her hand shook just a bit as she lifted the bottle. I wondered if reality had finally set in and Athena was realizing just how precarious her position was.

"They were always mean to me," she said. "I shouldn't have been surprised when they pushed so hard to have me charged with Beckett's murder, but I guess I still didn't expect them to take things that far. But like Tate said, even if I didn't pull the trigger, they always figured I was the ultimate reason. But the lengths they've gone to and are going to...I don't understand why Beckett didn't tell me just how bad they were before we—"

She stopped talking and took in a breath, staring out the window. I could tell she was trying to decide how to proceed.

"Are you ready to tell me now?" I asked.

She let out a single laugh. "I need to before I end up dead as well. But where do I even start?"

"When everything changed," I said.

She nodded. "I guess it all started to really go downhill a

couple months before Beckett was killed. I was always kept out of things for the most part, but I started noticing a higher-than-usual tension at the weekly family dinner at his parents' house. Don't get me wrong, Quentin always ruled with an iron fist and Beckett and Tate resented it—Beckett more than Tate—but things had pushed past uncomfortable and into confrontational."

"In what way?"

"Beckett started challenging his father, and not on anything that mattered. He would make a counterargument to a statement about the sky being blue even when it was crystal clear."

"So he was goading Quentin. Did you ask him why?"

"He said he couldn't spend the next thirty years or better being his father's servant. That the best of his life would be over before his father kicked off and he'd regret it every day until he died."

"A little dramatic," Gertie said, "but probably not inaccurate."

"Beckett said his father was insisting he divorce me. He said Beckett couldn't start a political career being married to me or ever run the family's firm. That my father's crimes were already tainting Quentin's business, and Beckett would never even move up much less ever be at the helm if he remained married to me."

"Is that when they started telling Beckett you were cheating on him?" I asked.

"Yes. I told him it wasn't true, and he said he knew they were just lying to get their way, like they always did. But...well, there must have been a tiny part of him that did believe it, or he wouldn't have punched Dixon. That whole thing was really weird."

"I agree," I said.

"The night of his fight with Dixon, after we got home, Beckett was so worked up. He was pacing back and forth and wouldn't calm down. He said we had to do something or his family was going to tear us and him apart. He said he'd been saving some money on the side—an account his father didn't know about—but it wasn't enough. He said in order to make a clean break we had to leave the country and we needed more money to do that."

She rose from her seat and stared silently out the window. I waited for her to tell me about Beckett misappropriating client funds, but I was unprepared for what she said next.

"That's when we decided that Beckett would disappear," she said quietly.

We all stared.

"I think you better explain," I said.

She turned to face us. "I told you about the life insurance policy."

"The two million dollars."

She nodded and sat back down. "That was more than enough to start a life somewhere that the Rousseaus could never find us. Beckett said he knew how to buy new identities, and with those we could disappear to a village on a beach or in a big city where no one would ever recognize us. It was my choice."

"What did you choose?"

She shrugged. "I told him I didn't care as long as I was with him. We decided to try both and see what we liked best. We were going to start with Rome. And then there was a village in Cyprus—a college friend had visited there once, and Beckett said it sounded lovely."

"So what was the plan?"

"Beckett was supposed to go out on that boat and disappear. Then once I collected the insurance money, I would declare my need to start over somewhere else and leave. It's not like anyone would care if I left. In fact, his family would be relieved to have me gone."

She leaned forward and looked directly at me. "He wasn't supposed to die."

CHAPTER TWENTY-ONE

GERTIE, IDA BELLE, AND I STARED AT ATHENA. OF ALL THE things I thought she was going to tell me, this wasn't even on the list. But as fantastic as it sounded, I believed her.

"But it takes five years to have a missing person declared dead," Gertie said.

"It takes five years for them to be automatically presumed dead," Athena said. "Beckett checked into all of that. He would stage the boat with the empty bottles of booze and cut himself to leave blood on the side—make it look like he'd been drunk and gone over. He knew the coast guard would do a thorough search of the waters because of who his father was, and Quentin would spare no expense in hiring private rescue teams, so the proof of trying to locate him would be apparent and immediate. Plus, we had an ace in the hole."

"Which was?"

"Beckett knew his father's company had him insured for a lot of money and that Quentin would call in favors to get Beckett's death pushed through in order to collect. He said Quentin needed a quick infusion of cash but never said why.

And then, of course, there was the added bonus of getting rid of me."

"Because your marriage legally ends at either death or divorce," Ida Belle said.

Athena nodded.

"And the money wired out of your account?" I asked.

"I still have absolutely no idea about that money," she said. "All I can figure is that maybe Beckett thought he'd need more than what he had tucked away. I can only believe that assassin being in the Bahamas then is just horrible timing."

"So all the calls to Beckett that he didn't answer—that was all part of the plan," I said.

"Yes. I was supposed to give him until the next afternoon, then sound the alarm. He'd bought a small inflatable raft and motor and took it on his dad's boat. He didn't take the boat out very far, so as long as the Gulf was calm, he wouldn't have had any issue making it back to shore in it. It just would have taken a while. He was going to buzz-cut his hair and dye it while he was on the boat, and he had an old untagged moped waiting to take him to the bus station. That would get him to Atlanta, where he'd get on an international flight using his new credentials."

"And Beckett Rousseau would effectively die," I said.

Athena nodded, starting to tear up. "Until the police came into his parents' house and said they'd found part of the body, I thought he was sitting on a beach somewhere, just biding his time."

I nodded. That explained everything that Casey had witnessed when she'd gone with her lead to deliver the news of Beckett's death. He was at war with his family, so his death was a way out for them—a final one. But my guess was Quentin had already started to write Beckett off and this gave him not only the freedom from the son who wouldn't toe the line, but the sympathy support from all his clients and constituents. Not to mention a big fat insurance check. But Athena had expected something entirely different from what the police found.

"There was nothing in the police report about finding Beckett's new identity," I said. "Where did he have those documents?"

"They should have been on him," Athena said. "I kept waiting for the cops to question me about them, but they never did."

"It's possible they were hidden well enough that the cops didn't find them," I said. "Or maybe he didn't take them on the boat at all and stashed them somewhere else—like a storage locker at the bus station. What about your documents?" I asked.

"I hadn't gotten mine yet. Beckett wanted me to, but I knew it would take time to get things settled with the insurance company. I thought it was safer to wait until closer to the time I would leave. To be honest, I was thinking by that point, no one would care, and I could probably skip the new identity altogether. Not like the Rousseaus were going to track me down after I left."

I nodded. "Is there any way Quentin could have found out what you were planning?"

She sucked in a breath. "Are you saying that Quentin found out about Beckett's plan? You think he killed his own son?"

"Is he capable?"

She ran one hand through her hair. "Good Lord. I figure he's capable of darned near anything, but I never thought... I guess I always figured one of Quentin's enemies had killed Beckett as a warning. You really think Quentin could have done this? Over stupid fights? Over marrying me?"

"No. I think if Quentin had Beckett killed, it was over

something much more serious than the things you knew about."

"Like what?"

"Did Beckett ever tell you that he was adopted?"

"What? No way! Are you sure?"

"I'm certain Lena didn't give birth to him. I have a very reliable witness who places her thin and in a bikini in Miami a couple weeks before Beckett's birth."

Her eye's widened. "Oh my God! The baby book."

"What baby book?"

"About a month before Beckett was killed, he asked me about starting a family someday. We knew we had to wait until things were better between him and Quentin but it was fun to think about it and plan. Because of the fire at my grandparents' house, I didn't have any baby pictures. My mom never saved any to cloud storage, and her parents were too old to even know what it was. But Beckett got his baby book from his parents' house, and we looked at the pictures and imagined what our baby might look like.

"The next week at dinner," Athena continued, "Lena confronted him about taking the book and demanded he return it. He refused and they got in this huge, ridiculous fight. Do you think Beckett found out about the adoption or suspected? And that's why Lena raised a stink when he wouldn't give the book back?"

"Well, based on the things I've heard, the Rousseaus don't sound like sentimental people."

"That's an understatement. Quite frankly, I was a little surprised that Lena even had a baby book, much less cared about Beckett returning it. But even if he was adopted, why would it matter to anyone but Beckett? I don't agree with parents who decide to keep it a secret, but plenty of them do it. It's crappy parenting but it's not a crime—"

She stopped talking and stared at me, her eyes widening. "They bought him. That's what you think, isn't it? They bought a baby and claimed Lena gave birth. And Beckett found out."

"It's a theory."

"If Beckett had proof and went to the media, Quentin and Lena would have been ruined."

I nodded. "I don't see either of them risking their cushy lives, do you?"

"So they killed him." Athena frowned. "But if Quentin found out about our plan, why not let us go through with it? Beckett and I disappearing forever solved everything for them."

"But they couldn't be sure it was forever. What would happen when you ran out of money? Beckett wasn't used to holding what one would consider a real job, and without references and proof of education, what kind of employment could he hope to gain, especially in another country? Certainly not one that allowed the standard of living he was accustomed to. As long as he had something on his parents, they would always have to worry about him coming back for more. And they wouldn't be able to say no, because if their long-dead son turned up alive, the insurance company would be certain to ask for that big payout back."

She shook her head in disbelief. "But how could someone raise a child from infant to adult and then do that? Even if he didn't come from Lena's body, he was her son. If they weren't capable of loving him because he wasn't their blood, why did they get him in the first place?"

"Politicians need families," Ida Belle said. "It's what voters like to see because it's representative of most of the population. It's something they identify with."

Gertie nodded. "And maybe Lena was all in on Beckett

until she had a biological child of her own. It's a crap move, but it happens."

"That's why they pushed so hard for me to be locked up, isn't it?" Athena asked. "They think I know."

"Actually, I'm pretty sure they're positive you don't know," I said. "If you had known, you would have brought it up during the investigation. Or—and this one is more likely—you'd have met an unfortunate end, like Beckett, before you'd ever been able to repeat it."

"Beckett always said he didn't fit in," Athena said. "I assumed it was because he refused to be Quentin's 'Beckett-and-call' boy, as he used to joke, while Tate was the eager puppy."

"I think there was a lot more to it than that," I said. "I just wish we had proof."

Athena smiled. "What if I told you I still have that baby book?"

"What?" I jumped out of my chair. "Talk about burying the lead."

"Well, until just now, I didn't know it *was* the lead. I'd completely forgotten about it until this conversation."

"Where is it?"

"My safe-deposit box. The Rousseaus don't know about it."

"Why would they?"

She laughed. "Because they insisted on controlling everything. All of our accounts were at a bank that a buddy of Quentin's manages. So last year, Beckett had me get the box in my name only at a small local bank that they don't have connections to. I thought maybe he was planning on hiding cash in it, but we never did. In fact, the only thing in there is the baby book. That's why I haven't thought about it until now."

"I'm thrilled that it's there," I said, "but *why* is it there?"

"The day after that fight over the book with Lena, Beckett gave it to me and told me to put it in the box. He said he wouldn't put it past her to come into our house and take it. I thought he was just being petty, but he was impossible to deal with when he was like that and Lena had been so rude about the entire thing, so I just did it and never thought about it again. Until now."

I smiled. I had a feeling this case was about to explode bigger than Gertie's purse.

———

THE BANK DIDN'T OPEN UNTIL TEN, SO WE PASSED THE TIME getting breakfast—a second time for all of us, but there was never a bad time for beignets and café au lait. Ida Belle didn't even complain about cleaning her SUV when it was necessary because of powdered sugar from Café du Monde.

Athena was worried that she'd be recognized now that the media had publicized her release, and I had to agree that it was very likely. And the last thing we wanted was for someone to spot her going into the bank and get a picture. If the Rousseaus were after that baby book, then that would tip them off that she might have it in her possession again.

But Gertie broke out her purse, which had more options in it than Walmart, and got her fixed up with a wig with a chin-length black bob. It was really amazing how much hair changed someone's appearance, but the short dark hair was in such a contrast to her long blond locks that I didn't think anyone in the general public would figure it out.

We kept our conversation over breakfast light and focused on anything but the case because it was too easy to be overheard. But despite the stellar beignets, the minutes crawled and I began to wish I'd suggested a jog or any other strenuous activity instead of sitting in wait. Finally, my watch hit ten till and I jumped up.

"Let's do this!" I said.

I went into the bank ahead of Athena—old habits of ensuring the room was clear—and pretended to look over the account options on a display in the lobby. Athena took off the wig before she went into the bank so as not to confuse anyone, and I could see the bank manager's surprise when he went to greet her, although he hurried to cover it up. They disappeared into another room, which I assumed housed the boxes, and a couple minutes later, she was back in the car with the all-important book in her tote bag.

It took all the self-control I could muster to wait until we were back in her hotel room to open up the book. I placed it on the desk and the four of us hovered around as I slowly turned each page for us to scan.

"Oh look!" Gertie said. "He was such a cute baby. Those dimples. Wait, I want to get a good look at the other pictures on this page."

"He wasn't killed for his dimples," Ida Belle said and motioned for me to turn.

The pages contained everything concerning baby Beckett —pictures, birth announcement, christening announcement, footprints, the standard lock of hair—but nothing that would raise suspicion about his birth.

"He really doesn't look like Lena and Quentin, does he?" Gertie said. "I know plenty of babies don't but even as an adult, there wasn't any resemblance to speak of. Seems odd with Tate looking like a carbon copy of his father."

I nodded and turned the last page, but it revealed no more than the others. Frustrated, I flipped the back cover over and the force of it dislodged a picture from its holder. It was the first picture in the book and showed Beckett wrapped in a fluffy blue blanket that probably cost more than my entire set of bed linens. His big eyes were staring up at the camera and I could already see the dimples in his porcelain skin.

"Aren't they supposed to be red-faced and crinkly looking?" I asked. "He looks like a Gerber commercial."

Gertie nodded. "Definitely not a newly newborn picture. His head is perfect as well. This was probably taken a couple weeks after the birth. And before you ask, no, that's not the norm. There's usually pics from the hospital. Heck, these days, people video the birth."

I cringed but I knew she was right.

"But this picture makes perfect sense if they bought Beckett," Ida Belle said. "If the mother sold him, then she probably didn't ask for or hang onto hospital birth pictures."

I opened the book to put the picture back in and sighed. The smoking gun I'd hoped for wasn't there. Maybe Beckett suspected and hoped to find evidence in the book as I had. Maybe Lena was afraid he might go down that route of thinking, and even though there wasn't anything damning in there, she would rather Beckett not have the book. Maybe Beckett *was* just being petty in holding on to it, as Athena had assumed.

As I went to put the picture back into its slot, I pushed too hard and it flipped over. There was writing on the back. I picked it up, expecting to see a date or name, but instead I found a strange sequence of letters and numbers and a website URL.

"That's Beckett's handwriting," Athena said.

My pulse shot up as I pulled out my phone.

"Look!" I yelled and showed them the screen. "That URL is for one of those genetic testing companies. And twenty bucks says this is a password."

"But why would he do that?" Athena asked. "He could just

grab some hair from his parents' bathroom at one of those dinners and have tests run to prove he wasn't theirs."

"And I'll bet he did," I said. "But once he was certain, he did this to try to find his birth parents. I assume you and Beckett set up new emails for your plan. Ones that the two of you could use to contact each other."

She nodded and gave me the email.

I tapped the email into the website along with the password on the back of the picture and within seconds, we were looking at a list of familial matches.

"Only two people," Athena said. "And I don't recognize the names at all."

"But both in Miami," Gertie pointed out. "Which is where Lena was spotted by Fortune's source."

"If Quentin bought Beckett, we have to assume he didn't come from great circumstances," Ida Belle said. "Poor families don't have money to spend on genetic tests, so it would be more surprising to find a lot of people on the list."

"I'm going to grab my laptop out of the SUV," I said. "It's time to work the internet."

It took another hour of searching to get a cell phone number for one of the matches. Obviously, I couldn't be completely truthful with the woman, so I told her I worked for a law office and was trying to locate a woman about a legal issue with an old adoption and that genetic testing had identified her as a potential relative.

She told me a man had called her the previous year saying he was trying to track down his birth mother. He said he had a serious health issue and was hoping she could help. He must have been convincing enough because she gave him the name of a distant cousin in Miami that her mother had told her had given up a baby. Unfortunately, she didn't know much more because the cousin had been an addict and had cut herself off from the family years ago.

"I hope your client is okay now," she said.

"Unfortunately, he's passed," I said. "Which is why we were hoping to locate his birth mother."

"Oh, I'm so sorry. Good luck."

I got off the phone, unable to control my excitement. We had a name.

Donna Miller.

Now I just had to find her.

CHAPTER TWENTY-TWO

We headed back to Sinful as soon as I got the name. Athena asked me to hold on to the baby book, which made me happy because I was going to ask anyway. I was really hoping that it would become evidence at some point and needed to ensure it was safe. I was still a little amazed at how things had unfolded so quickly but then, that's how cases often were. They dragged along, seeming to make no sense, then the smoke cleared and everything started falling into place. Now I just had to get home, grab my laptop, and start the search for Donna Miller.

Ida Belle dropped me and Gertie off at our respective homes before heading to her house to let Rambo out for a potty break. Then she was going to stop by the General Store to talk with Walter and pick us up some snacks. Ally had checked in on Francis while we were gone, but Gertie wanted to give him his grapes and sing with him for a while before getting back on the investigation. Apparently, singing with the bird was now a daily thing.

Given the common name, I had a lot to wade through before I narrowed things down to a list of ten women in

Miami and the surrounding area. I grabbed my phone and started making calls. By the time Ida Belle and Gertie arrived, I'd crossed six of them off my list and left messages for one more. The last three, I couldn't find a number for at all, but I'd found addresses.

I did searches on the addresses and started with the one for a sketchy apartment building in an even sketchier-looking area. I got the manager on the phone and told him I was trying to locate Donna Miller.

He snorted. "You and every other bill collector in Florida, including me."

"She skipped on you?"

"Yeah. Little over a year ago. Not a huge surprise. I tried to tell the owner we shouldn't rent to her, but he never listens. Bleeding heart, you know?"

"Any idea where she would have run off to?"

"Her useless son, Danny, was around a bit before she bounced. He used to turn up in between jail stints. He was always running his mouth—full of crap, you know? One of the tenants said he claimed they were headed to New Orleans to make their fortune. Like that was ever going to happen."

"New Orleans, huh. Thanks for the information. Sorry about the rent."

"Good luck."

"That has to be her, right?" Gertie asked. "Beckett has a brother."

"And they were coming to New Orleans to make their fortune," Ida Belle said, "which means Beckett got in touch with her."

"Which means they thought they were getting money out of the Rousseaus," Gertie said.

I blew out a breath and Ida Belle frowned.

"You think they're in the cemetery," she said.

"If the Rousseaus killed Beckett because he found out their secret, why would they leave loose threads like his addict mother and convict brother waving around?" I asked.

"Crap," Gertie said.

"Let's not start grousing until we know for sure," I said and started typing. "Not that they've made it easy with names like Donna and Danny Miller."

It took another hour of digging, but I finally located an arrest record in New Orleans for a Danny Miller, dated a couple weeks before Beckett disappeared. It was a minor offense—a scuffle in a bar—and he was released on bail within a couple days. I clicked on the mug shot and smiled. He looked like a really worn-out version of Beckett.

Ida Belle leaned in to look and whistled. "Those are some strong genes."

I poked around and got an address from the record and tracked it back to an extended-stay motel in the Ninth Ward. It was a huge long shot, but I called the motel, deciding on what angle I was going to go with as the phone rang.

"Hello," I said when a harried-sounding woman answered. "I'm with NOLA Bail Bonds and have been trying to reach Donna Miller. We issued a refund check to her at this location and it's been returned. I really don't want to spend another year chasing her down but there are rules about it, so I was hoping you'd be able to help me out."

"I appreciate your pain," the manager said. "After countless hours trying to chase down people for bounced checks, the owner finally issued a cash or nothing policy. Which only led to us being robbed...by the people who'd just paid up."

"Wow."

"Occupational hazard. Anyway, I remember Miller, but she hasn't been here for a year or so. She and her son were staying here for a couple weeks, then there was a drive-by shooting.

She caught a bullet in her arm—surface wound, but it will cause you to rethink your living quarters. Didn't even come back to pack up her stuff. I put it all in a box and met her in a parking lot downtown. I figured she was on her way back to Florida."

"You have an excellent memory."

"And I'm wasting it all here. I hope you find her. Drugs had gotten the better of her for too long, but she was always nice—had manners, unlike most everyone else here. Anyway, she didn't deserve a bullet, and I'm sure she can use the money."

"Thanks."

"Sounds like the hired help missed his shot," Ida Belle said.

I nodded. "If she went back to Florida and disappeared into cash-only rentals in areas where no one ever sees or hears anything, we'll never find her."

"Maybe she didn't," Gertie said. "Leaving takes money and I doubt she had any. And they probably needed to get Danny's arrest squared away. Maybe they just disappeared here. She wouldn't be the first, and the Rousseaus' connections are white-collar criminals. I doubt their reach extends to the cash-only type of living quarters."

I smiled. "No. But I know someone whose connections do."

Gertie grinned. "Friends in *those* places."

I called Big Hebert and told him that I thought I knew who Beckett's birth mother was and she'd been in NOLA but had gone underground. I told him I couldn't explain everything right now, but that I thought she might be able to shed light on Beckett's death. Then I gave him a rundown of her and the type of living situation she would gravitate to.

"Let me check with some people," Big said.

"It's break time," Gertie said when I hung up.

Ida Belle set out the snacks she'd picked up at the General

Store and we marveled over how much we'd learned in one morning. When my phone rang an hour later, I grabbed it so quickly, I chipped polish off one of my shiny nails.

"There's a Donna Miller in an apartment in Algiers," Big said. "No phone number, but she's lived there for about six months and is from Florida. The building is one of mine, and not the best of locations, so watch your back."

"You're incredible!"

He laughed. "I want the full story when you've finished with this."

"Absolutely."

We were already running out the door before I stuck my phone in my pocket.

———

THE APARTMENT BUILDING WAS AS OLD AS I EXPECTED AND the area surrounding it was as sketchy as Big had said, but the building itself was maintained decently. That's the one thing I could say for the Heberts—they weren't slumlords. Even their low-rent properties still had decent care. We parked in front of her unit, and I took a deep breath and blew it out.

"This might be it," Ida Belle said. "Have you decided how to pitch it?"

We'd discussed our angle the entire drive. If I just presented myself as a PI and wouldn't state my client, then Donna would probably assume I was working for the Rousseaus and would say nothing, then disappear again as soon as we pulled out of the parking lot. And I didn't think telling her that I was working for the woman who'd originally been convicted of killing her son was a great idea either. But for the life of me, I still hadn't come up with a better option. If Donna was involved in what I was beginning to suspect had happened, I needed to get it out of her.

"I'll decide after I meet her," I said. The CIA had trained me to read any situation in an instant. I needed to trust in those skills. Not everything in life could be planned.

I knocked on the door and heard someone moving around inside. Then the door opened and a woman peered out at me.

Late forties but easily looked ten years older, but her resemblance to Beckett was obvious. Five foot six, a hundred thirty pounds. A surprisingly good amount of muscle tone, her hair was clean and brushed and her skin clear. Overall, she looked far better than I expected but wasn't even a remote threat.

"Don't have no money to buy stuff and don't owe no one," she said.

"I'm not here for money," I said. "I'm here to ask you about your son."

She opened the door wider and glanced at Ida Belle and Gertie, clearly confused. "You cops? You know what happened to my Danny?"

"No. I meant your other son—Beckett."

She sucked in a breath and for a moment, I thought she was going to slam the door in my face, but she didn't. This was one of those times when I had a huge advantage over others, because two seemingly innocuous senior women seemed to automatically shift me into the not-dangerous category.

She glanced around the parking lot, now clearly scared, and I knew exactly why.

"I'm not working for the Rousseaus," I said. "In fact, I'm trying to prove they were involved in Beckett's death."

She narrowed her eyes at me. "You don't look like a cop."

"That's because I'm not. I'm a private investigator. These two ladies are my assistants." I pulled out my card and handed it to her.

She studied the card for a bit, then asked, "So who are you working for?"

"Athena Durand."

She stared a bit longer and I could see she was considering everything I'd said, then she stood back and motioned us inside. The living room was sparsely furnished and the furniture itself had seen its better days, but the place was surprisingly clean. Since Donna was an addict, I'd expected a completely different scene inside.

"I don't have nothing but water to offer you, and it's tap," she said as she motioned for us to sit. "Or I can make coffee."

"We're fine, thanks," I said.

She stood in the middle of the living room, looking at us for a bit longer, then finally perched on the coffee table and pulled a cigarette out of her shirt pocket. "Do you mind?" she asked.

"Go ahead," I said.

She lit up the cigarette, took a puff, and slowly blew it out, then she crushed it out in a clean ashtray on the coffee table and took another deep breath.

"Helps calm the nerves," she said. "But I'm trying to quit. I get one puff, then I have to think about whether or not it was worth it."

"And was it?" I asked.

"Probably was this time. I got clean from the meth last year. That was a hard ride, but it was worth it. Way I was going, I'd probably have been dead by now if I hadn't."

"Can I ask how you did it? Most people don't, especially after a lot of years as a user."

She shrugged. "Came here with big plans, but then I'm guessing you already have an idea about that. Then somebody killed Beckett, Danny disappeared, and someone tried to kill me. I guess you can say I was scared straight. If you're high, you can't watch your back."

"That's true, but you could have returned to Florida."

"Nothing for me there but the kind of people I needed to avoid. And I couldn't leave without knowing what happened to Danny. So I left the Ward and came here, figuring it was far enough away from where I was before that I might be able to disappear. I met my roommate at a motel not far from here. She worked for one of those commercial cleaning crews that did that motel and some others. We got to talking when she cleaned and hit it off. The company needed more workers—cash pay— and she needed a roommate, so here we are. She helped me get clean. She's a really good person. If things are about to go south for me, I need to know. I don't want trouble coming her way."

"I'm not going to lie to you—Athena Durand was attacked at her motel room a couple nights ago. I think her release has some people scared."

"You think they're looking for me?"

"Probably. But I don't think they'll find you. Your name isn't on the lease and doesn't come up anywhere online in reference to this address or even the area."

"*You* found me."

I smiled. "I have friends that the Rousseaus don't. What happened to Danny?"

"I don't know. We were supposed to meet up with Beckett that morning—the day Beckett went out on that boat. I was sick, so I didn't go. Danny left out of the motel that morning, and never came back. That evening, I went out to the vending machine for a soda, and someone took a shot at me. I thought it was random at first, then Danny never turned up, and I heard about Beckett the next night on the news, so I laid low after they cut me loose from the hospital."

"Did Danny have a cell phone?"

"A prepaid one. I called but it was turned off. I checked hospitals, jail, the morgue...everywhere a person can turn up and not be able to contact you, but there's nothing. I call around every month or so and check again."

"I want to be honest with you. I don't believe for a minute that Athena killed Beckett and I'm sure you heard her case has been overturned. What I think is that the Rousseaus are cleaning house, and they are very dangerous people. I want to find out who killed Beckett before all the evidence is erased, and I'm hoping you'll help me."

She shook her head. "There's nothing I can do against people like that."

"You can tell me the truth. From the beginning—when Beckett was born."

She fingered the spent cigarette again and finally nodded. "I wasn't a user then. Smoked a joint when I got the opportunity, but it was mostly alcohol and cigarettes. Did my best to stay off the stuff both times I was pregnant, and the babies were born healthy. But when I had Beckett, Danny was three. I was still waitressing but it didn't pay the bills, not with the cost of childcare. I got a little bit of aid but not enough to cover the bills in a place like Miami. I mostly depended on men making up the rest, and that wasn't a good thing overall. Anyway, the bottom line was I couldn't afford another kid. Hell, I couldn't afford the one I had."

"And Beckett's father?"

She shrugged. "Don't even know who he is any more than I know who Danny's is. I was a party girl. Could have been a regular or any number of one-night frat boys who blew through the bar I worked at. Bitch of it is, I was on birth control. Doctors wouldn't do anything better because I was too young, but after I had Beckett they finally agreed to lock that down."

"How did you meet the Rousseaus?"

"I didn't."

"Then how did they end up with Beckett?"

"A couple days after I had Beckett, I stopped by the bar to get my paycheck and told the manager I needed to be put back on the schedule. He refused, saying I had to be out for a while because he couldn't afford the liability. I tried to explain my situation, but he wouldn't listen and told me to go and let him know when my doctor cleared me. One of the waitresses followed me out and I told her what was going on. There was a group of suits standing nearby in the parking lot. It wasn't until Beckett turned up and showed me pictures that I realized one of those men was Quentin Rousseau."

"So he overheard your conversation."

"Must have, because the next day, some guy who said he was an attorney knocks on my door and says he has a client who's interested in a private adoption. That his wife had miscarried unexpectedly and this was an opportunity to do something that would make everyone's lives better. I wouldn't have another kid to consider, this couple would have the baby they were expecting to have, and Beckett would get a better life than what I'd ever manage."

"How much did he pay you?"

"Twenty thousand."

"That's a lot of money," Ida Belle said.

"A fortune to someone like me," Donna said. "And there was no downside. I couldn't offer Beckett anything. I was struggling with just myself and Danny. I could use that money to make a better life for us, and I figured Beckett would have it great because people that had twenty grand to buy him weren't hurting."

She paused and stared down at the cigarette, shaking her head. "I did all right for a while. Got a better job in an office and found someone to keep Danny during the day. I quit the bar and the men for a long time, but addiction is a hard thing to overcome. I stuck with beer and cigarettes, but living a normal life just wasn't for me. I was still in my twenties, and to my way of thinking, was living like I was fifty. So I started up everything again, blew through the rest of the money, and then I was worse off than when I'd started because for a while I'd had the cash to buy the harder stuff."

"When did you find out who Beckett was?"

"When he came knocking on my door. Gave me the biggest shock of my life. He and Danny look so much like my daddy when he was young. I guess the genes are strong in my family. Unfortunately, my daddy was also an addict, so you get the good and the bad."

"What did he want?"

"There was a lot of talk about finding out who he was and all, but the bottom line was he wanted to get away from the Rousseaus. He told me some stories about how they were and they weren't good people. I guess I knew that given how they got Beckett in the first place, but I always thought if someone went to those lengths to get a baby then they'd love them. I never figured him for being a prop for a politician, but that's what he said he was."

"That's probably true enough," I said. "But what did he expect you to do?"

"Just be on hand to tell the truth. He was going to confront the Rousseaus about how they came by him and tell them he wanted a lot of money and clear passage out of the country."

"So he was planning on blackmailing them," I said. "And using you as his leverage."

"He said Quentin had more money than God and we'd all

287

be set for life. All we had to do was sit here and wait. That's all I could do really. Not like there was any paperwork to prove what I was saying. Hell, I bet that guy who gave me the money and took Beckett wasn't even an attorney."

I nodded. "Your mere existence was the threat. A simple DNA test would back up your claim. I'm sure the Rousseaus would have faked some adoption documents, and some excuse why they were never filed, and brought up your addiction as the reason for your outlandish claims. But it still wouldn't look good for Quentin's next senate run, especially with Beckett as the driving force behind all the drama."

"That's basically what he said."

"What about Athena? What was her role in all of this?"

She shook her head. "Didn't have one. Beckett said she married him for his money and didn't deserve anything but what he left behind. Said she was cheating on him besides. I was surprised a bit when you said she hired you, but then I guess she doesn't want to go back to jail."

"She can't be tried again," I said. "She hired me because she wants to know who killed Beckett, and I have to tell you, I believe her when she says she loved him. The Rousseaus were dead set against her from the beginning and tried hard to convince Beckett that she was cheating, but I don't believe that either."

She blew out a breath. "Then it's a shame he left her to deal with his family. They really put one over on that girl. I never thought she did it, mind you, 'cause she didn't know nothing about all this. I always figured it was the Rousseaus."

"So what went wrong with the plan?"

"I wish to hell I knew. I got the call that morning from Beckett and he said he had the money. Danny left and never came back. I got shot. Then it was all over the news that Beckett was dead. I figured the whole thing had exploded in his face. And I know it's stupid for me to stick around because Danny is probably as dead as Beckett, but I need to know. The not knowing is harder than quitting the drugs."

"I'm sure it is. I'm going to be straight with you. You're probably safe enough here, but I'm going to keep making waves with this. If you want a foolproof place to hide for a while, I have one."

She gave a nervous laugh. "There's nowhere in this town that's completely safe from the Rousseaus."

"There is if you're with Big and Little Hebert."

Her eyes widened. "You move in strange circles, PI."

CHAPTER TWENTY-THREE

Donna called off work for a week, citing a family emergency, and I left money for the month's expenses for her roommate and Donna wrote her a note. Then after I arranged for Donna to be 'hosted' by the Heberts at their warehouse, Donna packed a bag, and we headed out. I knew Athena was sitting on pins and needles waiting to hear from me, but I didn't want to tell her what we'd found just yet, especially since it meant explaining that Beckett had lied to everyone and at this point, I was pretty sure his ultimate plan was screwing them all over.

Mannie took us up to Big's office where he and Little went straight about assuring Donna that she was safe there and welcome as long as it took. Big also told her that if things went on longer than expected, not to worry about the rent. He did own the apartments, after all. Donna looked somewhat over-whelmed, but then the most important and respected man in the southwest Louisiana underground had just offered up his home and protection. I could see where it was a lot to process, especially on top of everything else.

After that we headed to my house. I needed to do some

mental sorting and I couldn't do that dashing around from one place to another. Sometimes making notes had a way of prompting things to fall into place. I really hoped that would be the case because right now, I had a lot of damning information that I just knew could unlock everything. And the answer seemed to be hovering just out of my grasp.

Ida Belle and Gertie knew my process, so they headed to the kitchen to make themselves scarce. I went into my office, grabbed my laptop, then changed my mind and reached for sticky notes and started writing important points on them and sticking them on the wall in groups. At first, I grouped them in linear fashion based on how we'd uncovered them, but that didn't open up any new thoughts.

Ida Belle stuck her head in and saw me standing in front of the wall of sticky notes.

"I brought you a glass of tea and some cookies," she said when I looked over.

I glanced at my watch and realized I'd been in there for over an hour already. I sighed and stepped back to perch on the end of my desk. Ida Belle slid the cookies and tea on the desk and leaned beside me.

"Seems like you've covered all the salient points," she said and gestured to the wall.

"Yes, but I need them to make sense," I said.

Ida Belle shrugged. "Seems obvious enough, doesn't it? Beckett tried to blackmail his parents and they killed him."

"But what about his plans with Athena?"

"Blackmail was quicker, and he didn't have to share with Athena."

"The sharing part is harsh, but probably true," Gertie said as she walked in. "I'm afraid that marriage might have been as one-sided as everyone thought—they were just sympathetic to the wrong injured party."

I stared at the notes a bit longer, then jumped off the desk and started rearranging them in the order things had actually happened. I stood back and shook my head.

"None of this lines up right. Beckett got Donna and Danny to New Orleans a little over a month before he disappeared. So if the blackmail plan was such a good one, why make different plans with Athena weeks later?"

"Because Quentin found out and Beckett needed to disappear before they came after him?" Ida Belle suggested. "And he needed Athena to pull off plan B."

"Possibly, but if he was always planning on disappearing without Athena, then why did he get in a fight with Dixon the week before? Why would it matter? And look at the wire transfer to the Bahamas. It was before the fight with Dixon, which means it was before he pitched his idea to Athena. And then there's the whole boat setup. Do we really think he came up with the idea, then got fake documents, bought a moped, a raft, and a motor, and got all of that set up in less than a week?"

Beckett was a very flawed, very troubled young man. But he was also an extremely charming one.

You should write an old con movie like The Sting II.

You were angry that he was trying to play you.

The thoughts came into my mind like a hurtling ball and I couldn't stop the unraveling. "Beckett lied to everyone—his parents, his wife, his birth mother and brother—and by all appearances, he was trying to play them all as well. And I think he was playing the long con."

"I don't think that's a surprise at this point," Ida Belle said. "Veronique said he was looking for a way out with her and that was long before he cooked up all of this."

I nodded, getting excited. "Do you recall what Veronique said—that she thought Beckett chose Athena because he knew it would make Quentin mad? And Tate said their marriage hindered Beckett's political aspirations and cost them clients. And remember what you told me about that guy Athena dumped Dixon for—the one whose parents sent him off to get rid of her?"

Gertie perked up. "You think Beckett married Athena to try to get a payout and send-off from Quentin, because that's the way the Rousseaus always handled their problems."

"But it didn't work," Ida Belle said. "He couldn't get Quentin to bite."

"Or couldn't get him to bite enough," I said. "I think Beckett wanted a payout big enough to settle on some island and play the rich, cool dude for the rest of his life. And I think Quentin had his number and refused to play the game."

"A big risk on Quentin's end, especially if it was costing him clients," Gertie said.

"I think he figured he could handle the losses and that ultimately, he could wait Beckett out—that Beckett was more inclined to get frustrated with Athena and ditch her when he saw Quentin wasn't going to give in."

"And then he figured out that he was adopted," Ida Belle said. "I wonder how."

"I don't think we'll ever know unless Quentin or Lena admits it, but something got him on that track and then he acquired that baby book under the guise of 'family talk' with Athena."

"But Lena didn't buy it," Gertie said. "Because she knew why Beckett had really married Athena. But we've seen the book and know there's nothing in it that could have supported Beckett's theory of not being their son, much less any indication as to who his birth mother was. So why was Lena so upset he took it?"

"I think Lena realized what he suspected and panicked," I said.

"But why do they want the baby book now?" Ida Belle asked. "They couldn't have known that's where Beckett hid his password. They couldn't have even known he had it written down somewhere."

And then suddenly all the pieces fell into place—all the lies and betrayals and plans that overlapped or completely contradicted each other, and timing of things that seemed so off, suddenly made perfect sense. And I knew why a baby book that offered absolutely no clue as to Beckett's circumstances of birth was so important now.

I grabbed the baby book off my desk and motioned to Ida Belle and Gertie. "We have to get to New Orleans now."

Gertie grinned. "She's figured it out."

"I don't know for sure," I said. "But there's someone who can tell me."

———

WE MET DETECTIVE CASEY IN A PARKING LOT IN THE French Quarter where she was working surveillance. Her undercover car was parked at the end of a lot, facing an apartment building. We pulled up next to it and she motioned us over.

"If my target exits, I have to haul, so be ready to jump out," she said. "So what's this emergency?"

"I need you to do something for me," I said. "Do you have an evidence bag?"

"Of course, but what am I putting in it?"

I pulled out the baby book and showed her the name on the front, then turned to the page with the lock of hair. "I want you to run some of that hair against the DNA of the body you recovered."

Casey's eyes widened. "You're shi—you are not suggesting that body isn't Beckett's?"

"If it isn't, I think I know what happened," I said.

She ran one hand over her head. "Jesus H. Christ, Redding! Do you know what kind of shitstorm something like that would unleash?"

"I have a really good idea. But if you have to stick your neck out too far to do it, I'll find another way."

"Jesus," she said again and tapped her finger on the steering wheel. "I have a friend in the lab who owes me a big favor. If I log it as a test for a familial match based on evidence from another case, we might be able to pull it off without setting off alarms."

"Do you have a case you can pin it to?"

"We've all been assigned a batch of cold cases to work on in between the hot ones. If brass sees an old file number pop up on the lab list, they'll just think I'm working one of those and probably won't look any deeper. But if you're wrong and anyone gets a whiff of this, it wouldn't be good. The only thing that might be worse is if you're right."

I nodded. "I definitely don't want you to do it if it's too much risk. I'm not interested in costing you your job."

She blew out a breath. "How sure are you?"

"Sure enough to be here asking."

She cursed and shook her head. "I have to know. Everything about this case has bothered me since the day I had to sign off on it. I want the truth."

She removed an evidence bag from a kit in her center console, donned gloves, and carefully removed some of the hair.

"I've got another couple hours in the car on this

surveillance, then I'll take this over to the lab. My friend works third shift, which helps keep this on the down-low. I'll let you know when I have something—hopefully by tomorrow."

———

I'D SKIPPED DINNER WITH CARTER THE NIGHT BEFORE TO meet up with Detective Casey, and I knew he could tell by my voice that I was closing in on something. But he also knew it was smarter not to ask. I was anxious to share it with him, but now wasn't the time. When the whole thing had exploded and the NOLA police were left with the mess, then it would be safe for him to be in the know.

After a long, fitful night of tossing and turning, I was up before dawn. And I wasn't the only one on edge. Athena had texted me several times the day before and again this morning, asking if I had any updates. I told her that I was running down some leads but couldn't tell her about them until I had more information. No way I was going to attempt that conversation until I had answers to the questions she was bound to ask.

Everything hinged on what Casey's lab friend found.

Without that information, I wasn't making another move. But waiting to hear back was making me so edgy, I wanted to shoot something. I finally sent Carter a text and prepared to de-stress.

If you get reports of shots fired at my house, it's cool.
????

Decompression.

Got it.

Ida Belle and Gertie showed up while I was loading my spare magazines.

"Are we going to war?" Ida Belle asked. "Because I've only had two cups of coffee."

"And I'm not wearing my good underwear," Gertie said. "If I die in combat and the coroner sees what I have on, my mother will rise up out of her grave and kill me again."

"Since she hasn't already, you're probably good," Ida Belle said.

"No war," I said. "I need to burn off some frustration. There's some turkey necks in the freezer I've been saving for crab bait. Grab them and meet me at the bayou."

Five minutes later, I yelled, "Pull!" and Ida Belle tossed a turkey neck up into the air. I pulled my pistol, aimed, and the neck split into pieces and dropped into the bayou.

"The fish are probably wondering why it's raining breakfast," Gertie said and shook her head as I hit three more necks, one right after the other. "Your skill level never ceases to amaze me."

"What in the name of all that is holy are you doing?" Ronald's voice sounded behind me. "Good Lord, people need their beauty sleep."

"People?" I asked.

"Me! I need my beauty sleep."

"And I need to burn off some energy."

He huffed. "You assassins are so high-maintenance—always wanting to play with your weapons."

"It's 10:00 a.m. More sleep is not going to change things for you."

"Hurtful."

I tossed him a pair of noise-canceling headphones from my bag.

"Hmmm," he said. "Certainly not a fashion statement, but I'll give them a whirl."

I went through three more magazines and two baggies of turkey necks before I heard someone whistle. I turned around and saw Detective Casey hurrying toward us.

"I know your instincts are stellar, and I take some credit for mine as well," she said. "And I knew you wouldn't have asked me for that DNA run if you hadn't been pretty sure. But there's part of me that still can't believe what I'm about to say —it didn't match."

I smiled.

"You're certain that hair was Beckett's?" she asked.

"You saw the baby book. Beckett swiped it from his mother and asked Athena to lock it up in her safe-deposit box before he was killed. I have no reason to believe it's been faked or compromised. Can you take it to the DA?"

"No. He's in the Rousseaus' pockets. I thought so before when he charged Athena, but I'm certain of it now. I'll have to take it to the ADA. He's itching for a promotion and hates his boss, so anything to throw shade on the DA will make him happy."

"I'm guessing he'll be one of the few happy over it."

She snorted. "You think? The Rousseaus are going to level the NOLA PD for this."

"Let me ask you something—I know the original DNA test was done with hair found in a brush on the boat. Why not get hair from his penthouse? Why not run a familial against Quentin or Lena?"

"Because the Rousseaus said the brush on the boat was enough. Athena identified it as Beckett's, and the only person with access to the boat, other than Quentin, Lena, and Tate— who were alibied—was Beckett. That's why I asked you if you're absolutely certain that the hair in that baby book belonged to Beckett."

"I am. Because someone wants that book so badly, they hired Burkhead Security to retrieve it."

I gave her a brief rundown of what had happened at the motel and the storage unit.

"None of this is tracking for me," Casey said. "Why did Beckett ask Athena to hide the book?"

"At some point last year, Beckett suspected Lena and Quentin weren't his biological parents and took the book, probably hoping to find something that proved it. I don't think there was anything in it that would have helped but when Lena demanded it back, maybe he thought he'd over-looked something, so he asked Athena to secure it in her private safe-deposit box."

"Okay. So he's adopted and they didn't tell him. Happens every day."

"I don't think you'll find any adoption records for Beckett."

"You think they bought a baby. Obviously, that's illegal and reprehensible, but I still don't get why the baby book is so important."

"Because someone believes that baby hair is the last remaining evidence that could prove those body parts didn't belong to Beckett."

Casey stared at me, slowly nodding. "And the only people who would know about the book besides Athena are the Rousseaus. Holy crap!"

She threw her hands in the air. "Who the hell's funeral did I attend? And where is Beckett Rousseau?"

"I'm almost positive I've got the answer to the first ques-tion. Can you ask your friend for another favor? This one won't take long. I need him to run the DNA from the body parts through CODIS."

Casey stared at me for a long time, then blew out a breath. "This is going to blow up bigger than Hiroshima, isn't it?"

"You don't even know the half of it."

Then I asked her for one last favor.

CHAPTER TWENTY-FOUR

It was midafternoon before Casey's lab friend got everything pushed through, but since she'd gotten him out of bed to come back to work, we couldn't really complain. She was sticking her neck out at that point, and I knew the risks she was taking, even if the evidence supported her. I gave her the baby book and everything I had to support my theory, including a way to get in touch with Beckett's birth mother. She was still wearing a partially stunned look when she drove off. I couldn't blame her. Anything she might have thought was off during the original investigation hadn't come remotely close to what I believed had actually happened.

Now she was headed back to New Orleans to talk to the ADA and figure out how to proceed to drop the bomb she was carrying on the NOLA police department. The fallout was going to be epically bad, and her department wasn't going to escape unscathed. But I had my fingers crossed that Casey was going to be left out of any punitive measures doled out since she'd had no control over the original investigation.

Ida Belle, Gertie, and I were headed to New Orleans as well, to talk to Athena. I wasn't looking forward to the conversation because it was going to be an emotionally painful one for her. But Athena deserved to know what we'd found even though it completely rewrote everything she knew about her husband and her marriage.

While Ida Belle drove, I phoned her but I got no answer. I checked my watch and it had been thirty minutes since I'd left a message, but still hadn't heard back. Athena assured me that because of the media coverage, she was going to stay put. She'd already rescheduled a meeting with her attorney to virtual for that evening at my urging, so I figured she couldn't have gone too far. Maybe for bagels and coffee in the breakfast room downstairs or perhaps to the gym to work off some of the anxiety she must be feeling. Or maybe she was taking a marathon shower, as I did when I needed to take life down a notch.

By the time we pulled into the hotel parking lot, I still hadn't heard back and was starting to worry. Her phone was now going directly to voice mail, which meant it was either dead or turned off. Neither sat well with me even though we'd spotted her car in the lot. We hurried inside and I asked the clerk at the front desk to ring room 426. He complied and said there was no answer. I was about to ask him to check the room when the young lady who'd registered Athena walked out of the office and smiled at us.

"Hello, again," she said. "If you're looking for your friend, she came down about an hour ago asking about breakfast places nearby. I told her the diner next door was really good."

So that explained why she wasn't in her room, but not why she wasn't answering her phone. We hurried next door, but a quick scan of the few occupied tables didn't produce Athena. I stepped over to the hostess stand to speak to the older lady wiping off menus.

"Excuse me," I said. "I was supposed to meet a friend of

mine, but I'm really late. She's young, a little shorter than me, blond hair, blue eyes, annoyingly thin and pretty."

The woman laughed. "That's a perfect description, but at least she had manners. Most people don't these days. Your friend paid up a couple minutes ago and headed out."

"Thanks," I said.

I headed straight to the sidewalk and scanned the street. The hotel wasn't in a well-developed area. That had been one of the reasons we'd chosen it. There was a laundromat, tattoo parlor, and auto repair shop across the road and the hotel, the diner, and a gas station on this side. Everything was surrounded by woods. The nearest structures aside from these were a good half mile away.

"The gas station has a convenience store," Gertie said. "You think she went there?"

"She can buy chips and soda at the hotel," I said.

"There's a markup," Ida Belle said. "But that gas station is as old as Gertie and everything in it is probably stale. I don't see her putting her brand label clothes in a laundromat dryer and I'm pretty sure she didn't take this opportunity to get a tattoo."

"So where is she?" I asked.

"Is she a runner, like you?" Gertie asked.

"I don't know. I don't know anything about the woman except things concerning her dead husband. But this strikes me as a bad time to go out running, especially if you didn't bother to charge your phone."

I looked over at the hotel, my back starting to tense. Something was wrong.

And then it hit me. Tate had shown up at her attorney's office. I'd figured he was watching it for her arrival or paying someone else to, but I should have known. Burkhead had placed a tracker on her car, which meant the Rousseaus knew where to find her. They just had to wait until she came out of the hotel alone and they had an opportunity to grab her.

We had to find Athena now. I set off for the hotel and gestured to the parking lot.

"Burkhead put a tracker on her car," I said. "Spread out and look for anything that might tell us Athena was here."

Neither Ida Belle nor Gertie looked shocked at my announcement, but they were clearly as worried as I was. We spread out and started walking the lots in between the diner and the hotel, and then Ida Belle yelled.

"Over here!"

I hurried over and saw an open container of half-eaten pancakes on the ground in between two cars. I squatted and lifted up the container and found a receipt stuck in the leaking syrup on the bottom. Cash payment. And then I saw the note on the bottom of the ticket.

Order for Athena.

"They've got her," I said.

"If they kidnapped her, she could be anywhere," Ida Belle said.

"I found her cell phone!" Gertie yelled, and I saw her waving from the back of the parking lot, near the trees. "It's got those jewel stickers on it."

We hurried over and I recognized the phone, which was tossed in the high grass next to the dumpster. I was about to call the police and report a kidnapping when I heard a scream coming from the woods behind the hotel that led to a bayou. No need to risk being seen transporting Athena to another location, especially in broad daylight. It was easier to just drag her into the woods and dump the body in the bayou.

"Lag behind," I told Ida Belle and Gertie. "You are *not* qualified to take on Burkhead."

I set off into the woods in the direction of the scream,

pulling my pistol on the way. I located a trail and hurried down it, scanning the woods as I went. I spotted signs of recent passage and as the brush started to thin out, I figured I was getting close to the bayou so I slowed.

If they sighted me, I was a goner. No way a Burkhead employee was going to miss a shot like that. I stopped behind a large cypress tree and listened. I could hear the rushing water of the bayou nearby and just when I was about to move closer, I heard shuffling and a man cry out. Then a shot rang out and I left my coverage and bolted in the direction of the shot. I recognized that voice.

I burst into the clearing and saw Tate standing there with a gun trained on Athena, who was huddled on the ground about ten feet from him. I didn't see any blood, so I had to assume his shot had missed or it was only a warning. He glanced over at me and scowled.

"Put your gun down or I shoot her," he said.

I could take him out, no question about it. But his finger was on the trigger. Would he pull when he was hit?

"You don't want to do that," I said, keeping my weapon trained on him. "You'll ruin your life."

"She's already ruining my life," he said. "My mother and father are a mess. They'll never be right again as long as she's still alive. My mother isn't sleeping. My father is drinking. She has to pay for what she did."

"She didn't do anything," I said.

"She killed my brother."

"The man who died on that boat wasn't your brother."

Athena sucked in a breath, and Tate stared at me.

"What the hell are you talking about? Of course, it was Beckett."

"No. It wasn't. And technically speaking, Beckett wasn't

your brother because Lena and Quentin aren't his birth parents."

Tate looked at Athena. "Are you telling more lies?"

She shook her head. "I didn't know."

"I don't believe you," he said to me. "My parents wouldn't have kept that from me. Neither would Beckett."

"Beckett didn't know until right before he was killed," I said. "He found his birth mother. I spoke to her yesterday. Your parents bought him from her and passed him off as the baby your mother miscarried."

He shook his head. "You're lying."

"DNA doesn't lie."

"Then who was that on the boat?"

"Beckett's biological brother. Half brother if you're going by the DNA percentages."

"Then what happened to Beckett?"

"He ran off to another country—just like he and your parents planned for him to do."

"Why would they do that? It makes no sense."

"After arranging for his birth mother and half brother to come to New Orleans so he could use them as leverage against your parents, Beckett left. Your parents promised him a lot of money for keeping their secret, and money and a life free from them is all Beckett wanted. But your parents couldn't afford to leave his biological family alive, so Beckett hired an assassin and wired the money to him. The assassin killed Beckett's brother, took him out on that boat to set the stage for Beckett's disappearance, and tossed the body. But before he did it, he ran Beckett's brush through his dead brother's hair, just in case the body ever turned up."

"No!" Tate's face was red and contorted with rage. "That's all lies!"

But I could see a crack in his armor. I had no reason to lie about Beckett's parentage, and Tate knew that. And he had every reason to suspect his parents weren't always honest with him. Unfortunately, my declaration had torn Athena in two. Tears fell from her eyes like raindrops as she hunched over, sobbing, no longer concerned about living or dying.

"Beckett lied to you," I said. "And he lied to Athena. She was set up to take the blame if things went wrong. That's why he paid the assassin who killed his brother with money from their joint account. That's why he sent Dixon Edwards a note acting as Athena to get him to show up at that hotel the night you had an event. That's why he punched Dixon and pretended to believe Athena might be having an affair. It was all to shift suspicion on her if his disappearance ever turned into a homicide investigation."

Tate looked at Athena again and shook his head. "No. If my parents killed Beckett's family, then where did you get DNA?"

"She didn't."

Quentin's voice sounded to the side of me and he stepped into the clearing, the Burkhead man from the motel right behind him. Both had pistols trained on me.

My heart dropped. I'd made the wrong call. I'd thought I could talk Tate off the ledge, convincing him that he didn't have all the information and didn't need to ruin his life over lies his parents had told him. But I should have taken my chances and shot him when I had the opportunity. I could only pray that Ida Belle and Gertie hadn't crossed paths with Quentin already and if not, that they wouldn't try to be heroes.

"She's lying to you," Quentin said. "There is no DNA. Beckett died on that boat and Athena killed him."

"I had hair from Beckett's baby book and the police have that book now," I said. "And to back up my claims, I have

Beckett's mother stashed somewhere that you and Burkhead can never touch her."

His cheek twitched and I could tell he wasn't ready to completely discount what I was saying. "You're bluffing."

"Donna Miller from Miami," I said. "That's Beckett's birth mother, and she's prepared to tell a far different story than the one you want everyone to believe. Beckett was never on that boat. He was never intended to be."

"What's she saying, Dad?" Tate asked. "She's lying, right? It's all a lie."

Quentin looked at Tate and then back at me and smiled. "Of course she is. She's just trying to get out of here with that gold-digging whore Beckett married. They've caused us a lot of trouble but nothing I can't handle, especially since neither of them will be talking again."

I looked him directly in the eyes. "You know I'm not lying. A detective is going over all the evidence with the ADA as we speak. It's over. Whether I'm left standing afterward or not, you're finally going down."

Quentin's face turned beet red, and I saw his finger move to the trigger.

Rule of multiple enemy engagement—shoot the best shooter first.

So I put a round through the Burkhead man.

Then everything seemed to happen in slow motion. Quentin's expression shifted from determined to shocked as my bullet tore through the forehead of the hired gun standing next to him. As soon as the round had left the chamber, I leaped sideways, firing as I went, and I could hear their rounds whizzing by me.

The explosion rocked the clearing before I hit the ground.

I scrambled back up in the dusty haze, weapon pointed where Quentin and Tate had been standing, but now, both were on the ground, not moving. A crater was still smoking in the middle of the clearing, just a couple feet from where their bodies were now. Weapon at the ready, I rushed over to kick their discarded pistols out of their reach before leaning over to see if they were breathing.

That's when I realized that the specks falling on me—that I'd thought was dirt from the blast—were pink glitter.

I started laughing.

CHAPTER TWENTY-FIVE

IDA BELLE AND GERTIE RAN OUT FROM BEHIND THE TREES AS Athena sat upright and stared at the carnage in the clearing. But at least she was unhurt—by the bullets, anyway.

"Are they alive?" Ida Belle asked.

I nodded. "They were knocked unconscious by the blast."

Gertie whipped handcuffs out of her purse. "Then let's make sure that if they wake up, they don't go anywhere before the cops gets here. I don't have another glitter bomb."

"Where the heck did you have that thing?" Ida Belle asked. "I searched your purse before we left Fortune's house."

Gertie grinned. "I figured you wouldn't let me bring it, so I stuffed it in a sub sandwich. I got the blast perfect on this one, right? Although it's a little strong for parties."

I laughed again. "Yeah, maybe don't tell Carter you're working on those as party favors. The glitter was a perfect touch, although Ida Belle is going to hate me riding in her SUV."

"I'll probably get over it," she said, and I could tell by her expression that this one had come way too close for comfort. "You're bleeding."

I looked down and saw blood oozing out a rip in my jeans. "Looks like one of the shots grazed me. It's not a big deal."

Ida Belle threw her hands in the air. "It's not a big deal, she says. How about we let the paramedics make that determination?"

"We don't have to tell the cops about the pipe bomb, do we?" Gertie asked.

Ida Belle stared. "So where did that hole come from? Were we digging a grave? Were you sprinkling glitter on us while we worked like this was some macabre Disney film?"

I left them arguing to head over to Athena. She'd crawled a couple feet and was now leaned back against a tree. Her face was streaked with dirt and tears, and pink glitter glistened all over her head and body. I squatted beside her.

"Are you hurt?"

She shook her head. "Not physically, although my ears are ringing a bit."

"So are mine. It will go away soon."

She looked up and locked her teary eyes on me. "What you said—was all of that true?"

I nodded. "I'm sorry. I wish you hadn't had to hear about it that way, not that I think there was a good way to hear it."

"Beckett never loved me, did he? He thought Quentin would pay him off to divorce me, and when that didn't work, he pulled his birth mother and brother and used them as well."

"I'm really sorry to have to say this, but I don't think Beckett ever loved anyone but himself. He wasn't a good person, Athena."

"That's why he pushed me to get fake documents, isn't it? It was just one more thing that would have helped convince people I'd killed him and was going to flee the country. I can't believe he took things so far."

"It wasn't just with you. He tracked down his birth mother

and brother and set them up to be murdered. His mother would be dead already if she hadn't been sick the day Beckett's brother went to collect the money that was promised to them. The hit man tried to salvage the situation and took a shot at her later but didn't kill her. After that, she went off radar and stayed there until I found her."

"But I don't understand any of this. If Beckett wanted to leave so badly, why didn't Quentin just give him money and let him go? The Rousseaus have plenty. Why fake Beckett's death? Why kill his brother and try to kill his mother?"

"I'm just guessing here, but I think that around the time Beckett discovered he wasn't Quentin and Lena's son is when some shady investments were made that lost the firm's clients a lot of money. Remember, you said Beckett commented on Quentin needing a quick infusion of cash? Around the same time, there was some gossip that Beckett had made some unauthorized investments and lost, and Quentin made everyone whole to cover it up. But I think a forensic audit will show that it was actually Quentin who messed up. He didn't have enough liquidity to personally cover the losses. But Beckett was insured by the firm for five million."

Athena's face flushed with anger. "So they all won. Quentin made the clients whole and got to be the grieving father. And no one talked about the financial indiscretions because Quentin blamed it on Beckett and he was dead. Beckett got to ride off into the sunset with his bags of daddy's money, his brother and mother were no longer a threat to the Rousseau empire, and I got to rot in prison because I was as expendable to them as I was to my own mother."

Gertie and Ida Belle had walked up while we were talking, and Gertie dropped one hand on Athena's shoulder and squeezed. "Honey, you are and always were *too* good for the

Rousseaus, and your own family as well. You've just got to start believing that."

I heard shouting and a couple seconds later, a team of NOLA cops burst into the clearing, guns blazing. They stared at the scene in front of them, shocked and a little bit fearful. Quentin and Tate were starting to stir, and despite the layer of glitter and dust on them, there was no mistaking who they were.

The cops moved their guns to us as soon as they saw the handcuffs on Quentin and Tate, and the dead guy lying next to them, and we all put our hands up in the air. This was one of those times where you complied first and talked later.

"Put your weapons down." Casey's voice sounded behind them, and she shoved two cops aside to pass through to us. "These people are the good guys. They're doing the job we should have done and deserve a handshake, not a weapon pointed at them. Pick up those other two pieces of garbage and take them to booking."

"Detective Casey," one of the cops said nervously. "That's Senator Rousseau and his son."

"I know good and well who they are," Casey said. "And he's not going to be a senator for much longer—he's going to be Inmate No. Whatever. The ADA will meet you at the station."

The cops were obviously confused but weren't about to go against a direct order from a senior officer, especially when the ADA's position on the matter had been clearly defined.

Casey headed over to us and gave us all a good up-and-down look.

"You hit?" she asked me.

"Surface wound," I said.

She nodded. "Anyone else hurt?"

"Not physically," I said.

"Can you find him?" Athena asked. "Can you find Beckett?

He shouldn't get away with this—using people, destroying their lives, killing them..."

She sniffed, and I could see the tears were ready to fall all over again. I couldn't really blame her. I was tough, but Athena had been emotionally abused since birth. This was just one more horrific situation in her relatively short life.

Casey looked at Athena, her face full of sympathy. "Your PI already had me looking. She's one smart cookie. You hired well."

"Did you find him?" Athena asked.

Casey nodded, and I perked up because that must have happened while we were getting shot and glitter-bombed.

"Where was he?" I asked.

"In Cyprus, like you thought."

Athena's face flushed with anger. "Where he told me we'd go together. I don't understand how he lives with that—with everything he did."

"He doesn't," Casey said. "He was shot in the back of the head two days after arriving. It was a professional hit. But since he was using his new identity, no one knew who he really was."

"Quentin never intended to let him live," I said. "He knew as soon as Beckett blew through whatever money he'd gotten, he'd be back for more. And Quentin couldn't afford for that to happen for a lot of reasons."

Casey nodded. "I don't know that we'll ever be able to prove it, but I'm certain you're right. It doesn't matter, though. We have enough on Quentin to guarantee he'll rot to death in federal prison."

"So the ADA is ready for this?" I asked.

"He's practically frothing at the mouth. They're all the same—aspirations for either the bench or politics. Either way, this could be the hallmark case of his career."

"Good, then maybe he'll start cutting me some slack."

Casey laughed. "I wouldn't count on it." She looked at Athena. "I'm going to need a statement from you, but it doesn't have to be this second. Do you need to see a doctor?"

Athena shook her head. "The ringing in my ears is almost gone."

"Yeah," Casey said and glanced back at the hole. "That one is going to take some explaining."

I looked over at Gertie and grinned. "Tell the ADA it was a fluke."

———

SO MUCH HAPPENED ON FRIDAY THAT IT FELT LIKE THE DAY that would never end. I'd stayed up most of the night talking to Carter about everything that had gone down, and he was floored by the lengths Beckett had gone to and the amount of carnage in his wake. Nothing about Quentin's and Lena's roles surprised him but he was happy they'd finally be paying the piper.

Detective Casey had called me close to midnight and said the explosion at the DA's office had been monumental. The DA had attempted to backpedal on his role in Athena's conviction, but the dogs were already hunting. An investigation into his connection with the Rousseaus and rumors of jury tampering was already in the works.

What little sleep I had gotten was really good for a change. My mind was simply happier when things were back in balance, and they were, at least for the moment. So when Saturday evening rolled around, I happily donned my jeans, purple T-shirt, and Mardi Gras beads and headed out for the festival. I was going to swing by the Sinful Ladies booth and check on Ida Belle and Gertie, but first, I snagged a funnel cake and headed for a park bench under a big oak tree just shy of downtown.

Main Street was blocked off for the Mardi Gras festivities, and half of Sinful was already milling around even though the parade didn't start for an hour. I'd done an extra three miles that morning in anticipation of funnel cake and was determined to get at least two rounds in. Maybe even three. I had just taken my first bite when Dixon spotted me and headed my way. I motioned to a stump next to the bench and he took a seat.

"I heard what happened," he said. "With Quentin and Beckett and well, all of it."

"It's already on the news?" I knew it would be a big story, but I didn't think everything would be pushed out there that quickly.

"No. I mean, they're saying Quentin, Lena, and Tate were arrested, but the cops are being cagey about it. I'm sure most people figure it was something to do with money."

I nodded. "So how did you find out?"

"Athena told me. She was at my door at 6:00 a.m. this morning. Surprised the heck out of me given everything that's happened. I guess you know I wasn't exactly honest with you about her."

"I know you went to see her at the motel to try to win her back, and I'm guessing you gave a similar speech when you got set up to run into her at the hotel in New Orleans."

He nodded and stared at the ground. "I loved her. I know people said we were too young for it to be real, but they're wrong. I loved Athena. Part of me still does and I'm guessing part of me always will. I know she did me wrong, but we were kids. Everyone makes mistakes, and once I got older and understood her situation better, I got why she did the things she did."

"That's very mature and empathetic of you."

He shrugged. "I loved her and I didn't want to give that up. I guess I thought one day she'd realize who was really there for her and who wasn't. I just didn't consider that she never loved me—or didn't want to admit it. I'm not sure which."

"So what did she have to say?"

"She apologized. Said that of all the rotten things she'd done, hurting me the way she did was her biggest regret—even bigger than marrying Beckett."

"That's pretty big."

"Yeah. I told her that we both had our battle scars, and there was no use hiding from them or we'd just be in the same place in two years or five or ten. Better to tend to them...see if you can reduce the size and color..."

"But learn to live with them."

"Yes, ma'am. I want to thank you for everything you did for her. Regardless of the things Athena did wrong, she didn't deserve what the Rousseaus did to her."

"No. She didn't."

"I think she's a different person now. We both are. When I saw her again, I hurtled right back into the past, but things are never going to be that way again. And every time I get frustrated with that, I'm going to remind myself that I like who I am now. I like what I've accomplished, and there are even better things ahead."

"Count on it."

"Anyway, I've decided to stick around Sinful—take that job with the boat builder. This place is weird but it's home."

I smiled. "I feel the same way."

"Then I guess I'll see you around," he said and headed off.

I did a mental tally of all the cute single women in their twenties in Sinful and predicted that the very eligible Dixon Edwards wouldn't be alone for long.

"Is this seat taken?"

Athena's voice sounded behind me, and I looked over, more than a little surprised to see her. Her beautiful face was marred by the dark circles under her eyes and the shiner on her cheek that even great makeup and a skilled hand couldn't cover, and her eyes were still bloodshot and had that strained look of prolonged crying, but her face and shoulders weren't tense anymore.

"I heard you made the early rounds," I said. "I'm surprised you didn't flee the state as soon as you got police clearance. At least until you have to testify."

"I thought about it. Even packed my bag, which took all of about thirty seconds since most of my belongings are at your house."

"Oh yeah. I could have shipped them."

She smiled. "And you would have without question because that's just the kind of person you are. You know, everyone thinks you're this tough girl, and I'm not saying I doubt that for a minute, but you've got a big heart, Fortune Redding. I saw the way you looked at me in the clearing, when I'd just learned my entire marriage was not only a sham but that I was set up by the man I loved to take the rap for killing him if things went south. You felt sorry for me. Even after everything I've done and all the lies I told you. The truth of what Beckett did still made you sad."

I nodded. "To say it was unfair sounds trite. It was so far beyond unfair. When I finally put it all together, the first thing I wished was that you really had married Beckett for the money."

"But I thought that's exactly what you believed," she said, clearly surprised.

"No. My instincts are really good. I knew you were holding back some things from the beginning and outright lying about others. But the three things that kept me on this case were that a man was dead, I believed you loved him, and I didn't think you'd killed him."

"I wish I had your instincts."

I felt my heart tug at the sadness in her voice. "I'm sorry for what the Rousseaus did to you. Even more sorry you had to hear it all while literally staring down the barrel of your own mortality. And I'm beyond sorry that you've had to live with so much tragedy in so few years on this Earth."

She gave me a small smile. "Life isn't fair, right? That's what they always say."

"*They* could do with a good butt whipping."

"I agree."

"So what are your plans? You picked out that beach town yet? The insurance company won't be able to deny that life insurance claim any longer. You'll have cottage money."

"That's true. But I think I'm going to stick around for a while."

"Really?"

"I thought about what you said—about how I needed to give serious thought to the way I lived my life or I was going to find myself at odds with people until I died. You were right. I invested way too much into trying to create the perfect life— the one I felt I'd always had dangling just out of reach. But my desperation for security and love made me an easy target for Beckett. And on the flip side, I closed myself off to people who might have actually cared about me because they didn't fit what I had envisioned for myself."

"I think that's a good observation."

"It got me thinking about the way I lived before I met Beckett. Before I was tempted again by the idea of a Hall-mark life. I realized that what I'd had before I met him was actually pretty darn good. And I had options for making it better—ones that didn't require a rich man. So this morning, I talked to the manager at that hotel I used to work at and I laid it all out on the table. I didn't want him to have any surprises with the media storm that's sure to be coming. He said he'd hire me for the kitchen. I have to start at the bottom, of course, but the chef said if I showed promise, he'll work with me. Who knows? Maybe one day I'll even go to culinary school."

"I think that's great."

"I saw Christi, my old roommate, while I was at the hotel. She told me the Rousseaus had paid off her and Juno so they wouldn't testify as character witnesses for me. They didn't want the jury to know that I worked hard, paid my bills, and was actually in love with Beckett. Some suit with a gun told them they either took the money and kept their mouths shut or he'd set them up—plant dope on them or something."

I nodded. It was pretty much what I'd figured, although I hadn't realized that Christi had been one of Athena's roommates.

"She was apologizing all over the place, and I told her it wasn't necessary. I mean, I know better than anyone what they were capable of. Anyway, I told her that when I get my insurance money, I'm buying a condo—three bedrooms—and she and Juno are welcome to live and just split utilities and association fees while we all figure out a better future for ourselves."

"You've been busy this morning. That's a lot of serious decisions in a short amount of time."

She shrugged. "I had a year in prison to think about things. The most important thing I learned was that tomorrow isn't guaranteed. If you sit still long enough to let grass grow under your butt, you're likely to die that way."

"Well, I think all that sounds great. And I wouldn't worry about taking some time now and then to smell the roses.

You're still young with plenty of time to start over. If I did it, you can too."

She laughed. "You weren't exactly old when you came here."

I smiled because she was right. I hadn't been much older than Athena when I'd turned my back on one lifetime and opted for a completely new and different one.

"There's something else I was thinking about, but I wanted to run it by you first," she said.

"What's that?"

"I want to give Beckett's mother half the insurance money. She lost her son—the one who mattered, I mean—and would have lost her own life if things had gone the way the Rousseaus wanted them to. But given what you told me about her, I'm not sure how to do it and make sure she doesn't mess things up again."

I felt my chest tighten because it was easy to say the words of contrition and growth, but it was clear that Athena had done more than that. She was not only thinking about the big picture, she was taking action to change the way she'd done things in the past. Given everything she'd been through, it was beyond admirable and was a great indication of her future.

"I think that's a wonderful thing. Let me talk to some people and we'll find you an attorney and a financial adviser. Maybe the money can be in a trust that she draws on and she has to meet conditions to continue the draws."

"That sounds great," she said. "Well, I'm going to get out of here. If you wouldn't mind keeping those boxes for me a little longer, I'll get them when I find a place."

I nodded. "No problem."

"See you, Fortune. And thanks."

I polished off my funnel cake and headed for the Sinful Ladies booth. The line was long, and Ida Belle and Gertie looked happy as they took money and shoved cough syrup at the enthusiastic customers. I noticed the supply of grape was seriously depleted and shook my head.

"I don't think there are enough cages set up for the amount of grape that's been sold," I said.

The sheriff's department set up giant cages downtown to hold the drunk-and-disorderlies until they could behave properly. Given the strength of that grape syrup, this year was looking questionable for Carter and company.

"That taste test last Sunday really brought in the customers," Gertie said, looking entirely too happy about all of it.

"Do you need help here?" I asked.

"No, thanks," Ida Belle said. "In fact, our shift is over. We were just about to find you and go check on Molly and Ronald. Parade starts in ten minutes, and I figured you wanted to get a look beforehand."

I grinned. "I'll probably never say these words again, but I'm actually dying to see what he's wearing."

We headed for the far end of Main Street, where the parade was staging, and into the giant tent set up to house the king and queen before the event. There were ropes to keep the crowd from approaching, and even though people could easily go under or around, everyone respected the boundaries and looked forward to the surprise. Walter had picked both of them up, given them masks to wear, and driven them in from the other side so that no one could see them entering the tents. It was all very CIA in a Sinful sort of way.

Molly grinned at us as soon as we walked in. She wore a black tux with purple sequined vest and bow tie and dress shoes with purple sparkly laces.

"I brought some crab dip to snack on while we waited," she

said and pointed to a table in the corner. "There's a whole tub left if you want it."

"You don't have to tell us twice," Gertie said as she scooped up the container and deposited it into her purse. "It won't make it past midnight, I assure you."

Molly laughed. "That dip is going to single-handedly fund my retirement." She looked toward a divider in the tent and yelled, "Ronald, get out here. It's time to load up!"

The tent divider opened and Ronald stepped through.

"Wow!"

"Holy crap!"

"That is awesome!"

"Best. Dress. Ever."

We all spoke at once, but with good reason. Ronald's dress was unlike anything I'd ever seen. It was a straight sheath with simple straps and first it was purple, then green, then gold, then all three. Then it started sparkling all over like stars, then the colors shifted to lines that grew bright and faded, as though they were running up the dress. I took a step closer and leaned over. His wig was a long straight silver and the colors of the dress reflected off it.

"Are those LED lights sewn into the gown?" I asked.

Ronald nodded. "Genius, right? The seamstress will probably have arthritis and it took forever to program it, but this dress will be the most spectacular thing the Mardi Gras parade has ever seen."

"It's absolutely gorgeous!" Gertie exclaimed. "And your hair just sets off everything. You're the best queen ever!"

Ronald laughed. "So much covered in one sentence. But I'll take it." He looked over at Molly. "Now, if my dashing escort will assist me onto our throne, we'll make this happen."

We helped them get set up on the float—tradition called for all floats to be constructed on bass boats—then we headed out to watch the parade. As we approached our usual spot, I saw Carter leaning against the wall of the sheriff's department, talking on his cell phone. And he didn't look happy.

I crossed the street and stepped up just as he disconnected and slipped his phone back into his jeans pocket.

I gave him a pointed look. "Are you going to tell me about it before you leave or do that trendy thing and send me a text afterward so I can't argue with you?"

He had the decency to look guilty. "I should have known you'd clue in. But I didn't want to say anything until I'd made a decision."

"And have you?"

He nodded. "I don't think I have much choice. The Marines need me for a mission—not as an operative but for intel. I'm the only one who's been where they need to infiltrate who's still alive."

"How long?"

"Three weeks, maybe four. I leave Monday."

"Monday? That's cutting it close."

"Things evolved faster than they originally thought they would."

I nodded. It was an unfortunate aspect of that type of government work. You couldn't exactly schedule the right conditions. You had to be ready to go when they occurred.

"What about your job?" I asked.

"I've contacted a retired sheriff from another parish. He's agreed to fill in while I'm gone."

"Where will you be stationed?"

"An aircraft carrier, can't say where." He took my hand and squeezed. "If there was another option, I'd turn them down. But I don't want those men going in blind. They tried that once already and it was bad. Really bad."

I nodded. I got it. More than most people would.

I leaned over to kiss him. "You're a good man, Carter LeBlanc. The country is lucky to have you. But so is Sinful and so am I, so get your butt back here safely."

"I plan on it. I was thinking that maybe while I'm gone you could take some time off. A vacation maybe. Learn to knit or take up basketball. Maybe art lessons with my mother."

"You mean stay out of trouble?"

"Just a thought."

"It's like you don't even know me."

He grinned. "More like I know you too well."

WILL FORTUNE MANAGE TO STAY OUT OF TROUBLE WHILE Carter's away? Or will her next case have her in the crosshairs? Another Miss Fortune mystery is coming later this year.

GET YOUR OFFICIAL MISS FORTUNE MERCHANDISE AT THE newly launched Jana DeLeon Store at janadeleonstore.com. (Currently open to U.S. residents only) For readers outside of the U.S., a limited amount of merchandise is available through Zazzle at zazzle.com/store/janadeleon.

Made in United States
Orlando, FL
02 June 2023

33746899R00180